COLD HEARTED

By Jamaica

Self-Published with help by
MIDNIGHT EXPRESS BOOKS

Out of Sight, Out of Mind Publishing
Presents

COLD HEARTED

ISBN-13: 978-0692399682 (Midnight Express Books)
ISBN-10: 0692399682

Self-Published with help by
MIDNIGHT EXPRESS BOOKS
POBox 69
Berryville AR 72616
(870) 210-3772
MEBooks1@yahoo.com

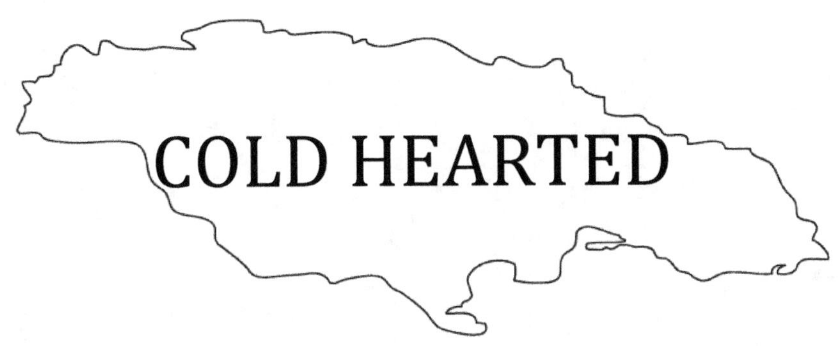

COLD HEARTED

By Jamaica

ACKNOWLEDGMENT

To the man above, all my blessings comes from you! Without you there would be NO me. Thank you for keeping me sane and stable, for giving me another gift. I'm forever BLESS! I love you...

Tameia and Tamaine Jr... The two of you are my motivation; ya'll the reason why I push myself like I do. Even tho I am away know that everything that I do, I'm doing it for ya'll. I love and miss ya'll with all of my heart. LOYALTY is a must, don't ever forget that! I rather lay it down than tell on anyone, so PLEASE forgive me for not being there. I'll try to make it all up in due time!!! I'll be home soon so please make mommie proud... I love Ya'll...

My grandparents, Oswald and Julia James, Ya'll raised me well. I am who I am today because of ya'll. I'm so bless to have grandparents like you two. I love you guys with all off me.

Leather, lady I don't even know where to start. If it wasn't for you I don't know where my kids would be. I owe you my life because they are my life. Anything you ask for, I swear I m going to find a way to give it to you. I thank you from the bottom of my heart and I love you.

Donna & William, thanks for the love and support. I appreciate everything, Mom... I love ya'll...

My father, I know that you are mad but you have to remember, I am still your child.

My siblings, I am still a James breed, we have daddy's blood running through us but it is all good... I am not mad...

My loyal little sister, I love you, even though you're in the UK, you still show me love and I love you for that, Chessan!!!

Doneille, thank you for everything, it's all love...

A.D... Shit is crazy, but thank you also...

Gevetta, I love you!!! Thanks for telling me to put my thoughts on paper. Look at me now!)

Jerry Obi, don't hate me for that... These past years, you have shown me a lot. The love and support is real, don't forget me !!!

Kemper, you keep me updated with everything, ha!ha! Thanks a lot.

Gutta Pot, thanks for keeping me alive from the outside.

Kala Buchanan, thanks for being there for me... You put up with a lot but yet you know that you are my HITTA for life. This time has made our bond so strong that it is unbreakable. When I put the pen down, you always there to remind me of Kids... I know the light and the music gets on your nerves so bare with me... Amanda, Kala loves you a lot... Zaimen, Arionna and Dolla she loves and miss ya'll... I love you dawg four life!!! Real Talk...Brooklyn, you mom loves you!

Spgetti, thank you for putting up with me. I know I get on your nerves but you're the best editor/typer ever... I love you. I know you ready so, LET'S GET IT!! !

Wheat, friend how can I say thank you... When I ask you to do something for me, you get it done... Thank You and I love you, oh yea you know I do the best roller set EVER. :)

Punkin, I can't wait for 50/50 to open up! They hate on us'cause they can't do hair like us, but it is all good'cause it makes us better. I love and miss you friend...

Kiara Culpepper aka Miss Polo, you a fool for that one!!! Keep your head up, blood does not make us Family, LOYALTY does!!! I love you!!! Jasmine Rucker aka Juicy J, yo I heard you all the way turned up...

Kim W, Lucy D, Beverly M, Shannon R, Christine H... When I am down and out, or just need an ear to talk to... Ya'll are there... I love all off ya'll... Thanks for just being yourselves!!!

Asia D, Shonda H, T Davis, Tiffanie B, Joyce L, Linda F, Diana E, Veronica D, Lady Dee, Shelly, Vanessa, Candice, Frankie, Tony, BP, Keshia, Boz, Cherly C, Cherly H, Jackie, Kiwi, B, Lantia, Ila, Hydie, Leslie, Tracey S, Jersey, Michelle(6), The Thunder Cats (Amanda, Virginia, Cassie). Amber, and every person head that I do. I can't remember right now but if I forgot your name, don't charge it to my heart just put it right here. Stay up!!! Myecia "Face" Lucas and Anisha "CT" Wilson; I hope ya'll happy now…

To the Williams family: Nicki, Shandura, Dee... Keep ya'll heads up...I will never forget ya'll, Real Recognize Real all the way...

Pierre Pennix aka Big P...lol ... Yo Keep your head up, don't stress just make sure you keep your word with your kids... And to all your home boys "Loyalty is all I Know!!!" Stay free and duck them HATERS.

T. Paige, you did 0-100 real quick but hey it is life, RIGHT?...

Jeremiah Scott, funny huh? I know... Keep your head up... I don't hold the past over your head'cause I am a real woman...You know this... I'm always going to keep it real with you, I hope you do the same with me...I'm a rider!!!

Jolon C aka Jo, mane oh mane only God knows!!! If we would have crossed paths... We know the rest...

C. Lara, no words need to be said but Death Before Dishonor!!!

Sir Finch, do the right thing believe me it will pay off!!!

Angella, thanks for everything girl... Love Ya'll

Yadira Avilez Lopez, thanks for the book cover; I knew I could depend on you. You the best!!!

Leonard Sango, thank you for the love and support you and your family show me all away from Canada... Thank you again and again!!!

Chanelle from Canada and Carola from Sweden, thanks for all the love that ya'll show me through the mail...

Tara and Skip... Rest in peace!!! I miss ya'll so much, I am ready to break down now but I know ya'll would not approve...

Not a day goes by that I don't think of ya'll... Gone but not F0RG0TT0N...

To the realest Rappers ever: Young Jeezy and Lil' Boosie...

To the snitch that told on me and 18 more, God forgives". . . I pray that I can forgive you but I know deep down in my heart that I could Never.

Esha thanks for helping your grandma raise my babies... I love you for that...Real talk... Do the right thing...

LOYALTY is a MUST and we all should live by it!!!

REAL RECOGNIZE REAL...

Officers (CO)... Even though ya'll have those badges you guys still treat me like a human...Ms. D Holmes and Mr. D. Jackson, don't ever change stay the same...

Victor and Linda Huddleston at Midnight Express, you guys are the greatest. The work is amazing!!! Hands down, ya'll the BEST EVER…

This is me:

Julian James #16692-084
F.C.I Aliceville
POBox 4000
Aliceville A1 35442

Chapter 1

My name is Sweets...

Bad Bitch! Yup, that's me. That shit ain't even in the dictionary, but know if it was my picture would be right beside it.

I was born and raised in the best state ever, where the city never sleeps and everyone minds their own damn business. New York is the place to be, but not for me.

Daddy was thirty years old when my Momma was seventeen. She was a track runner, and he was a water pump operator. Shit, that ain't keep them from makin' me, thank God! I was born September 6, 1986 at Kings County Hospital located in Brooklyn, New York. I am my mother's first and only child, but I am my father's second girl. My parents nicknamed me Sweet Pea because they said I was the prettiest little girl they'd ever seen, but hell, my real name is Corona Cocaine Cash. Yea, that shit sounds crazy, but my name was a statement that was ready to hit the world. It sounds like a damn serial killer, but hey, only time can tell, right?

My mother left when I was only three days old, so I never

knew her. My father said he came home and found me sleeping in my crib with a note attached:

Richie, I am tired of your lies, tired of taking care of your child. I know all about the other seven children you have. You have turned my life into a living hell, and I am just tired of it all, so you can get one of your other women to raise her. She don't even look like me.

Yvette

I only know what my mother looks like, and that's from pictures. Truth be told, I don't look like that bitch at all.

I'm the spitting image of my father, and for that I am very thankful. I've got his honey dip complexion with big brown eyes and shoulder length black hair. For everything else, I hate my father to the fullest. Once my mother was gone he found someone else to perform the motherly duties.

Her name was Vesta King, and she also had a child by my father. His name was King Cash, and he was six years older than me. Vesta was beautiful inside and out. She did everything she could to make my father happy, but one thing she couldn't control was whether or not he kept his dick in his pants.

Her love for him was pure and real. No matter how many kids he had, her love for him never changed. King was her only child, but she loved me like I was her own, so when she died of cancer I cried my heart out. I wanted to die with her. That didn't stop my father though. He kept having babies, and different women kept taking care the two of us. King was twelve when his mother passed, and I was seven. Even though she wasn't my real mother, she'll always be my mother in my heart.

One of those women was Carlenee Carter. She was ugly, and I hated her with a passion because when Daddy was home she would treat us like gold, but once he was gone King and I were her doormats. She would call us ugly, retarded, wicked and stupid.

She had a son of her own, but he didn't belong to Daddy. Anyone could tell, 'cause the mother lover look just like her: UGLY! His name is Damien Fuller, and he was older than us. He was seventeen, and I hated how he would look at me when I was home with him.

One night King had gone to spend the night over at his best friend Shawn's house. Daddy and Carlenee had gone out too, so it was only me and ugly ass Damien at home. I was doing my homework when he came into my room.

"You act like you all that."

"Get out of my room, Ugly!"

Before I knew it, he was on top of me ripping my pajamas off. I tried to fight back, but I was too small, and he was so strong. I just couldn't. I prayed that King would come through the door, but that never happened. What did happen next would have you crying, and I ain't about to start that shit. I couldn't even speak I was crying so hard. Not with emotion, but with hatred, feeling that my father allowed all this to happen to me.

When King came home the next day he found me in my room just sitting on my bed shaking and staring into space.

"Sweet Pea, what's wrong? Why you lookin' like that? And why you smell like that?"

I kept my face still, with no signs of anything, but my heart was telling a different story.

"Why the hell is blood on the sheets? Corona, I'm talkin' to you!"

Then tears began to fall from my eyes.

"Come on Corona. Tell your brother what happened."

I took a deep breath, and I spoke the unspeakable, "He raped me, King. He came in here and he took my pride, my joy, and my soul."

Daddy and Carlenee were in the living room watching television, and we could hear them laughing from my room. King ran out, leaving my door wide open.

"How the hell can you have this woman in here with you when her son raped my sister?" King yelled at our father.

"Boy, shut the hell up and get away from me," Richie told him. Carlenee didn't say a word. She just sat there like a dumb, ugly bitch.

Now you see why I hate my father with a passion. That day it was my brother King who bathed me, and made me soup to eat.

He nurtured me back to life. He slept on the floor by my bed at night, guarding the door at night as I slept. Our father never even came to see if I was okay. I didn't matter to him at all. I missed Vesta so much, but I was so glad that King was there to protect me.

King would walk me to and from school, and help me with my

homework. He even cooked and cleaned for me. I loved my brother very much.

Two days before King's nineteenth birthday he became extremely ill and it seemed serious enough that Daddy dropped us off at the hospital.

"King, you gotta get better! Please!"

"I'm gonna try, but if I don't, I want you to take care of yourself. Be strong; don't let anyone take advantage of you. If you have to, turn your heart cold to protect yourself, then do it."

Those were my brother's last words. Come to find out, King had had cancer, and it had already spread all the way to his brain. By the time they got to him, my brother was gone. Carlenee and her ugly ass son moved out soon after King passed, so it was just me and Daddy. We barely spoke to each other, and that was fine with me. I didn't know who my real mother was, I'd lost the only mother who had ever loved me, and I also lost my protector and brother, King. I had a father who wasn't into raising me, so I mostly raised myself. School and church became my getaway. I worked hard in school, and I graduated one year early with a full scholarship to attend Liberty University in Lynchburg, Virginia. I wanted to move away from home, far away so I could be free from the past that tried to hold me. I didn't even say goodbye to my father.

I just packed up all my clothes and left. I was damn sure going to miss New York, but New York wasn't going to miss me.

Liberty University is a Christian college, but its location was crazy! The damn name of the town had a bitch scared! Lynchburg! Well, Virginia was about to be my new fuckin' home, and I was ready.

In August of 2004, I left Brooklyn, New York behind. I took the train, and even though the ride was eight hours long, it was fun. I knew that Vesta and King were watching over me, and just thinking of that brought a smile to my face.

Adjusting to a new environment was hard, but you gotta do what you gotta do, and that's what I've always done. My roommate's name was Hannah, some shit. I don't remember her last name, but she was from Germany. I remember it tripped me out that people from all over the world were there to get an education.

"What's your name?" she asked me.

"Corona Cocaine Cash, but you can call me Sweets."

"Sweets. I like that."

"Yea, my name is Sweets."

College was fun and exciting in the beginning. My major was computer science, and I was a beast in Math, so my Math professor asked me to tutor some of the students, which I did.

In need of money, I decided to get a job off campus. Working while going to school was tough, but eventually because I'd been going to school all my life, I got bored with it, and I started failing classes.

"Girl, you need to get your education. Without education, you ain't nothin'!" I could hear King's voice loud and clear. Instead of just allowing myself to fail I decided to take a break. One year in college and that was that. I used the money that I'd saved to get my first apartment. I worked at a Kroger gas station on Timberlake Road. Shit, I loved that job! That's where my whole life started to change from that good little girl to this bad ass bitch.

Chapter 2

Virus

In June of 2005 I caught a virus like you wouldn't believe; a BAD one. I had just finished eating lunch with my co-worker, Dimples. As I strolled across the parking lot to get back to the booth, I heard someone yelling.

"I ain't never seen you before."

I ignored the voice completely and put a little more swagger into my step. On some real live shit, I've got a bomb ass shape, and standing right at 5'4", a killer body. I guessed that's what they were hollering at. When I got back to the booth I thanked Pam for holding things down while I was gone.

"Have a good evening," she told me on her way out.

"And you do the same."

Pam was an elderly white lady who worked so she could get out of the house and away from her husband. She didn't have any children, but I could tell she wanted some, 'cause she would always say how other people's kids were a blessing. I felt sorry for her 'cause she was sweeter than honey. I wondered why she really wanted to work at seventy-five years old, but she never told me and I never asked.

"Can I get twenty on pump seven and a box of Grape Dutches, please?"

"Yes, you can, but do you have an ID, sir?"

He gave me his ID and I noticed that his birthday was April 21, 1986. He had just turned 18.

"When's your birthday?" he asked me.

"What?!"

"Since you know when my birthday is, when is yours?"

Now don't get me wrong, this nigga was fine; had to be 190 solid, around 5'11", thick black hair, plus he was sharp. Light skinned men ain't even my type. I didn't really have a type back then, but hey, he was on point.

"Since I can't get your birthday, can I get your number?"

"No!"

"Why?"

"You don't have a shirt on, and you should never approach a woman when you have a hat on," I told him.

He looked at me with surprise and walked away. He got his gas, left and I kept doing my job. Shit, he was fine, but he had to have some respect at least! "Just a straight up hood nigga," I told myself, but yo, this nigga blew my mind. A few minutes later he was back wearing a shirt and no hat. All I could do was smile.

"You ain't from around here?" he asked me.

"No. I'm from Brooklyn, New York."

"My name is Traymon, but everyone calls me T."

"Okay," I said, wondering what else he wanted.

"I see your name tag says Corona."

"Yea, that's my name, but I go by Sweets," I thanked God no one was getting gas. I wanted to see where this was headed.

"I ain't tryin' to be rude, but I gotta run. Can I get your number before I go? Please?"

Call me what you want to, but I gave it to him! He had just impressed me to the utmost.

"I'm gonna call you tonight," he told me.

I got off work at eleven pm, and since I didn't have a car, my co-worker Dimples gave me a ride home."

Dimples is 5'6", white, with blue eyes, auburn hair and a gorgeous body. Her breasts stood up just right, with a small waist and a plumed ass.

"Were you born like that or you paid for it?" I asked her one day.

"Ha! What do you think?"

"I mean, damn! Your shit is perfect!"

This bitch knew her body was all that.

"I was born like this. With the help of some black dick!"

We both started laughing. Ever since that day, me and Dimples lived in a world by ourselves. Her name is Dimples Marshall, and she was born and raised right here in Lynchburg, Virginia by both of her parents. She had dropped out of college when she turned 21 'cause she figured it wasn't for her.

"So, the saying is true then?" I asked her.

"What saying?"

"School is not for everyone?" I told her.

"I guess you could say that, 'cause it sure ain't for me."

"That's exactly what I say."

Both of her parents are pastors at their own church, who want nothing but the best for her, but she wanted to be different. "Thanks for the ride home," I told her when she pulled up in front of my apartment.

"No problem! What time do you have to be at work tomorrow?"

"Seven fuckin' o' clock," I was mad just thinking about it.

"Me too, girl. Do you want me to pick you up?" she asked me.

"It's up to you, either way I'm gonna be there."

"Girl, you crazy as shit! All I want is a yes or no," she said with a laugh.

“Yes, and thank you.”

“A’ite, I’ll be here at 6:30, okay?”

“Okay! Thanks again for giving me a ride home. I’ll be waiting on you in the morning,” I told her as I got out of the car.

I lived in a two bedroom apartment all by my damn self. I mean, I wasn’t doin’ it big or nothin’, but it was mine. My apartment was pretty much empty. All I had was two TV’s and a bed. The stove and fridge came with it, and every room was carpeted except for the kitchen and the bathroom. As I did every night, I fixed something to eat, took a shower, and then I let the TV watch me sleep. At times like this I missed my brother King.

King had had long hair, and I used to braid it every day. He would never complain he would just sit there and sing.

“King, what you want to become in life?” I would ask him.

“Mane, I don’t know. What you want to be, Corona?”

“I want to be rich, live good, be happy, and just enjoy life.”

“Well, only you can make your hopes, dreams, and future come true, Corona. Only you, little sister.”

“Damn, who the hell is callin’ me this time of night?” I asked myself as I headed to the phone.

“Hello?”

“What you doin’?”

It was Traymon. I already knew his voice, from anywhere.

“Nothin’. Ready to go to bed.”

“ Why so early?”

“‘Cause it’s almost 12:30 in the morning, and I have to be back at work by seven.”

We ended up talking till three o’ clock anyway. He told me all about himself. He was the oldest child, his mom died two days before his high school graduation, and he had three brothers and a sister. Unfortunately he’d lost all four of them in a bad wreck, and he didn’t know who his father was. He didn’t have a steady place to call home either, ‘cause he was living from place to place with his friends. His life sounded all fucked up.

“Damn, that’s crazy,” Dimples said.

“I know, yo. That is crazy.”

I considered Dimples a true friend ‘cause she would listen to me while I talked her ears off. We got our schedules changed so that we could work together. We even took our lunches together.

T would come to my job every day and kick it with me, and we would talk on the phone every night about everything. Over the next month or so our friendship started looking different. I knew Traymon Davis was a virus I couldn’t get rid of.

Chapter 3

Show Me

Dimples had moved out of her parent's house to become my roommate. We already did everything else together, so why not?

I told her everything about my past and the things that had happened to me. I swear, every time I would tell her something she would cry.

"Sweets, you are so strong! I probably would have killed myself."

"Girl, only the strong survive. Yea, I used to be weak, but being weak didn't get me nowhere, so strong is all I know."

"Girl, I love you."

"I love you too, Dimples."

We made a pact to always be there for each other, no matter what. No man or woman could ever get between us.

"Let's not forget money," she said.

"Nothin', nada, will ever come between us, I told her."

One night Traymon asked if I could do his hair.

"How you know I do hair?"

"Shit girl, you black, plus you come from New York, and people from New York know how to do every fuckin' thing."

I couldn't help but laugh.

"You funny as hell," I told him.

"So you can do my hair for me?"

"You gotta come to my apartment then."

"A'ite, what's the address?"

"122 Landover Place, apartment B-11."

"See you in a minute then," he said before hanging up the phone.

Dimples had gone to her parent's house to visit. Thanks to them, our apartment was beautiful, and nowhere near as empty as it had started out. They had given us a kitchen table with matching chairs and a living room suite. They'd also bought Dimples a brand new bedroom suite. In a way I felt like I was their child also.

I was cooking crab legs when I heard the doorbell. Traymon is sexy from head to toe. He was wearing a fresh white t-shirt blue Roca Wear pants, with some white dope mans and his hair looking wild all over his head.

“Can I come in?”

I was just standing there looking at him. I was in some boy shorts and a wife-beater, with my hair pulled up in a ponytail

“Yea, come in. I’m in the kitchen cookin’.”

“Lead the way, I’m right behind you.”

I could feel his eyes on my body, and I wondered if he could feel the heat coming from me.

“Are you hungry?” I asked him.

“Only if you plannin’ on feedin’ me.”

“Are you hungry?”

“Yea.”

“You can go watch TV in the living room while I finish cooking.”

“Okay.”

I finished up and fixed our plates at the table. I was dishing the crab legs out when Dimples came through the door.

“Girl, everything you cook smells so good, it could wake the dead up!” she said as she came towards the kitchen.

“And who the hell is that?” she asked as she noticed Traymon making his way to the table.

“Girl, this is Traymon. Traymon, this is Dimples, my best friend and roommate.”

"Nice to meet you. I've heard nothin' but good things about you, Dimples."

"Same here." Dimples responded.

"You gonna eat with us?" I asked her.

"Naw, go ahead. I just ate. If you need me, I'm in my room," she said, leaving us alone at the table.

We talked a little as we ate.

"Damn, you sure can cook."

"Well thank you."

When we were finished I put the dishes away, and told him to wait on me in the living room while I cleaned up the kitchen. When I was done I went and got a comb to do his hair.

He watched TV while I freaked his braids out. Boy, he had a head full of hair! I had to work the next day, so I decided that I should give him a little design, nothing major, but nothing too simple either. Let's just say it was sweet. It was around eleven when I finished his hair. I had a very long day of work ahead of me, and was mad that I had to be there at seven.

"Can I spend the night?"

I wanted to tell him no, but I couldn't. I thought about not having a place to stay.

"Yea, but you have to sleep on the sofa, 'cause my bed is mines only."

He laughed at me before saying "Okay."

I went into the hallway closet, 'cause the air was jumping.

I walked into Dimples' room, where she was on her phone.

"Girl, he gonna spend the night."

"WHAT?"

"Yea, but he's sleepin' on the sofa."

"Okay, bitch, but you is crazy," she told me, and started laughing.

"I love you," I tell her

"I love you bunches more," she replies.

I closed her door and went to give Traymon the blanket that I had pulled from the hallway closet.

"Have a good night," I told him when I handed it over.

"You, too."

I went into my room and left my door open a little so I could hear. Was I scared? Hell naw! He was harmless. I didn't even remember my dream, but six o' clock came quick. I got up, looked in the living room, and he was still there, sleeping peacefully, like a baby without any problems. I must say, he looked damn good.

I jumped into the shower, handled my business, and was out by 6:15. I woke Dimples up so she could get ready, because we had to leave by 6:35 if we were going to make it to work on time. When Dimples went outside to warm up the car I woke Traymon.

“Look, you can sleep till you ready to get up and leave, but it’s too early to go now.”

“Okay.”

“Just close the door behind you,” I told him.

“A’ite, have a good day.”

“I hope you have a great one.” I told him, and left.

When I got into the car, Dimples had the nerve to say, “How you know he won’t steal what we have?”

“Girl, you act like we rich.”

“We ain’t rich yet, but we will be one day,” she said, and then she turned the music up. Young Jeezy had become our rapper, and listening to him on the way to work motivated us.

Traymon was on my mind all day that day, and I couldn’t wait to get off at 2:00. When we went on break we talked about him.

“Be careful, Sweets. Don’t rush into anything.”

“Dimples, thanks for just bein’ here for me.”

“That’s what friends are for.”

When we finally got off work I couldn’t wait to get home. I wondered why Traymon didn’t come see me that day.

“Girl, my damn feet hurt like hell!” Dimples complained when we got into the car.

“I can only imagine! Where they have you workin’ now?”

“Sometimes I run the register, sometimes I run the floor. I mean, it all depends on who’s working for that day, but I know this for a fact though: I am tired of working in a damn grocery store.”

“I can’t really complain, ‘cause I sit on my ass all the time, but the paycheck ain’t shit.”

“Don’t worry, things will get better.”

“Dimples, I really hope so,” I said, looking out the window.

Dimples had a really good heart, she stayed positive, but you could tell that deep down inside of her she was a monster.

As I turned my key in the door we could hear music playing.

“Sweets, did you leave the TV on?”

I heard Dimples talking, but I couldn’t answer, ‘cause what I saw when I opened the door had me stuck. On top of the table there was a vase with some red flowers in it.

“Roses?” big mouth Dimples had to say.

I went straight to my room ‘cause that’s where the music was coming from. Let’s just say I wasn’t daydreaming. Traymon was posted up in my bed watching music videos.

“What is wrong with him? Girl, you can’t tell me you didn’t give him some last night.” Dimples’ crazy ass had to say before she went into her room. All I could do was just look at him.

He never once took his face from the TV.

"What the hell happened between last night and today?" I asked him. He didn't answer, so I took off my shoes and I went to put them in the closet, but when I opened the door my heart stopped. This nigga done moved all his clothes, shoes, hats and jackets into my damn closet! Fuck the closet, he done moved into my apartment.

"I ain't leaving. You're my girl now, and I'm living with you."

All I could do was look at him. My mouth didn't work, but my mind was racing, like, "Damn, who is this nigga?"

Before I could say anything, he spoke again.

"I'm gonna make you my wife."

I was speechless.

How was I supposed to live with this nigga, not knowing if he was mentally challenged or what? I guess you could say he showed me that he was truly a virus.

Welcome

Traymom had a couple of friends who I thought were completely crazy. Terry and Tori always kept me laughing.

Terry was in love with Dimples, but since he wasn't black, she damn sure didn't give him any play.

"Traymon, look, living here, you're gonna have to respect both Dimples and myself."

"I do respect you."

"Yeah, you do, but when we ain't here, I don't want your friends over here. And, no smoking either, 'cause I know damn well you smoke weed. Do all that shit somewhere else."

"I can do that," he said.

"Oh, and one more thing..."

"What's that?"

"We are not having sex."

"I'll wait as long as you want, baby."

Traymon was working at the pipe company with his grandfather back then. Grandpa A, as Traymon called him was a deacon, and he was so black that he looked damn near purple, but he was an awesome man. Living with Traymon and Dimples was both good and bad because they would bump heads every now and then. Traymon would work from 6am-6pm, with Thursdays and Fridays as his days off. The paycheck was a beautiful thing, and everything went a little further having three people splitting up the bills. I was damn sure saving up for a rainy day!

I remember one night Traymon wanted to fuck so bad that he held my ass and beat his dick off.

"Damn! We been together for almost five months, and you can't give a nigga none?" he asked me one night when we were in bed.

I looked at him and told him, "I am just not ready."

He didn't say anything, or get up. He just held me and then we went to sleep.

"Dimples, you think he's gonna fuck someone else?"

Traymon was at work, so it was just me and her at home.

"Sweets, what I am about to tell you is nothin' but the truth."

"Go ahead, I'm listening."

"What you don't do, another bitch will. He's got needs, too. He probably used to fuck every day, and now he ain't gettin' none at all, so yea, he's gonna do what he's gotta do."

"Meaning?" I asked.

"Not saying he's cheating, but not having sex when he's used to it will get old, and then you might not have him at all."

"I work, I cook, I clean."

"Yea, you do all that, but you not givin' him any."

"He said he'll wait on me."

"That's good, but Sweets, it will get old."

Dimples had left me thinking hard. I just wanted to make sure I was ready.

The remaining members of Traymon's family are crazy, crazy in a good way, and a bad way. They all loved me, and they loved the way that I talked with my New York accent. Since his mother wasn't alive, he called his second cousin, an older woman, 'mother'.

Bella was a good woman. When Traymon's mom died, she had just had newborn twins, and Bella is the one who raised them. She kept a door open for Traymon, but he loved everywhere else. Bella also had two kids of her own, but they were grown. The oldest of her children was off the chain, and doing time in prison for shooting her own damn brother in public. With Virginia being a common wealth state, they pressed charges on her and sent her to lock up for two years. The brother she shot, he was on his way to prison for shooting his uncle. I'm thinking to myself, "Damn! This family is fuckin' crazy for real! Shootin' up their own people and shit."

But I can either love them or hate them, and I chose to love them ‘cause they had a crazy way of showing their love. I knew soon, and very soon, they would consider me family. That’s all I needed, ‘cause I was falling in love with Traymon. We used to visit his mom’s gravesite and take her flowers. We did crazy things and we had fun with each other, but shit... all that was about to change...

We finally ended up having sex, and boy oh boy, was it whack! YES! Straight up whack! He came in one minute. I never thought that would happen to me, but it did.

All I could do is lay there in pain, and the whole time I was laughing in my head, my thoughts were so loud.

“Damn! Did you just bust in a minute?” I asked him when he finished. He was so embarrassed, but I had to know.

“Am I your first?” I asked after I had cleaned myself up.

“Naw, but I know I’m your first.”

“How you figure?”

“There’s blood on the sheets.”

Seeing the blood brought back memories of a different time and a different place, and just like before tears started rolling down my face.

“Baby, what’s wrong?” he asked as he reached for me.

“Nothing,” I lied, “I just want to go to sleep.”

He helped me into the bed, wiped my tears, and held me. He wrapped his legs around mine and started rocking me to sleep.

I guess he thought I was asleep, ‘cause after a while I heard him say “I love you.” I didn’t respond, but I thought “Welcome to a heart of pain, Traymon.” This is hard for me. I gotta let go of my past. I gotta give him a chance to love me like I’m supposed to be loved. I have to leave my old life behind. One day I’ll tell him everything. One day.

Jamaica

Chapter 5

Really?!

The next time we had sex, I can say that nigga put a show on! He won't no King Kong, but he was a good size seven. Dimples would tell me what to do. She would let me watch porn and take notes. Yea, that bitch is a super freak!

"You gotta let him fuck you in the ass, too."

"Bitch, you done lost your motherfuckin' mind! That's an exit, not an entrance!"

She shrugged her shoulders at me and rolled her eyes.

"What you don't do, the next bitch will. I'm just sayin'."

"Well, I guess I ain't doin' it, so he can hit the door!"

She busted out laughing at me, and I felt I had to ask, "Do you do it in the ass?"

She turned around to display the seat of her jeans, and said, "Why you think my ass so fat and plump?"

“Ugh, you a nasty bitch.”

“Call me what you wanna, but you can’t call me horny.”

I couldn’t help but laugh at her. That white bitch was plum crazy.

Traymon had quit his job, but still somehow stayed with money in his pockets. I kept working, ‘cause I loved my job, and’cause King had told me to never depend on anyone, especially a man, ‘cause then he would feel like he owned me.

I never asked him any questions, but I was damn sure curious. His phone would ring at 3, 4, 5 o’ clock in the morning. I mean, the shit NEVER stopped ringing.

“Who’s callin’ you like that?”

“My cousin, Yacc.”

Yacc was wild and loose in the streets. Anyone could tell; the way he carried himself was out of this world.

I trusted Traymon. If you don’t have any trust in a relationship, then you don’t have anything at all, so I kept his word close to my heart, but you know when you got that feeling that something ain’t right? Well, I had that feeling.

“Dimples, I think he’s cheating on me.”

“Why would you say that?” she asked me while I laid up in her bed.

“I don’t know. I just got that feeling.”

“Well, whatever you find out and need help with, know that I got your back all the way."

One night while we were sleeping, I had a dream that he was cheating on me. I woke up out of my dream, and went straight for his phone. Once I had the phone, I went into Dimples' room.

"Bitch, wake up!"

"What time is it?" she asked, still mostly asleep.

"3:45 in the morning. Get the fuck up, already!"

She sat up in the bed.

"What's wrong?"

I showed her the phone, and she read the screen out loud.

"Thirty missed calls, five new texts messages, and voice mail is full. What the fuck he got goin on?" she asked me.

"Bitch, I don't know."

There were no outgoing messages, but there were 20 old messages. Sounds crazy, right? No number had a name attached to it, so I didn't know who was who. I went straight the fuck to the text messages. One number kept calling back to back, and then they'd text. One text said "call me now. I got all the money."

Me and Dimples looked at each other.

Then another text said: "Are you comin?"

But the ones that blew my mind were: "So since you home

with your bitch now you can't respond to me"

and: "Fuck you don't call or text me no more"

I wasn't worried about Traymon, he was fast asleep.

"Fuck that, call the number," Dimples said.

I called the number from his phone, but no one answered. "Bitches like to play games, Sweets. Just wait a minute and then call back."

So that's what I did. I waited for a minute or so, and then I resent the number.

"Hello?" A bitch answered the phone.

"Who is this?"

"Ask your man, don't ask me," then she hung up.

Tears ran down my face, and Dimples wrapped her arms around me to hold me. Thank God she was there.

"I feel played. He betrayed me," I said between sobs.

"Girl, you been through worse, you can get through this too."

"I m not going to work in the morning, but I know you are, so go back to sleep," I told her.

What she said next had me bawling.

"Sweets, I'm your friend, your best friend. You don't go to work, I ain't goin' either. You stay up, I'm up with you. Best friends help each other. It's what we do."

“Well, help me kill this nigga then,” I told her, and as soon as the words left my mouth my mind went wild. I went into the kitchen and got a butcher knife. I grabbed a pair of yellow latex gloves out from under the sink and put them on. Dimples got the dish rag of the counter and poured bleach on it.

He never heard us coming. I walked directly to his side of the bed, and stabbed him right in the heart.

“Push the cloth in his mouth,” I told Dimples. I used the knife to slit his throat, and I watched as his life’s blood ran out of the hole that I’d opened in him to soak into the sheets.

“Bitch, did you just ask me to help you kill him?” Dimples asked me, bringing me back down to reality.

“Yea, I have it all planned out in my head,” which was true. I did.

“Think Sweets! Use your head before you act it all out.”

I left Dimples’ room and went back to my own. After I put his phone back where I’d gotten it from, I crawled back into bed beside him like nothing had happened. Like my whole life hadn’t just changed with a phone call.

“I love you,” I told him as he slept, which I truly did.

For the rest of the night I couldn’t sleep because I couldn’t stop thinking, couldn’t stop questioning myself. Had I done something wrong? Could I have prevented this from happening? What the hell did I do to this nigga to make him cheat on me? But God only knew, and I guess he wasn’t in a speaking mood that night. Eventually I fell asleep despite my thoughts and questions.

When I woke up it was around eight in the morning, T was already up. It was cold as hell outside. He was in the living room on the X-Box and Dimples was still in bed. I got up and got straight to the point.

“Please don’t lie to me, T. Just tell me the truth.”

“What are you talkin’ about?”

“I went through your phone, and some girl texted you, so I called her. She said, “Ask your man.” I’m not even mad, ‘cause it takes two people to commit a sexual crime.”

“Look, I’ve always kept it real with you, so I ain’t even about to start lyin’. Me and my cousin J been in the trap... He asked me if he could use my phone so he could call this shawty.”

“I’m all ears.” I told him. Men nowadays seem to be pathological liars, but hey, I couldn’t prove him wrong. So I had to choose to either believe him or not.

“And what the fuck is a trap?” I had to know.

“A place where you sling work.”

I was completely lost, so I looked at Dimples, but from the way her face was looking she was no better off. When T got up and went to the kitchen we both followed him. He went into a drawer next to the stove, pulled out a zip lock bag, handed it to me and walked away. The shit inside it looked like butter. A solid chunk of butter.

“What the fuck is this?” Dimples asked him.

“That’s fifty-six grams of crack, otherwise known as work.

The trap is a house that has crackheads and drug dealers, so I be slingin' work all day at the trap."

That's how I really and truly began to be introduced to the street life.

Chapter 6

New Mission

“Look, Sweets, I don’t want ya’ll sellin’ drugs,” Traymon said, referring to me and Dimples.

“Well, I’m tired of working. I’m tired of wearing the same clothes and shoes. I wanna wear shit I can’t even spell or pronounce,” Dimples said.

“Me too! I wanna be happy. I wanna be rich, you know, live like Jay-Z and Beyonce,” I said, looking Traymon dead in his eyes.

“Don’t get me wrong, selling drugs can get you killed or in jail. The real money is robbing the niggas who hustle their asses off,” he said.

“So where do we come in at in this?” Dimples asked.

“Since ya’ll new to this, no one knows ya’ll, so settin’ niggas up won’t be a problem. I’ll show ya’ll who to talk to. Ya’ll get close to them, find out everything ya’ll can, then me and my homeboy Terry will do the rest of the work.”

“How much do we get paid?” Dimples asked.

“Say we hit a lick,” he began, but I had to cut him off.

“What’s a lick?” I asked.

“A lick is the same as sayin’ you gonna rob somebody, but you cut it short and say ‘I got a lick to do’.”

Me and Dimples just looked at each other and shook our heads. Back then we didn’t know nothin’.

“Ski means you wearin’ a mask to cover your face. Burner means gun. A bench is a scale, white is cocaine, hard is crack, boy is heroin and poppers is pills. There’s a lot that you’ll know, just give it some time.” Traymon schooled us on almost everything, especially how to get and keep a nigga on track.

“Okay, so what do we get?” I had to ask him again.

“Okay, say we hit a lick for forty stacks.”

“Stacks mean thousands, right?” I wondered if he was tired of me cutting him off. Too bad if he was.

“Yeah, it does. So, $40,000 divided by four means we each get 10 stack a piece.”

“Free money! Hell yeah, I am down!” Dimples spoke up first.

“Count me in,” I said.

Since that day, we didn’t show our face back at the Kroger where we worked. The money we made was beautiful. The lifestyle became addictive and crazy. I loved it, and I just couldn’t give it up, but with money comes problems, and that’s when they started for us.

After going strong for two years only one person was in jail, and everyone was still breathing. Terry was the only one of us who went to jail, and that wasn't even for hustling. He caught a DUI that cost him a year, so we took turns sending him money. We couldn't leave a man when he was down, so we did what we could to keep him sane and comfortable.

Chapter 7

Are You Serious?

"Baby, I'm 'bout to take a shower," Traymon said to me.

As soon as he closed the bathroom door his phone went off.

I waited to see if he was coming back out to get it, but he never did, and me being myself, I got it for him.

TEXT MESSAGE FROM REGINA I pressed open to read the message: "I can't wait to kick it with you again, Boo. I really miss you, Traymon."

My whole body went from cold to hot. I kicked the bathroom door wide open. Hell yeah. That shit really scared his ass.

He should be scared. REAL fuckin' scared.

"What the fuck is you doin' you dirty dawg motherfucker?"

"What the hell wrong with you?" he asked. He ain't even have his clothes on yet.

I swung on his ass, but he grabbed my hand and pushed me out the bathroom.

“How you gonna cheat on me? What the fuck I ever do to you?”

I headed back to the bedroom to find his phone, and when I got my hands on it I threw it at him.

“If you go lookin’ for shit, you’re gonna find what you’re lookin’ for!” he had the nerve to yell at me.

“Get your shit and get the fuck out.”

As soon as I said that he turned around and punched me dead in my right eye.

“UGH!” I started screaming. Dimples flew out of her room and into mine with her gun in her hand.

“Yo! You heard what the fuck she said! Get your shit and get the fuck out!”

“Dimples, I can’t see!” I cried to her.

When I moved my hands from my face and realized there was blood everywhere, I panicked inside. I pushed my hands back to my eye.

“You got one minute!” I heard Dimples telling him.

“Bitch, you done lost your mind!”

“I may have lost my mind, but you gonna lose your brains.”

I guess he grabbed his phone and left. I couldn’t really tell one way or another since I couldn’t see too well. All I knew was

Dimples' gun was bigger than his pride, 'cause he was most definitely gone.

"We goin' to the emergency room."

"Dimples, I don't care what we do; I just wanna keep my eye!"

She got me to the emergency room in record time. The lady at the front desk asked me what was wrong, and when I removed the cloth I was holding against my eye, she asked, "How did that happen, and when?"

"We were playin' football, and I caught it with my face."

Then she wanted to ask me fifty questions. All I wanted to do was get my damn eye fixed and leave. They took me to check my blood pressure and pulse. Again with the questions!

"Are you pregnant?"

"No."

"When was your last period?" Shit. I couldn't remember.

"I don't know." I started crying; I couldn't keep the tears from falling anymore. I felt Dimples squeeze my arm.

"Sweets, get it together," she said.

I was moved to a room and told to lie on the bed as they hooked me up to some machine. I hated hospitals because they reminded me of losing King, but my eye needed serious help. Eventually a doctor came in and told us that I needed to have an x-ray, but before I could do that I needed to have a pregnancy test done.

A nurse came in to run a catheter and get a urine sample. Then I was shipped to the x-ray room where I was told that part of my eye socket was broken and that several blood vessels had burst.

"Am I going to lose my eye?" I asked the nurse, but she didn't bother to answer me. I couldn't even cry anymore. Come to find out, I had to have surgery to remove the blood from around my pupil, which is why I couldn't see.

"That nigga's lucky," I heard Dimples say.

We were moved back to the room that we'd been in before the x-ray while the operating room was prepared.

"Are you scared?" Dimples asked me.

"Naw, bitch, what the fuck you think?"

She started laughing at me, and I felt some of the tension leave my body. That's one reason why I loved her so much. She knew how to hold me up when I was down.

"Miss Cash, you will be put to sleep for this procedure," the doctor said when he came back in.

"Sir, I don't care what you do, just make sure I can see again." I heard Dimples laughing, and almost against my will I felt the corner of my mouth tilt upwards in a half-ass smile.

"Love you, Sweets. I'll be right here waiting on you."

I don't remember shit else.

"Bitch, you need to wake up is what you need to do!"

I tried opening up my eyes, but only one of them worked.

My right eye had a patch on it, and I wondered for a second if I looked like a pirate. Must be that sleepy juice making me stupid. Damn drugs.

"My fuckin' head hurts, yo."

Just then the doctor walked in.

"Miss Cash, how are you feeling?"

"Okay, I guess."

"When you remove the patch to clean the area, make sure that it is done in the dark. More light will damage your pupil.

No use of cell phones, drink plenty of water and take Tylenol or aspirin."

"Why can't I get no Percocet?"

"Because you're at least three weeks pregnant."

"Um... What did you say?"

"What you say?!" Dimples and I asked both questions at the same time.

"Congrats, you're three weeks pregnant. Take care of yourself'."

A nurse came in to take over the discharge and the doctor left the room. "After you sign the release form you're free to go."

Hell yeah, I was ready to go home. Ready to take a shower, and go to sleep. Real sleep, not that drug induced darkness. Feeling shocked, I turned to Dimples.

“This shit can’t be serious?” I asked her.

“Girl, yes it is serious.”

Chapter 8

Shall we?

I took a shower in the dark while Dimples hung sheets over the windows in my room.

"Girl, he came and got all his shit," Dimples said to me. "Good. I'm glad he did."

"You gonna take him back?"

I wanted to punch Dimples in her damn mouth for asking me something so stupid.

"No."

Dimples tried to cook us dinner. The chicken wings were burnt, but I ate them anyway. I loved Traymon, but I couldn't use love as an excuse to be with him. Not only was he cheating on me, but he had busted my eye up. Dimples slept in my bed with me that night.

"Do me a favor, Dimples?"

"What's that?" she asked, sounding puzzled.

"Text him, and say that every dog has its day and his is coming. And by the way, I'm three weeks pregnant."

She did that, and he never texted back. He never came, or called to apologize. It was like I never mattered at all.

It took four months for my eye to fully heal, and my belly to start to show. I had even seen Traymon a couple of times at the mall with a girl. Not one time did I act a fool. I'm a lady. I carry myself as a lady, so why would I act any different? Dimples was doing a great job of keeping my mind off of him.

Thank God we had saved our money, 'cause it came in handy.

"Today is the day I'm gonna be a father!" Dimples shouted.

"What you say, crazy bitch?"

"Quit playin'. Sweets! You know I'm this baby's daddy!"

I couldn't help but laugh at her. That day I gave birth to a little girl who weighed in at 7 lbs 10 oz, and was 21 inches long.

"She's so beautiful," I heard Dimples say.

Beautiful wasn't the word. She had Traymon's complexion, his eyes, lips, and even the dip in his chin, but she had my nose and hair.

"What are we gonna call you?" Dimples asked while looking at the new bundle of joy, and that's when it hit me—the perfect name, for my perfect child.

"We gonna name her Ex'Quisite."

"Huh, Sweets?"

“Ex’Quisite Queen Cash!” and my baby smiled when I said her name.

“When do I sign the birth certificate?”

“What you say, Dimples?”

“I’m the father. They got to have my signature on the birth certificate. Duh! So when do I sign it?” She had the nerve to say. We all smiled at that. Even Ex’Quisite.

“Whatever, girl!”

Three days later, I was ready to go home, and so was Dimples.

She had been taking showers in my room, and I know she missed the tub. After I signed the last page of my release paper work, I looked at Ex’Quisite’s little face and asked her, “Are you ready?”

Looking at her, I couldn’t help but wonder, how the fuck could my mother have left me the way she did? And why? Just fucking why?

“Bitch, let’s go.” Thank God Dimples had interrupted my thoughts. Strapped into a pink car seat, Ex’Quisite looked like she was ready to roll.

Chapter 9

New Members

A whole nine months had passed, and I still hadn't heard from Traymon, so I called his mother to let her know that I'd had the baby. She was super excited, and couldn't wait to see her. We talked for a few minutes, and I ensured that she would see the baby soon.

Dimples and I took turns taking care of Ex'Quisite. I was glad to have a friend like her to help me.

"How about I give Ex'Quisite a nickname?" Dimples asked me one day.

"Shit, go ahead, since you the daddy and all." We both started laughing.

"How about Beauty?"

"Beauty it is then. Ain't no need to second guess the father!"

Beauty had a doctor's appointment, and Dimples, being the best daddy ever, drove us to and from.

"She's perfect," the nurse told me.

Beauty ate, slept, smiled, shit and pissed with no worries in the world, and I was cool with that.

"Dimples, I just want to say thank you. Thank you ain't even enough."

"Girl, go ahead with that bullshit!" she responded.

"Naw, for real though! I owe you my life, plus more."

She started crying, and her tears ran from her eyes like a runaway river.

On the way home we stopped at Hardees's to get something to eat. As soon as we pulled into the parking lot we saw a light green magnum on 22's, and we could see a nigga beating on someone around the side of the car. From afar it looked like it was another nigga he had down on the ground, but when we got closer we could see that it was a female.

I'm not down with that shit, and I won't never be down with it. "You got that on you?" I asked Dimples.

"Yea, glovebox." she answered.

I was out of the car in 2.5 seconds, straight hopped the fuck out. The girl was on the ground in the fetal position, no screams or tears, just taking a nigga's beat down. I couldn't even see her face. That nigga was so busy he didn't notice me until I shot him dead in his ass. Suddenly he was bleeding, and I watched him fall to the ground. I ran over to the girl while he was distracted by the bullet in his ass, and with my gun still in one hand, I helped her up off the ground with the other.

Dimples helped me get her into the backseat. Honestly, I wanted to go back and put another bullet in his ass. Or head, either way. A man beating on a woman ain't no damn good and don't deserve no better. We got in the car and left.

Thank God we were only a minute away from home. Dimples got Beauty out of the car, and I helped the young lady that I had picked up off of the ground. She'd been beaten bloody and both of her eyes were black and swollen. She looked like a raccoon, and it seemed like her clothes were barely hanging on her.

"Take your time and walk," I told her as I supported her and helped her to the door.

When we got inside the apartment, Dimples went to put Beauty to sleep while I started cleaning the girl up. I added a little bleach to the water, but she took the pain like a real G. I noticed that her head was still bleeding.

"Damn, what the hell?" I said looking up at Dimples when she came back after putting Beauty down. "I should've killed his ass."

"Look, we don't even know you, but girl, you can stay with us as long as you need." She hadn't said a word since we picked her up, or speak right then either. She just started crying. "Don't cry... You gotta stay strong." I said, hugging her.

Next thing I knew, Dimples was hugging us both.

Envy Simone Moss is her name, but she'd rather go by Black, and yes, Black fits her perfect. She's not an ugly too dark black, but she's that pretty dark chocolate black, so I understand where her alias came from. She was 22 years old the day we found her in that parking lot, and she had no children. She told us that her father had died in a club when she was only four years old and that her mother had raised her, but not in a loving way. She said her mother hated the ground that she walked on and never gave her a reason why. Her mom got herself hooked on drugs when Black was only twelve years old, so she basically raised herself. She said she used to run away from home when social services would show up. One day her little brother wasn't fast enough, and they took him away. She never saw him again.

Her fucking piece of shit mom would send drug dealers into her room when she was sleeping so that they could have their way with her to pay for her drug habit. Not knowing what to do, Black had left home at sixteen and never looked back. Her first boyfriend was a pimp who beat her and treated her like shit.

One night while he was asleep she took all of his money, and left Roanoke, Virginia and moved to Lynchburg. Living at the Salvation Army wasn't for her, and she got a job working at McDonald's as she struggled to get on her feet.

For six months she did everything, and learned how to do the things that she didn't already know how to do. She used the money that she saved to get a two bedroom apartment. A few days before Christmas her boss called her into his office.

"Envy, you work so hard. You're always on time, perfect attendance, and the register is always correct when you work. Since I am leaving this branch, someone will have to replace me. I gave your name to Regional, and they said okay!"

With that, Black became the new manager, not only of her job, but of her life. Things were finally looking up for her.

On Christmas day she met Terrence Morris, aka Spring. He seemed so perfect to her, and they started a friendship that eventually evolved into a relationship. For a whole year things seemed to be superb. Good job, good man, good life. But things are rarely what they appear to be.

Terrence Morris, aka Spring, was a very well known drug dealer in the state of Virginia, and everyone feared him 'cause he was about his business. He changed his name to Cake, claiming he was about that bread. He had three children by three different women, and the youngest child's mother was completely cuckoo. Her head doesn't even attach to her body.

Two years into her relationship with him he started putting his hands on her. Black started missing work, and eventually they fired her. Yup. Fired the damn boss. Ain't that some shit? Crazy. She stayed with him, thinking it was love, but the pain she felt began to destroy that love. She stood 5'7" and was skinny as a stick, with short hair like Kelly Rowland. She had no confidence in herself, and ended up staying with that man for another two years. She continued to tell the story of her life leading up to the parking lot where we had found her.

"I went to the store to do a little grocery shopping, 'cause his last baby ma was supposed to be dropping their son off. I came back too soon. I found Cake ramming his dick into her from the back in my living room, on my damn sofa! That was the last straw there for me."

"What did you do?" Dimples asked.

"I stood there and watched until he bust his nut, and then he turned around and saw me. That bitch went and got the kid from the room, and walked right passed me smiling."

“And?” I asked her.

“I just looked at that ho and smiled back. I know I was blessed to see that for myself.”

“Then what happened?” This girl’s story was crazy.

“Then he said we should go get something to eat. By the time we got to Hardees’s I finally had the nerve to say something.”

“What did you say?” I couldn’t stop asking this girl questions.

“I told him it was over, and he went cuckoo times cuckoo.

Thank goodness ya’ll saved me.”

“I wanted to kill him. I should’ve just kept pulling the trigger, but don’t worry, every single dog has it’s day coming. Welcome! You’re the new member of our family.”

And that’s how Black, Dimples, Beauty and myself all became one.

Chapter 10

Flash Back

Mane, it was crazy how we all met, everything that happens is always a blessing, even if it doesn't seem like it at first.

We all ended up moving into a three bedroom house on Tate Street, 'cause Black never went back to Cake, and Dimples was still single even though she had sex partners.

We used to struggle really hard, so we all three got jobs. Dimples worked' at an Applebee's as a hostess, Black became a stripper doing private parties, and I got a chair at a salon called Layers. Traymon's mother would babysit Beauty for me while I worked, and if she was busy then Dimples and Black would take turns playing Daddy.

Sometimes when I used to pick Beauty up from Bella's house Traymon would be there playing with her, and he would ask if he could keep her for the night. It used to hurt me to know that he'd walked out on us when we'd needed him the most, but instead of holding his child against him, I showed him the real woman side of me. I'd always tell him he could keep her when he asked. He never came to my house, and I never went to his.

We always used Bella's house as neutral territory to pick up or drop off Beauty.

Beauty loved her daddy to the fullest. Da-da was her first word, and as she started getting older she couldn't do no wrong in anyone's eyes. In every way Beauty was safe and loved, and that's all I wanted for her.

Traymon has moved on with Regina, the one he had cheated on me with. I haven't had sex since the last time I was with him and that's been almost three years now. I'm talking to someone now, but he's in jail and will be for another two years.

Tired of Bein' Broke

Beauty was spending the weekend with her father and soon- to-be stepmother.

"Mane, I am so fucking tired of working," Dimples said as we watched TV one night.

"Shit, I'm tired of shaking my ass," Black replied.

"Why the fuck can't we start getting money like we used to, Sweets? Why we can't get back on the hustle?" Dimples asked as she looked at me like I had the answers to life. We had already told Black about how we used to get down before Beauty was born. Traymon had trained us well, but I had quit after having Beauty, and I didn't think that Dimples could handle it on her own.

"What you sayin, girl?" I asked her.

"Shit! Ain't it obvious? We struggling like a motherfucker! I'm not sayin' we deep down, but damn, we broke, bitch!"

"Even if we go back to our old ways, we still gotta keep our jobs."

Don't get me wrong, I loved working at the hair salon. Doing hair has always been a passion of mine, but having some more money and planning for Beauty's future was bigger than a passion.

"Shit, that's cool with us," Dimples said while Black nodded her head in agreement.

"A lotta shit gotta change though," I told them.

"C'mon and lead the way," Black said.

"Okay... we can't live together. We gotta split up. No one should know where we live. Not even your mama! We must be in control of everything that we do. We keep our business to ourselves, stay low, and continue doing what we started doing best."

And just that quick, we was right back to making mad money, 'cause we was damn sure tired of bein' broke.

In Training

If you see one of us out, please trust and believe the other two ain't far behind. Not during the week, since we all have different jobs, but come Friday, Saturday, and Sunday we're like bread, peanut butter and jelly, 'cause we're on the same hustle together. This is what we do.

Club 2 is our destination tonight. Doctors, lawyers, teachers, dope boys, doesn't matter. You name an occupation; they there too... just like us.

I'm ready to get off work, and I've only got thirty minutes left, so I take a bathroom break to call my bitches and let them know the plan. Dimples must be in a meeting, 'cause she doesn't answer, so I hit Black up. No matter what's goin' on I know she's gonna answer her phone.

"Yo, what you doin'?" I ask her when she picks up.

"Mane, you already know."

"Ugh. You a crazy bitch." That bitch is shakin' her ass while she's on the phone with me.

“Yeah, you already know I know!” I laughed,

“You still good for tonight, Black?”

“Hell yeah, and I can’t wait either. Dimples called me earlier on her break, and said she isn’t getting off till six, but she said that she had everything with her.”

“A’ite, so I’ll see ya’ll later.”

“You got a babysitter?” she asks. For a bitch to be stripping she sure is talking a whole hell of a lot.

“Yeah, her daddy picked her up from school already, talkin’ “bout how they goin’ out of town this weekend.”

“Shake that ass!” I hear a male voice holler in the background. “Bitch, I’ll let you know everything later! Bye!”

I can’t help but laugh, ‘cause I know she’s been steady shaking her ass this whole time. I will say one thing though, the girl can dance.

I love my bitches, will ride and die for them no matter if they are right or wrong, and that’s just the way it is. There ain’t no changing that. The love we’ve got for each other is unexplainable. Ain’t no nigga or bitch in existence who can come between us.

I clean up my station and tell my co-workers to have a beautiful weekend. The clock says it’s time for me to go. I hit the back door, and head to the black 2013 Impala that I’m leasing at the moment. I only live about ten minutes away, so I jump on the highway, bumping TM:103, ‘cause that nigga Jeezy ain’t nothin’ but the TRUTH!

I check the mail box, but there's no mail.

"Really," I say to myself. I'm surprised there isn't a bill in there. Beauty's with her dad, so I have the house to myself.

I lay my Gucci pocketbook down on the computer stand, put my phone on the charger and check my caller ID; no new calls.

It's almost 4:00pm, so I know "my nigga" behind bars will be ringing soon. I pick up the cordless and head into my bedroom to change my clothes, so I can get started on cleaning this house.

I put on some boy shorts and a wife beater before I start to straighten my room up. I know Beauty's room's off the meat rack; clothes, toys and snack wrappers everywhere. I prepare myself for the tornado that I am about to see by putting on some music. As always it's a whirlwind in her room. Once I finish with her room, I head straight to the kitchen to start cooking dinner, 'cause neither Dimples nor Black can cook, even though they both stay hungry. Then again, maybe that's why they're always ready to eat, 'cause they can't cook for shit.

I take some chicken wings out of the freezer, and put them in the sink in some warm water to thaw out. Then I grab my phone to text both my bitches to let them know that I'm home and I'm cleaning. That way if they call or text me and don't get an answer they know to call the house phone. They know nine times out of ten if I'm cleaning the stereo is on.

It's 3:59, and my house phone is ringing. The caller ID confirms that it's the Department of Corrections. I answer the phone as I head back to the living room.

“You have a collect call from,” The operator paused and a recording of Jay’s voice came on the line saying, “Your baby.” Before the operator continued it’s own recording…”... an inmate at Dillwyn Correctional Facility. Press zero to accept the call. Press nine to hear the rate.”

I press zero.

“Hey, baby.”

“You miss Daddy?” He asks her.

“You know I do, baby. How is your day so far?

“Same shit, different day.”

Me and Jay been “kickin’ it” since my daughter was almost two. He’s got one more year to do, and I been riding faithfully with him all the way. He wants me to marry him, but I’m not quite sure yet. I’m gonna wait to see how this works out before I change my last name.

I clean the living room and the bathroom while I talk, and it doesn’t seem like it takes very long for his 15 minutes to run out, but I know he’ll call me right back. I enjoy hearing stories from inside jail. Him and his homeboy Bunny are getting paid behind bars. They know how to hustle their asses off.

“Babe, you gonna get a surprise from me tonight.”

“What is it, boo?”

Yeah, he wants to know what it is, but I won’t tell him. Even though “my man” is behind bars I still make him feel special.

“If I tell you then it won’t be a surprise anymore.”

"Boo, when I come home I'm gonna take you to the moon and back!" he declared.

"I'll be waiting on you."

"Corona, I love you so much, girl! You don't even have an idea of how much I truly love and appreciate you, but I've got a lifetime to show you."

He's so sweet all I can do is smile. Time flies by when you're having fun. We were lucky to get our I love you's in before the system cut us off.

Now that the house is clean, I turn up my Trey Songz mix tape and head back to the kitchen, but before I start cooking, I call my sperm donor to talk to my daughter.

"Yo, nigga," I say to him when he answers the phone.

"What's good, yo?"

"Shit, chillin'. Where's Beauty at?"

"Ex'Quisite! Your mom on the phone!" I can hear her in the background, probably talking shit. That's my girl. I smile at the sound of her voice, even though she's not in my ear yet.

"Hey, baby! I miss you," I tell her when she gets the phone.

"Ma, I miss you too, but I'm playin' with my toys."

"You havin' fun?"

"Yea! I love you this much, Ma! Bye!" Just like that, she's gone. Damn. I remember when she couldn't even talk or walk.

Now my baby's rappin' and flyin'. Traymon gets back on the phone, but I ain't tryin' to talk to him, so I just tell him my friend is beeping in and I've got to go. He keeps talking anyway, so I hang up on him. It ain't my fault the nigga's deaf. Our relationship won't go beyond our daughter.

If it ain't about her, then we ain't got shit to say, and nothin' in common.

"Fuck!"

It's almost five! The time is moving fast, which means that I need to move fast too. I season up the wings. I guess curry wings with white rice will have to do. Them bitches don't ever complain. They go crazy over my cooking. Come to think of it, I should open up my own damn beauty salon and a restaurant.

I am so lost in my thoughts and daydreams that I don't even hear Black come in, and she scares the fuck out of me. "Sexy and you know it," she says to me.

"I try, you know!" I shake my ass a little and we both start to laugh.

"Damn, that chicken smells good! I need to learn to cook, 'cause one day I'm gonna cook for my husband," her crazy ass has the nerve to say, knowing good and damn well she can burn boiling water! I just look at her and burst out laughing again.

I damn sure don't see her getting married anytime soon. The only dick she claims is hitting that at the moment is her dildo, "Black Kong".

"So, deadbeat got my niece, huh?"

"Yeah! Him, Beauty, and his girlfriend are goin* out of town for the weekend. I think he said North Carolina, some shit like that."

"Really?"

"I guess. As long as Beauty's good and well taken care of, fuck the rest."

"I still can't believe that nigga traded you in for that bitch." "It's all good. I damn sure ain't losin' no sleep or weight over his bitch ass." Every time I get to talking about that shit I get mad. Black must have noticed, 'cause she changes the subject fast.

"What's Jay doin' besides time?"

"He good, ready to come home and beat this pussy up," I told her as I grabbed my crotch. She just shook her head at me.

"For real though, he's a'ite. He got his G.E.D., so I'm proud of him. He keeps talkin' about us gettin' married, and I just agree with him, 'cause I don't want to hurt his feelings or make his time any harder, but on some real shit, Black, I ain't goin' there anytime soon. Then he gets to talkin' crazy about me havin' another baby. Fuck that!"

"You know what to do for that though, right?"

"Damn right! Birth control!"

Our conversation is practically drowned out. We can hear the system beating from all the way down the street. I turn the stove down, and follow Black to the front porch. Dimples is pulling up in front of the house. She's got her hair and windows down, but her swag up. Our white friend is so hood it's unbelievable. She's just a black girl trapped in a white girl's body. This girl keeps her Suburban clean, but her rims even cleaner.

"Chevy so tall lookin' down on ya'll. We all love us some Young Jeezy! We would fuck him in a heartbeat!"

Black starts shaking her ass next to me. That's the only thing she's got on her that isn't small. This bitch stays dancing; it's her life. May as well get paid to do something she's gonna be doing anyway. No wonder she's a damn stripper!

"Ya'll bitches miss me? 'Cause I damn sure miss ya'll!" Dimples says as she climbs out of her truck.

"You know we do," Black responds.

All three of us hug each other and repeat our motto: "Until our caskets drop, we shall stand together."

"The food's almost ready," I say, and that's all it takes to get them headed for the door. I go to the kitchen to get shit together so we can grub.

Dimples and Black are in the living room talking about who's going to pull the best lookin' nigga tonight. I'm always laughin' at these two.

"Where my baby at?" I hear Dimples asking. Beauty loves her some Auntie Dimples and Auntie Black. They let her get away with murder, they spoil her, and whatever she wants she gets, no questions asked.

"Black, fill Dimples in on everything while I get the plates together."

We don't keep anything from each other, and we know everything about one another. Yeah, we're friends, but we are also sisters. Blood couldn't make us any closer. We're family, and nothing will ever change that.

"Dinner's ready, and I know ya'll bitches hungry too!" I yell from the kitchen.

"Hell yeah," Dimples says, and Black is right behind her. "Can't nobody cook like you, girl," she says. That makes me smile, 'cause I know they ain't lying. I love the kitchen. It's my favorite room in the house.

"Hell fuckin' yeah! My favorite! I love curry chicken!" Dimples famished ass says. We sit down at the table and link hands with one another.

"Who gonna pray?" she asks.

"You the pastor's kid," I say to her.

"I'll pray," Black laughs.

"Don't take too long either, 'cause a bitch is hun-gry," Dimples says, stretching the word hungry out.

"God, thank you for today, thank you for everything, guide and protect us, bless this food, amen. You didn't think that was too long?" Black asks her when she's finished praying.

"You stay with the jokes."

"What time we leavin' tonight, ya'll?"

Nobody answered me 'cause they both had their faces head deep in their plates. After about thirty seconds, Black finally says,

"We leavin' at 10."

I remind them that we ain't pulling any stunts tonight.

"We just checkin' shit out, a'ite?"

We ate, laughed, and talked shit about what we're stuntin' in tonight. They slap each other high fives when I tell them that I'm gonna be the one doing all the driving.

"I ain't drinkin', so ya'll bitches can have all the fun in the world."

"I love it when Jay don't make you mad," Black tells me.

They know me so well, it ain't even funny. When he makes me mad, all I wanna do is drink and act a fool. Dimples scrapes the last of her food off of her plate and into her mouth before telling us she's headed to the shower to start getting ready. Black finishes next and goes to put her shit together in Beauty's room while I start cleaning the kitchen.

Time is definitely flying by. I didn't realize it was eight until I heard the house phone ringing. I know it's Jay calling. "Baby, I miss you."

"How much, Daddy?"

"I miss you this much, like our princess say."

He keeps a smile on my face most of the time. We talk about Beauty for a minute, and then he asks about my girls.

"Where's them crazy ass bitches at?"

"Dimples is in the shower, but Black's right here. You wanna holla at her?"

"Yeah."

I hand the phone to Black.

"What's craccin', nigga?" she said.

"Put him on speaker phone," I whisper to her.

She does so, and his voice fills the room.

"What ya'll doin tonight?" he asked her.

"Shit, nothin' major. Goin' to Club 2, and havin' us a girl's night out."

"Okay, ya'll have fun and be careful."

"You already know we will, plus your wife drivin', PLUS she ain't drinkin', so you know me and Dimples are gonna have a ball."

She hands the phone back to me and leaves the kitchen.

"Baby, what you wearing tonight?"

"I don't know yet for sure, but I think I wanna wear my white Polo dress with my pink pumps."

"You heavy like that?"

"Boy, quit playin'! You know I'm gonna send you some pictures ASAP, so relax and breathe!"

I know you are, baby. They just called my name for mail, so hold on."

"When he gets back on the phone a few seconds later he says, "Baby, I love you! You the fuckin' best I swear!" This makes me smile, because I know that he just got his surprise. I had sent him like twenty cards, and $250.00.

"You make me feel like a king."

"You know that's my job," I tell him.

The recorded system operator comes on the line. "You have sixty seconds left."

"I love you, girl. Have fun and be careful."

"I love you too, Jahmain. Call me first thing in the morning, okay?"

"A'ite, baby. Love you."

"I love you more," I say before I hang up the phone.

I do love him. He makes me happy and he keeps my attention. I think we have a good relationship. He trusts me, and I'm learning to trust him.

"I am so gone over you," Black says, mocking me.

"Shut the hell up."

"I'm done," Dimples just came out of the shower, hair wrapped in a towel.

"'Bout damn time," I tell her.

"I'm next!" Black shouts and takes off running for the

bathroom. “You know what they say about the best!” I shout after her,

“They save it for last!”

“We sharper than a motherfucking razor blade,” Dimples says, and I have to agree. She’s wearing a blue Roc A Wear outfit, with some red bottoms. For a white girl, she’s got a banging body.

My bitch is fly. Black’s in some shorts, looking like a hooker with some class. That bitch hates clothes, and clothes hate her. She loves showing her body off. I grab the nina from my drawer and put it in the waistband of my skirt, so the neighbors can’t see it. I leave the light on in Beauty’s room and the television on in mine. I grab Dimples’ keys. We’re taking her white Suburban, riding on them 26’s.

Dimples is up front with me, ‘cause Black loves to ride in the back. She hits that big ass flat screen as soon as we get in. Don’t no bitches do it like us! We put our seat belts on, and I hit the music. You already know who coming out the speakers...

“One thing about me, yeah I got swag”

Young Jeezy!

I have Dimples put the strap in the glove box. We never leave home without a strap. Niggas and bitches grimey nowadays, so we stay on top of them. We jam the entire way to Club 2. The place is only 20 minutes away from my house doing the speed limit, but if I’m in a hurry I can get there in 10.

Finding a parking space is always hard, so we always park on the side of the building. Fuck getting a ticket. We don't care. We'll just pay that shit. If shit goes sour, then our ride will be nearby instead of out back, plus we can see a good section of the parking lot.

"All types of cars out here tonight," Dimples says.

"Hell yeah," I agree with her.

"Who the fuck drivin' that all white 760 with white 22's on it? THAT'S what we need to know." Black eyeballs the car hard.

One thing for sure, they got some bread. Some extra good looking bread and Black wants some. Then again, well, we all want some.

We can hear the music from outside. Thank goodness there isn't a long line. Four men are behind us, so you already know they're checking us out.

"Damn, shawty in the all white."

I don't even budge to look back. I put some attitude in my waist and let my ass do the talking.

"Damn, she fat!" I heard him exclaim. Dimples looks back and laughs at them. Banging body and all, she's still got that innocent look to her.

Nicki's coming through the speakers, and I randomly wonder how she came up with that song, "Stupid Ho."

"Hey Brandon," we all three say at the same time.

He's one of the security guards here, but he collects the money sometimes too. This pussy looking dude called Pat is doing the searching.

“Ya’ll tryn’a hurt ‘em tonight,” Brandon says as he looks us up and down like he likes what he sees.

“Naw, we just tryin’ to have some fun,” Dimples says to him. Black pays our way in and we all get searched. One day though, we ain’t gonna get searched at all. I gotta start working on that.

Pat’s in love with me, but he ain’t my type. Then again, anything to have my way, you best believe I’m on it. I wink at him and tell him I’ll holla at him later. Word on the street says he’s a dope boy. I wonder how much weight he’s pushing though. I’ll find out everything I want to know in due time.

Chapter 13

Party Time

It's almost 11, and the place is super packed. All eyes on us as always. A couple bitches from around the way are present. They're clocking us, trying to see what they can learn. You can see the difference between them bitches and us. They fuck to get paid. We have jobs. Don't no nigga pay our bills.

"Hey, Sweets," this bitch Nichole says to me.

"Hey, what's up with you?"

"Tryna have some fun."

"Hell yeah. Me too." I wish this bitch would get the fuck away from me.

"I'm comin' to the shop on Thursday, 'cause that's my day off. You think you can hook me up?" Knowing damn well her ass ain't got no job.

"Yeah, slide through. I got you."

Her baby daddy, Steven, is on my ass hard, but I don't want

him ‘cause everyone says he’s got that House In Virginia, HIV. His money is supposed to be mad long, but I just can’t chance it. The money might have the monkey too!

“See you Thursday then,” she says.

I walk away to find my bitches, but I don’t get too far ‘cause a nigga grabs my arm.

“Damn, ma, you look sexy.”

I scan him up and down. He looks like he’s in his late 20’s or early 30’s. He’s handsome, and looks like his smile is perfect, but his eyes tell a different story. A story of fear, emptiness, and loneliness. They seem cold. Super cold. He’s got long dreads past his shoulders. He’s in blue jeans, a denim shirt, and some Polo loafers. Damn!

“And you lookin’ quite good yourself,” is all I can come up with. He’s got me stuck.

“What’s your name?”

“Corona, but everyone calls me Sweets.”

“Oh yeah? I’m thinkin’ I’ve got a sweet tooth right about now.”

“Really? I wonder how many girls you use that line on?”

“None, ‘cause I never met one sweet as you before.”

He’s got me smiling, I can’t even lie. He is trying his hardest. “Who you here with tonight?”

“Me and my girls.”

“Who you leavin’ with?”

“The same people I came with.” I know I sound like I got a slick mouth, but at least it’s honest.

He smiles at me. Yup, his smile is perfect.

“Playin’ hard I see.”

Even though I already know it, I ask him his name to make him feel comfortable. His real name is Cedrick, but they call him Ced for short. I start scanning the club for Dimples and Black. I wanna make sure they’re good.

“Who you lookin’ for?”

“My girls.”

“You not scared are you?”

For what? I want to know, but I keep my smart mouth to myself this time.

“I’m a big girl, and I can take care of myself. Remember that.”

“You got me failin’ for you already,” he says as he smiles at me again. Perfect.

“So quick?”

“Yes. I love your style, and you’re beautiful. You look different, you seem different, and I like different. And to be honest, no other girl has grabbed my attention.”

“Save me the story,” I tell him, and he laughs at me.

“Girl, what you doin’?” Black comes out of nowhere, fucking up our conversation.

“Nothin’. Just talkin’, and tryn’a find ya’ll bitches. Ced, this is Black, Black this is Ced.”

They shake hands, and I see Dimples over Black’s shoulder talking to one of Ced s homeboys.

“Let’s go dance,” Black says, grabbing my arm and pulling me away “See you around, “I tell him. I can tell he doesn’t want me to leave him. His eyes, they’re a story all by themselves! When we get across the room Black grabs Dimples the same way she got me, only she’s got a drink in her hand. Dimples bucks the cup in 5 seconds and puts it on a table as we walk past. Truth is, that bitch is an alcoholic. I turn back around, and Ced is still watching me walk away. Mane, I bet money makes him look radiant! We finally make our way to the dance floor. I see Ced not too far away. A light skinned bitch tries talking to him, but he brushes her off like hair. He’s busy watching me watch him.

The DJ is killin’ it. “Hard in the Paint” by Wacka Flocka comes on, and Black is going crazy, this is her shit. We all start dancing, and the next thing I know I feel someone on my neck. I turn around thinking it’s got to be Ced, but it isn’t. Some lame-ass-tryna-be-pretty-nigga wants to get his dick hard off me.

“Get the fuck away from me!”

“Fuck you, bitch!” He says, and moves on to the next woman.

That dusty bucket bitch bends over in front of him! Females kill me. A dance for free and you ain’t hit his pockets? Not from one of us! I tell my bitches that I’m gonna sit down and scope the place out, but they know me better than that. Cedrick is on- my mind.

His swag a trillion, could have any female in here, but he wants me from what it looks like. I leave the dance floor, even though by now it's my shit that's playing. I sit at the table nearest the dance floor, and I scan the room for Ced. I spot him at the bar with the same light skinned bitch from earlier. I watch him give her some money, and I wonder who she is. I take my eyes off him, and watch my bitches having fun. I'm so deep in thought that I don't hear him until he touches my back.

"Can I get a dance?"

"No!"

"Why not?"

"Because I don't want no problems with your girlfriend," I tell him while I look her up and down.

"Oh, so you funny too." He says, following my eyes.

"She ain't nobody special to me."

"How am I supposed to believe you?"

"Take my word for it."

"Take your word?"

"My word is like my balls. Real and authentic."

"How nice," I want to say something else so bad, but for the second time tonight I hold my tongue.

"She's my nigga's baby ma. He got killed four years ago, so I told her not to ask any nigga for shit while I am around. I gave her some bread to have fun."

I wonder if he's telling the truth, 'cause I know nigga's swear on their momma and still lie.

"Oh yeah? That's what's up."

"Can I get you a drink?"

"No thanks."

"You stay shuttin' me down."

"Naw, that's not it." Them bitches look like they having a jolly ol' time.

"Your girls havin' fun. Too much fun," he says to me as I watch them.

"Are you havin' fun?" I ask him.

"As a matter of fact, I'm havin' the best time of my life."

He's got all the right answers. I hope the Patron ain't got him talking, 'cause I can smell it on his breath. I get up to walk away, but he moves to step in front of me.

"Can I ask you out sometime?"

"I gotta think about it, Ced."

His short response gives me goosebumps.

"I'll be waitin'," he says as I walk off.

I have to give it to him. He seems determined to the fullest.

Dimples stays talking to a sexy ass nigga, and Black is on the dance floor with a nigga twice as black as she is. All I can see is his teeth, and I have to shake my head at that.

Black and Blacker.

"Damn, take my ass off with you," I say to the dude who bumps into me as he walks past. To my surprise it's the dude from the dance floor who tried to get up on me.

"Bitch, you ain't all that."

He don't know who he's fucking with.

"Nigga, fuck you and the bitch you came from."

Next thing I know this dude is all up in my face. I see Ced behind him, and he's got a couple of his niggas with him.

"Now apologize to the lady," I hear Ced say to him. Dude doesn't move, his whole body's straight like an arrow.

"I apologize."

"Fuck you and the bitch you came from." I tell him again. I don't know what Ced tells him, but dude bounces. Ced is strapped, I can see the joint in his waistband. He must have put it in dude's back, 'cause that nigga was scared.

"I told you I'm a big girl. I can take care of myself."

"Why do that when you can have me, baby?" He wants to leave an imprint on my heart, but he's leaving a dent in my brain for the night. I decide to leave him with a hint to see if he'd follow up on it.

"When you need your hair done, come holla at me at Layers." I tell him and walk away. He's sexy, handsome for real, drop dead gorgeous and shining brighter than a diamond, but it's time to go. This is too much for one night. That nigga I got into it with has got me nervous, 'cause I can't get to the strap fast enough. I wonder how Ced got his in.

My bitches ain't looking for me, but I find them at the bar buying drinks.

"Ya'll ready?"

"Yeah, one more drink," Dimples tells me.

"We seen the little commotion over there, but your new BF had your back," Black says.

"Yeah, he did," I respond proudly.

"Who's the nigga I got into it with?"

"Oh, that's Marcus! I got the rundown already," Dimples downs her drink, and we go through the back door to walk around the side of the building.

"Damn, bitch! Your boy drivin' that?" Black exclaims.

Ced's in the driver's seat of that all white 760! The real

question here is: Did I hit the jackpot?

We stop moving so he won't see us and we watch him drive away before we get in the truck. Dimples gets in the back this time, 'cause she's out for the night. I tell Black to open up the glove box and get me the nina, 'cause if I see this Marcus dude again, I'm gonna blast his ass.

Once we hit the highway, I let Ced settle on my mind. Black must be feeling good, 'cause she's pulled her seat back.

Dimples is talking trash in the back thinking she's rapping.

I laugh at my bitches, 'cause they are the shit no matter what. Instead of bumping some Jeezy, I pull Drake's CD out, ''Take Care*', and put it on my jam, "Practice". Cedrick is on my mind super hard. It's been a long time since a man has made such an impression on me. Don't get me wrong, I love Jay, but he's locked up and ain't gettin' out no time soon. This is too damn much for one night. Whatever else happens just fucking happens. We finally make it home around 3:30 in the morning. I wake my bitches up, and tell Black to open the front door 'cause I got to get Dimples out.

""I don't feel too good, Sweets." she moaned as I pulled her from the backseat.

"Bitch I ain't tell you to get white girl wasted!"

"I gotta throw up."

"Dimples, let's try to make to the bathroom."

When I get her inside I help her out of her shoes and she staggers to the bathroom. Black goes straight to my bedroom to lay down. I know it's a wrap. I can hear Dimples pouring her guts out. I grab a blanket from the hallway closet, and flop my ass on the sofa. Dimples will crash in Beauty's room.

I have a long day ahead of me. I got to be up in less than three hours, 'cause it's Jay's visitation day.

Chapter 14

New Day

I don't even hear Dimples when she leaves the bathroom, all I hear is the alarm going off in the bedroom.

"It's seven already?" I drag myself from the couch and peek in on Dimples on my way to my room. She's still sleeping. I am tired as hell! Black starts moving around in the bed when I turn the light on.

"Damn, bitch! Turn that shit off!"

"Wake the fuck up! Ya'll comin' with me to see Jay today?"

"If you drive, yeah, we'll go."

Dimples comes into the room and plops down onto the bed.

"Ya'll bitches and hangovers don't mix."

I've got to get moving. I take a shower, put on my apple bottom jeans with a v-neck Polo shirt and grab my Air Force 1's.

This is gonna have to do, ‘cause time ain’t on my side. I forward the house phone to my cell, and tell them hungover bitches it’s time to go.

The ride to Dillwyn is almost two hours long. Visitation starts at eight, and I’ll be there by nine. I want to sleep so bad, but sleep has to wait. At 8:45 my phone starts ringing. Yup. It’s Jay.

After I listen to the operator, I press 0. “Hello?”

“Hey, baby. Where you at?” he has the fucking audacity to ask.

“On my way to see you! Stop askin’ questions you already know the answer to,” I snap at him,

“You woke up in a bad mood, I see.”

“Naw, just tired. Ready to see you though.”

“Where Dimples and Black?”

“In the car with me. They sleep.”

We talk about last night. I tell him about the situation with “Marcus” and how Dimples threw up.

“Was it packed out there?”

“Yeah. Same people, just a different night, baby.” I wonder why people who are locked up always worry about what people on the outside are doing.

“Look, I’ll see you in a minute. I hate talkin’ and drivin’.”

“A’ite, baby. Be careful.”

It's almost nine, so I call my daughter right quick to see how she's doing.

"Hello?" Regina answers the phone.

"Hey, how you doin'?"

"Fine, and you?"

"Chillin'. Where Ex'Quisite at?"

"She still asleep."

"Where Traymon at?"

"Sleep too."

"Okay, let them know I called, please and thank you."

"I will," she says.

Hearing her voice makes me sick, but shit, it's reality. I gotta accept her, but not right now. She is one sneaky bitch. I can just feel it.

The parking lot is always packed.

"Ya'll bitches wake the hell up!"

"We gonna get something to eat and do a little shopping,"

Black says with a yawn.

"Tell Jay don't drop the soap," Dimples giggles.

"Ha, ha, bitch, you got jokes."

I hate coming out here, and I hate how they search me from head to toe, but I want for him to be happy. I've been coming out here for a year now, faithfully. Rain, sleet or snow, I'm here. The line isn't long today, so going through the process isn't too bad. I'm placed at the fifth table in the fourth row, but instead of sitting down I go to the vending machine to get us a drink. These niggas down here always checking me out.

Even some bitches are giving me the eye.

When I get back to the table, the couple behind me are having a huge disagreement. Dude only has six months left, and his shawty says she's moving away. Crazy, right? But even though niggas are behind these walls they have more than one bitch. You don't know if what they tell you is the truth.

There's a thing called 'jail talk', and the men are excellent at it. Jay knows that I have more sense than that, so running that jail shit by me would be a complete waste of time. He always says, "You think and act like a nigga so much, where the bitch part at?" I have it in me, but I just don't bring it out. We're living in a cold hearted world.

His swagger is on point. He's got a white tee under his blue button up shirt, and he's wearing Levi's with some black Timbs. My nigga is fresh to death, and doesn't need or want for shit, 'cause I make sure he's straight.

"Damn! My baby lookin' like a bag of money! Turn around for Daddy," he tells me.

"Boy, you is crazy! Give me some sugar."

He puts his lips on mines, grabs me ass, and tilts my head back with the force of his kiss. This is the best part. Just touching him, and having him touch me has my pussy dripping.

What I would do for some of this dick; only God knows.

“You smell good, boo.”

“Shit, girl, I could eat you right now, right here if they would let me!”

“Since that can’t happen, what you want to eat?”

“You know, the regular.”

I walk away to get some chicken wings. Not only is he watching me as I go, but he’s also watching other niggas clock me.

Knowing that he has me makes him happy. We spend four hours talking, eating, and laughing nonstop. Visitation is over at three .

I hate leaving him here, but I can’t change it. Only time can.

We end the visit the same way we started it.

“Damn. I need some dick bad.”

Jamaica

Chapter 15

Get Ready

Dimples and Black keep their conversation rolling when I get into the car, and it almost seems like they don't even know I'm there until Dimples pulls me into it.

"Anyway Sweets, that nigga who tried that bullshit with you last night? His name is Marcus. He's from Madison Street, and he's pushing mad weight, too. He just came home four months ago. He's got two kids with different baby ma's, and he keeps all the bread. He works out of his mother's house. She lives on Old Forest Road, and she works as a private sitter at night."

"How sure are you?" I ask.

"Well, his younger brother, Pooh, fuckin' with a girl from church, so she got the rundown for me. Plus ol' girl say the nigga stay strapped."

Church people some shit, I tell you!

"Last night his ass was slippin', almost got smoked."

"Fuck that nigga, yo!" Black says.

"Damn right! Let's see if he at the bar tonight. If he is, then

Black, I want you on him, cool?" I ask.

"Comprende!"

"Anyway, I got this other nigga who lives on the other side of town, his name is Whyte. He's sexy as fuck, plus he got a big dick." We all start laughing when she says that.

"Dimples, how the fuck you know his dick is big, bitch?" Black asks her. I wanna hear this shit for sure!

"Last night when he grabbed my ass, I grabbed his dick. Grab for grab, you know! I ain't shy, shit!" We laugh real hard when she says that. When I say that bitch is crazy, that bitch is crazy!

"I am tired as hell, and don't feel like drivin' back."

"I got you," Dimples says "Get your ass in the back then."

"Ya'll ain't get me shit to eat?"

"You know we didn't know how long your ass was gonna be inside, and your shit would have been cold anyway, so relax!" Black says to me as I get in the backseat.

"We can go to the little country store and get you some hot dogs if you want, Sweets." Dimples speaks over the music she put on as soon as she hit the driver's seat.

"...She walks like a boss... Talks like a boss..."

"Turn that shit down, my phone ringin' ya'll." 404 area code. Who the fuck can this be? When I answer a male voice responds to me.

"Can I speak to Sweets?"

"This her. Who this?"

"I see you've forgotten my voice already."

"How did you get my number?"

"I have my ways. Especially when I want something."

"Who is it, bitch?!" Nosey ass Black hisses from the front seat.

"Hey, Cedrick, how are you doin'?"

"Good, and you?"

"I'm good, but for real... please tell me how you got my number.

"A friend of a friend of a friend."

"You went through all that for me?"

"Yeah, only for you though."

"I hear you talkin'" I wonder if he can hear my smile in my voice.

"So, Miss Lady, are you busy?"

"Naw, if I was I wouldn't have answered."

"Has anyone ever told you how reckless your mouth is?"

"Naw, but you can tell me."

“You have the most sassy mouth that I have ever run across, but I like it, and I know that I can live with it.”

“You ain’t gotta put up with it, ‘cause we ain’t together.

“N-O-T-Y-E-T,” he says, spelling the words out. Now at a loss for words, I really don’t know what to say.

“You still there?”

“Yeah, I’m still here. Just listening to you.”

“Good! You got any plans for tonight?”

“Me and my girls are goin’ out.”

“Oh, okay. Mind if I ask where?”

“We’re not sure yet.”

“Are you just tryin’ not to let me know?”

“Probably a bar, but as I said, we ain’t sure yet.”

“I love that mouth of yours,” he tells me.

“Me too. If I do see you out tonight, I’ll speak.”

“Sweets, I would really like that, and now that you have my number, make sure you save it and use it.”

“I won’t lose it!”

Conversation over, I hang up. Black may as well have climbed into the backseat with me, ‘cause her whole body’s practically already here. I tell them everything that was said. They are both quiet, but smiling like crazy until Dimples says, "Don't forget about us."

"That will never happen!"

Just like that I lost my appetite. When we stop at the country store, the only thing we get is gas. The ride home is silent. Black goes back to sleep as Keyisha Cole's song 'Enough of No Love' plays. I'm tired as hell myself. I don't even hear my phone ringing, but I miss my daughter's call. I don't even wake up until I hear the car door slam when we make it back to the house. My first thoughts are of what Dimples said earlier about not forgetting them. That had me mad. Why does she think that I would forget them just like that?

She must have known it pissed me off, 'cause she apologizes for saying it.

I tell her it's cool, I ain't trippin' "all that anger you got built up inside of you, you need to release that shit," she tells me.

"I will. As soon as Jay gets home."

"The way you lookin', I think Ced will be the one helpin' you with that!"

"You got jokes, too?"

"I agree," says Black.

"Do you really think if Jay was out and you was in, he'd be holdin' you down like you holdin' him down?" Dimples asks me to make a point. I hate that question, 'cause I know the answer like I know the back of my hand.

“Naw.”

“You mean, hell fuckin’ no!” Dimples says, correcting me.

“Preach, girl!” Black had to put her five cents in. I should just be glad she didn’t give me change for a dollar. They keep it real and raw with me all the time, no matter if they hurt my feelings or not. I’d rather my feelings hurt than have my heart broken again.

“You need to get some dick in your life for real!” Black informs me.

“When you last had a nut? I mean a real nut, too!” Dimples asks. “Since you ain’t gettin’ no dick, you need to get yourself a toy, ‘cause four bitches on thumb street ain’t cuttin’ it!”

Black laughs.

“Don’t worry, when I do ya’ll bitches will be the first to know! I gotta call Beauty, so ya’ll shut the fuck up with that language.”

My sperm donor answers.

“What’s good, nigga?”

“Shit, our daughter wanted you, but she and shawty went to get their nails and shit done.”

“Oh, okay I”

“What you doin’, Sweets?”

“Nothin’. What you doin’ Traymon?”

"Missin' you, babyma."

"Boy, you crazy as hell! When Beauty gets back tell her to call me."

"You ain't gonna let me hit that again?"

"Bye, nigga!"

Just because he is my baby daddy he thinks that he can and should fuck me at any given time. He's got the game truly fucked up! I will never, and I mean NEVER let him see or touch this pussy cat again!

"You should at least let him bang you out one more time," Dimples says like her opinion is gonna change anything. It won't.

"At least let him give you some head," Black suggests. Another opinion that doesn't matter.

"Ya'll fuckin' crazy. Ya'll can miss me with that bullshit."

Come to think of it, I should at least get some head and record it. That way if his shawty ever gets out of line, I can put her ass back in her place, and let that bitch know no matter what, he will always want this pussy. Even though my mind tells me to get revenge on her, my heart still says no. I discard the idea as soon as I have it. He is old meat, and I need new spice and flavor in my life.

Ready!

Buffalo Wild Wings is the spot to be on Saturday nights.

It's free to get in, a place where you can chill and watch games, or just hang out with your friends. Where there's sports, there's men, and where there's men, there's usually money. That means me and my bitches are where the money's at.

We aren't dressed to impress or draw attention. Just some jeans, fitted tee's, and sneakers. Black is the driver for the night, and she has a job to do, so she needs to be sober, but me and Dimples? SHIT! We're gonna get it in! I need a drink, too.

When we pull up, the clock on the dashboard says it's 10:30. BWW's closes at 2, and three hours is plenty of time to do what we came to do. As soon as we get inside I ask Dimples if she grabbed the nina.

"Have we ever left home without it?" she raises her eyebrow at me.

I just smile at her. I love my bitches.

Black spots Marcus first. She walks off and leaves us standing where we are. Dimples with her alcoholic ass wants a drink, so we move towards the bar. Marcus and Black are over by the bathroom. She's definitely got his attention. On some real shit, it looks like pussy rules his ass, and if that's the case then we have him exactly where we want him. This is gonna be fun. Black's got an ass like WOW, and Marcus is on her.

"What can I get you tonight, ladies?" the waitress asks. She's pretty, but she's got Assatall Syndrome: she ain't got no ass at all. Her name tag says her name is Brittney.

"Two Jamaican lizards, please," I tell her.

Dimples places her order too. "One Jamaican lizard, and a Long Island iced tea."

"Okay, I'll be right back!" She disappears to make our drinks.

I glance over at Black to make sure she's cool. She is, so I relax a little. I watch as a white boy starts talking to Dimples. He's cute, but he ain't her type unless his money's right. Then he'd be just right for all three of us! I excuse myself and sit at an empty table. I'm not seated for two minutes before I hear: "Excuse me, can I have the seat beside you?"

I know that voice.

"Yeah, you can." He sits, and I ask him, "how did you know that I'd be out here tonight?"

"An angel told me, and I followed the stars," Ced explains.

The waitress interrupts, "Your drinks," she says as she puts two glasses down on the table between us.

"How nice of you to buy me a drink," he sounds like he's teasing. "Naw, they both for me," I tell him, smiling," but you can drink one if you want."

"What else can I drink?" he winks at me before turning his attention to Brittney. "Two Patron and a Redbull, please."

Mane, he is so sexy. Damn! All white tee, black jeans and white dopeman's, with an all white fitted hat that says Heats on the front.

"Who you goin' for, the Heats or the Celtics?" he asks me.

"I love green, so the Celtics get my vote."

"Damn! That hurt! I thought you would at least like James."

"Naw, La'Bron too cocky for me. I like Randoo. He seems humble."

"Good, so we can bet each other when they play?"

"You got it!"

I look around, and Dimples is nowhere in sight, but Black is still in the same spot with Marcus. Ced is very entertaining, and he keeps me smiling even though his team is winning.

"Don't look so sad, it's just a game," he says, winking at me. "Yeah, if you say so."

We slip conversation in on the commercials while watching the game. We laugh and mean mug each other for the next forty-eight minutes. 104-98 Heats way...

My phone is ringing and the screen says it's Jay. It's almost time for lockdown, so I know he wants to tell me goodnight. I have to answer, so I tell Ced that I'll be right back. By the time I get outside it's time to press 0.

"You looked so sexy today, after that visit I had to beat my dick."

"Well, hello to you too, darling."

"I hear music."

"I'm at the bar havin' a few drinks and watchin' the games. Boston lost, so you know I'm mad as shit."

"We know they ain't goin'" nowhere, but we're rootin' for 'em 'cause the Lakers ain't shit nowadays."

"Oh, so you a traitor now?"

"Naw, boo! I'm just ridin' with you!" he laughs.

"At least you pick right."

"You seen or talked to my brother lately?"

"Naw, what's wrong?"

"Shit, just checkin' on him."

On some real shit, Jay's family loves him, they just don't show it. He doesn't let that stress him, 'cause he knows I got his back all the way.

"Well, baby, have fun. I ain't gonna hold you," he says.

That's weird for him to say. We've only been on the phone for seven minutes. I'm missing Ced's company, but I want to know why Jay wants to hang up so quick.

"What's wrong, baby?" I ask.

"Shit, gonna play some poker real quick before they lock us down."
"Oh, okay. Well, I love you, Jahmain Jones."

"I love you too. I'll call you tomorrow."

This shit is weird. This is the first time he's ever wanted to get off the phone early. He hangs up before I can say anything else. Damn. My feelings -are hurt. Maybe I'm trippin' 'cause I got Ced in there waiting on me. My mind is racing. I wonder what's goin' on between Black and Marcus, and where the fuck is Dimples at? I've got a lot going on, and I need to get back inside.

Ced is still at the table where I left him. I glance across the way for Black, but I don't see her. Where the fuck is Dimples? "I'll be right back, I gotta go to.the bathroom."

Ced acknowledges me with a nod.

My eyes are everywhere as I cut across the room. I need to find them fast, so i rush into the bathroom to call her ass.

"Damn, bitch, where the fuck you at?" I ask when Black picks up.

"At BDubs, chillin' with my friend Marcus outside."

When the hell did they go outside?! I was just out there!

"You in the car with him?"

"Yeah, I miss you too mom."

"He wanna fuck?"

"Yeah, look in the kitchen drawer. It's under the mat."

"You ready to go?" I near her ask Marcus.

"Okay, girl, just stall for a minute," I tell her. I hang the phone up. I have to find Dimples fast, and I've only got 2 minutes to get this together. I leave the bathroom and squeeze my way back to the table where Ced is still waiting. My eyes are still on the prowl for Dimples. I finally spot her ass on the other side. I tell Ced that I've got to go, and that I'll call him as soon as possible. When he asks if everything is okay I tell him I'm good, toss a hundred dollar bill on the table, and tell him to tip Brittney well. He doesn't have time to get a word out before I'm gone.

"Bitch, I'm sorry, but we got to go." When I get to Dimples I grab her arm, pulling her away from her friend.

"I'll call you," Dimples says over her shoulder to dude.

As soon as we get out the front door we see a car leaving the parking lot. We run to our car at full speed. I know that's him.

I fill Dimples in on everything as I start the car. This sucka for pussy nigga gonna need help when we're done with him. Dimples starts changing her clothes, and she pulls her hair into a pony tail. I can see the BMW ahead of us, and I know Black is talking her ass off. I hang back to keep enough distance so that he doesn't notice that he's being followed.

If he's headed to his mom's house we're only 20 minutes away, and it looks like that's where he's going. I still have to change my clothes, but Dimples is ready. We don't say shit. She puts the Flocka CD in and puts it on our motivation song. "I fuck my money up and now I can't re-up, ran up in his spot just to get my stacks up." Flocka says.

"I need to get my clothes changed."

"I hope this dumb ass nigga stop at the store to get some condoms at least." Dimples states.

"Damn right!"

This nigga does just that. Me and Dimples switch seats, and I start getting myself together. Everything's black, so you know it's an all black party goin' down. Black Dickies outfit, skully caps, Timbs and bandanas. The nina's even black, and the duffle bag too. The nigga comes out of the store with a six pack and a Four Loco. That's gotta be for my bitch.

He pulls out of the gas station and makes an immediate right onto Jackson. Dimples hits the headlights and stays back. It's a dead end ahead, and that's where he's headed, so we park the car and keep track of his tail lights. He turns into a driveway. We can't see the house number, but we also can't miss that light blue BMW he drives either.

We watch as Marcus and Black both exit the vehicle. Black knows her part of the job. We wait five minutes before we start walking toward the house. Even with 20/20 vision, you still can't see us. We're as close to being invisible as we can get without being air. This is a quiet neighborhood, and it looks rich. We're ready and in position. Now all we're waiting on is for Black to text us to let us know it's okay.

Twenty minutes go by before we finally hear from her. Her text says, "Let's Get It."

The front door is unlocked. Job well done, Black! Thank God this place has carpet to muffle our footsteps. I guess no one else is home. I have to give it to whoever lives here. The place is beautiful.

The mouth piece we have in our mouths make us sound like men. Black sees us before Marcus feels the nina at his head. She's on her back looking up and making loud ass noises. He's on top of her, doing whatever it is he thinks he s doing.

"Nigga, if you move I'm gonna blow your motherfuckin' head off,"

I tell him. Black starts screaming her ass off. It's pretty good acting. It's also irritating as hell.

"Shut the fuck up, bitch! Another sound and I'll mute you forever," I yell.

Dimples tells Black to get dressed. "And put your cell phone in this bag, too!" Dimples sounds pretty good when she's givin' orders. Maybe it's just the mouthpiece. Marcus has a limp dick, but it's less than average. I wanted to laugh, but I'm a professional, and I hold my composure.

"Get your shit and leave, bitch. If you call anybody or say anything, I'll find you and kill you." Dimples says.

And you know what? That bitch Black starts crying REAL TEARS! Yo, this bitch deserves a Grammy for tonight! She rushes into her clothes, and runs out the door.

"Move if you want to, and watch me send you to meet your maker,"

I tell Marcus who's still laying on the bed where he'd rolled off of Black. He looks like he doesn't even give a fuck, he's ridin' cool, but I want him to know that for right now, I am his master.

I tie his hands behind his back with a sheet off of the bed. Then Dimples passes me a rope out of the duffle bag, and I use it to tie his ankles together. Black had left her panties. I pick them up off the floor and shove them into his mouth.

"You look like a newborn baby waitin' on a bottle: helpless," I say to him.

Dimples throws her head back and laughs. This is a good time, and it's bound to get better.

"Fuck you!" His defiance is muffled by the panties in his mouth, but I know what he said. Attitude. I know how to fix that.

I pistol whip his ass, and blood splatters on the headboard and blankets. He starts screaming through the gag, and it sounds pretty loud, so I stuff the panties even deeper into his mouth.

"Where the money and work at?" Dimples asks him. He doesn't answer, so she starts to tear shit up.

"Ain't no need to answer, nigga! I already got you."

There are six Jordan boxes full of money, two boxes full of bags of white powder, and one pound of some sticky looking weed. I keep my gun trained on his ass. Dimples pulls everything out of the closet, and starts transferring it to the duffle bag. This nigga's lookin' like he wants to cry. When I push him off the bed Dimples helps me flip the mattress over on him before we run for the door.

No one is outside except Black. She's parked right in front of the house. We jump in the car and she pulls off like nothing even happened. We take our ski masks off at the stop sign, put our seat belts on, and watch Black hit the highway.

We ride in silence the whole way home, which seems to take forever 'cause Black is doing the speed limit. Ridin' dirty is a life sentence, and we ain't goin' down that road. When we make it to the house, she parks the car in the backyard, and we go in through the back door. Mission accomplished. As soon as we get inside we let loose and jump for joy.

We count the money twice to make sure our numbers are correct. $42,450, a whole chicken of cocaine, and a pound of some good ass weed.

"What a fuckin' lick!" Damn, I like those numbers!

"Fuck havin' a nigga, especially when we can have his money," Black comments, serious as hell.

"Damn, Black! You look real good layin' on your back." Dimples says, and even I had to agree. She did that.

"The dick was a'ite, but the money, the work and the smoke is even better! I gotta wash this pussy juice off me, ya'll" Black tells us as she heads to the bathroom.

"Next time make sure you get a nut," I can't help but laugh my ass off. What a fuckin' night!

One mission down, and plenty left to go. We each had $14,150, 12 ounces of coke, and I'm gonna sell the whole pound of weed to my boss's baby daddy and split the bread between us. We've accomplished so much, in just two days! Shit is lookin' real good.

Damn! Now that things have slowed down Ced's back on my mind. I wonder what he's doing and thinking, so I get my phone and text him: Just wanted to let you know you're on my mind heavy. Shit, for all I know, he's laid up. Oh well. I can't figure out if he's gonna be a victim, a lover, or both. All I can do is give it time.

It's eight in the morning when I hear the toaster going off. Dimples is making her a bread and butter sandwich. Crazy ass bitch!

"We only have two hours to get ready for church. Mom and Dad will be lookin' for us today," She says when I walk into the kitchen. Sunday is the Lord's day, and our family time. We go to church to thank the Lord for all of our blessings, go out to eat after, and then come home to chill. Church is as great as it always is. Mr. and Mrs. John Marshall know the word of the Lord, and they know how to show it. They love me and Black like we're their own kids.

We finally get home around 4:30. Jay hasn't called me all day, but Ced did text me back. "You had me worried last night, but I'm good now 'cause I see that I'm on your mind."

Yeah. I think I like that.

"That nigga Whyte's our next lick," Dimples informs us.

"A'ite, what's the details?" That's our Black! On top of it already!

"Well, this bitch who works at the restaurant with me used to fuck with him, but he dawg her ass and force her to have an abortion, so now she puttin' all his business on front street. Ol' girl says she gonna get him set the fuck up, and get revenge on him ‘cause he broke her heart.”

“Hmm” snorts Black, “Karma is a bitch, and you always want that bitch to be beautiful!”

“Damn right!” I agree completely.

“Ya’ll think Karma will get us?” the pastor’s kid had to ask.

We all look at each other. It’s just reality. Do unto others as you would have others do unto you!

“Fuck that! When the time comes, we’ll think about it, but for right now money’s on my mind and should be on ya’ll’s!” I tell them, meaning every word that came out of my mouth.

“Anyway, back to business, ya’ll,” Dimples proceeds with the info on our next victim. “This nigga Whyte got at least four baby mothers. He works for a construction company on Westbrook Ave. and he lives in Timberlake with one of his baby ma’s. I think she’s the most recent one, but he’s fuckin’ with this yellow bitch named Spooners who lives on Campbell Ave, so he’s back and forth. Plus he’s got a white girl named Dove who drives him everywhere. The most important thing is that this nigga keeps all the money in a storage unit on Park Ave. Mad nigga’s want to get at him, but he moves too fast, and he stays on the low. No clubbin’ or bar hoppin’, so it’s hard to keep a GPS on him.”

I had to stop and think. This nigga HAS to have some serious bread. He is ballin’ hard. Just imagine who his plug is. Damn!

I wonder if we could get at that.

“Well, ol’ girl says he’s got at least seventy stacks in that bitch!" Dimples is pink with excitement, and I know she's thinking about her cut already. I do the math right quick in my head; we'd each get a little over twenty stacks if it's an even seventy. I know this guy's got a lotta money, 'cause having that many women costs, or the dick is absolutely astounding. I'm a thinker, and I think good, long and hard on this, but on some real shit, it wasn't nothing to think about. Seventy stacks!

"It's not what you do; it's who you know that can help you do it. That's the key to success or failure," I school them a little. You learn something new every day.

"Shit, I'll go around and find the address from his old joint. I'll follow him around for a couple of days to see what's up." "Ain't no need for that, Dimples," I tell her," Jay's cousin A'dasia works at the storage on Park Ave. She's gotta know this nigga! Black, get me my phone off the television stand."

Dimples is smiling like a faggot with ten bags of dicks. It's time to make a phone call.

"Hey, baby girl. What's good?" I say when she picks up.

"Shit, just chillin' cousin-in-law. How my big cousin doin'?"

"He good. Can't wait to come home, you already know. How's the family doin'?"

"They good, the babies sleep, thank God!"

It's time to cut to the chase.

"I need your help real bad on something that you can't tell anyone about."

“What’s good?” she asks, sounding like she’s down.

“You ever heard of a nigga named Whyte?” I put her on speaker phone so my bitches can hear too.

“Yeah, I know of him, but I don’t know him like that. He comes every month to pay his bill on this storage unit he’s renting where I work.” she says.

Now we’re all three smiling like we just seen the dentist.

“Yea.” I’m excited like a motherfucker, but I keep my voice cool.

“Why, what’s up?”

“See, he got one of my bitches pregnant and ain’t tryin’ to help her. He put her out of their house and took all their shit. So now she don’t know how she’s gonna start over. Plus’, having their baby on her own is hard. Everything is in the storage unit.” I hope she believes me, ‘cause that right there is all lies, but it just flew out of my mouth.

“I could get in trouble or lose my job.”

“Shit, I know, but I promise you I’ll make sure she don’t tell shit, and you already know my mouth is closed.”

“A’ite, I’ll text you the number tomorrow when I get to work.”

“That’s a bet. I got you, too.” I tell her.

“Tell my cousin I love him and I can’t wait for him to come home.”

“You already know I will.” I say with a smile on my face.

Dimples and Black are dancing like two little girls in a candy store.

"A'ite, we doin' this shit tomorrow night, late night shit, like some John Creeper type shit," Dimples says when I end the call with A'dasia.

"Damn, I gotta ask Regina if Beauty can spend the night." Asking my sperm donor to watch his own child is a problem. I either have to pay him, or he's gonna say, "You know I'm gonna be missin' money." Fuck it. I'll just pay her ass a couple hundred, 'cause this lick is gonna be right. Shit. 'Sometimes it seems like I stay on this damn phone.

"Yo, what ya'll doin'?"

"Shit, on the way back home. What's up?"

"Nothin'. Where's your wife at?"

"You got jokes. She right here." Word on the street is they're getting married. He claims it ain't that serious, but you already know niggas and bitches lie.

"Let me talk to her real quick."

"Hold on." I hear the phone change hands, and I hear him saying, "Sweets wanna talk to you."

"Hello?"

"Hey girl. How was ya'll's trip?"

"Good, we had fun. Beauty had a blast, but she out cold in the back seat."

“Yeah, I know she had a ball.”

“Hell yeah. We all did, ready to be back though, for real.”

“Can you do me a favor?”

“What’s that?” she asked me.

“You think you can keep Beauty for me until Tuesday? I’ll pick her up from school that day.”

“Yeah, I can do that.”

“Thank you so much, girl.”

“No problem.”

“Give her a kiss for me when she wakes up, and tell her I love her this much.”

“I will.”

“Ya’ll be safe, and thanks again.”

“Okay.”

She wants to be wifey, then she better act like one.

“Smooth operator!” Black says as she does Michael Jackson’s moon walk.

We eat and watch the football games; play some cards and talk some shit. Sunday’s our day. Come to think of it, Jay hasn’t called me all day. He sure is occupied, but with what?

I can’t be mad. Even though he’s locked up, he’s still got a life to live, but I usually speak to him twice a day at least, and on my days off we're talking from 8:00am to 11:30pm. Yeah!

I miss his voice, but hey, I miss Ced's presence too. Damn!

I think I'm in big trouble. Fuck it. I'm human.

Dimples and Black have crashed. They're both sleeping. I dial Ced's number around one in the morning.

"Can I speak to Ced?" I ask when he picks up the phone, even though I know it's him.

"He out of town."

"Oh, okay. Tell him Sweets called, please." Just when I am about to hang up the phone he stops me.

"Girl, stop playin' with me."

"You play too much, I thought I'd play back."

"I been waitin' on your call all day, sexy lady."

"So why didn't you just call me then?"

"I texted you, but you didn't text back, so I let it be. Ain't tryin' to cloud your space or be a stalker."

"Oh, yeah?"

"What you doin' this time of night, anyway?" He asks.

"Nothin'. Can't sleep even though I have to be at work at nine in the morning."

"Can I come get my hair done in the morning, then?"

"I'm booked in the morning, but you can come at one. I'll be done with you before three."

"Damn, you must think I'm just a two hour nigga?"

"Naw, I don't know! But I gotta be off at 2:30, 'cause I gotta get my little girl from school." Yeah, I'm lyin' to him. I ain't gotta get her till Tuesday, but what am I supposed to do? He don't need to know my business.

"You got a little girl? How old is she?"

"Yeah, she's almost four, goin' on twenty-one."

"I know; kids nowadays are a trip. I have three my damn self. Two girls; one boy."

"How old are they?

"Christina is seven, Gobra is five, and Jr. is six."

"Back to back, I see."

"Yeah, maybe one day your little girl can play with Cobra?"

"One day." This conversation is too much for me. I got to get off this phone, not that I am tired, but because he's getting to me... in a damn good way.

"Anyway, Ced, I'll see you tomorrow at one, and don't be late either."

"Believe me, the only time I'm late is when I'm havin' my way." This man is a smart ass for sure! Sex is on my mind, so everything he's saying sounds potentially sexual to me.

"Sweet dreams."

"You too, baby girl."

I hang up the phone so fast it's crazy. Boy, oh boy, he had me hot.

Where U Came From?

As always, Black is the first one up, and the first one gone. Since it's Monday, I have to start the week off with a terrific breakfast. Scrambled eggs with cheese, fried apples, honey bacon, grits, toasted bread, with a nice tall glass of orange juice.

"Girl, you gotta teach me to throw down in the kitchen, 'cause you could break up a happy home just by seasoning up some food," Dimples proclaims to me.

"Bitch, you a damn fool for that one!"

It's seven already, which means that Beauty's up and getting ready for school. I wonder if Traymon and Regina take her together? Thank goodness for Dimples running her mouth. She takes me out of my thoughts, and brings me back to the obvious.

"I wish I could stay with you all day, but a girl like me gotta go make an honest livin'," she mutters.

"Love you, too, crazy ass," I yell at her as she's on her way out.

Damn. I've got a love/hate relationship with Mondays. I get to work extra early, 'cause I need to holla at Talena about the weed. She's already here.

"Hey, Miss Boss Lady," I say as I enter the shop.

"Hey girl. How are you doin'?"

"Good, and you?"

"I'm okay, just a little stressed out."

"Damn, Talena, you seem down and out. You sure you're okay?"

"It's just me and Twan. Every time he gets stressed out he takes his problems out on me, and I am gettin' tired of that shit."

Word on the street, and from my own eyes, I know Twan lives in the streets. The streets is all he knows. His older brother Jerome raised him because their parents died, and since Jerome's been locked up for four years now, Twan's been holding shit down by himself. I kind of salute the nigga, 'cause he didn't give up on life even though his father killed his mother, and then himself right in front of his sons. Jerome taught him the street life at an early age, so he took advantage of it, and he opened up a salon in Talena's name.

"Girl, as long as the nigga ain't cheatin', don't have no rugrats on you, and ain't beatin' on you, then you good. Stress will fly by, just keep standin' by him."

"Sweets, I want him out of the game. Look what Jerome's doin'! That nigga's never cornin' home! He got life plus 20 for drugs!"

The system is fucked the fuck up. Kill a motherfucker, and you get ten, no more than fifteen, but sell drugs if you want to, and you can watch them throw dirt at you from the bottom of a shallow grave.

"Talk to him. Explain it all to him, Talena! Let me ask you a question though."

"What's that?"

"What's he sellin'?"

"Weed."

"Well, that ain't so bad. It's that white shit that's the devil, but that green is a different story, and now that they makin' it legalized, he's gonna be good. He might do a little time, but nothin' big."

"We got kids to raise, Sweets. What happens if the system don't get him? His enemies will?"

"Ya'll just have to talk this shit out."

"It's a drought, and he's mad that he can't supply his workers, and he's takin' all his stress out on me."

"Well, I might can help out in a way."

"How, Sweets?"

"I got a pound of some icky shit, and since you my peoples, I can help him out, but only if he wants to though."

"Girl, you a blessing, but you know that shit stays between me and you."

"Come on now, Talena! You been knowin' me for how long now?"

"Three years."

"That's a damn long time. Have you ever heard my name in any shit?" That upsets me, but I don't let her see it, 'cause this bitch's really got me fucked up.

"Naw, I ain't never heard your name in any shit, so I know for a fact you good."

Hell yeah! Until your ass cross me! If she only knew... I can't really blame her, 'cause she's protecting herself and her man.

"Well, I got that shit nearby, so you can call Twan and let him know."

As I finish my sentence the door to the salon opens.

"Look who the wind blew in here," I say with a smile on my face. Twan comes in and heads in Talena's direction.

"Hey, baby," he says to her, "I got you some breakfast while I was out, and thought I'd stop by to see you."

"What's craccin', Sweets?"

"Nothin', just livin'"

I leave them there, kissin' and shit. Too much of that

sentimental stuff ain't no good for me. About ten minutes later I see him walking towards my car. He's looking good and he seems cool. I've heard about him in the streets. As I sit in my car, I brush the little devil off my shoulder that keeps talking in my ear, but damn, he looks useful. Four fingers on thumb street is getting old for real. Got me thinking crazy.

He opens the door and sits in the passenger seat.

"You must be workin' hard, 'cause you damn sure ridin' clean," he says.

"Boy, you got jokes! Cutting grass on Saturdays and Sundays ain't no joke." I reply with a straight face.

"Let me find out you know how to work a lawn mower?"

"You'd be surprised at what I know how to do," I tell his ass.

I can get smart, too. Shit. I pull the bag from the back seat, and toss it in his lap, eyeing him closely.

"Damn, Sweets. I never thought you'd know about this part of life."

"I told you, you'd be surprised at what I know." Damn, he smells good!

"So, you want it or not?"

"Bossy, I like that!"

Is he hitting on me? I wonder.

"Girl, where you get this sticky icky from?"

“Loose lips damn sure sink ships.”

“What you want for it?”

“2,500 and it’s yours.”

“Damn, ma! You can’t cut me no slack?”

I speak with my eyes. Hell no!

“I only got two bands on me now.”

“Twan, this one time only. Next time I’m gonna tax your ass to the white meat.”

“Alright! Alright! I get the point,”

He’s straight cheesin’. Damn, his smile is pretty too. Calm down, girl, I keep having to tell myself. He hands me the money, and looks me up and down. I don’t count it, ‘cause there ain’t no need to. I know where to find his bitch if the shit ain’t straight. Don’t nobody get spared in this game called L.I.F.E.

We both get out of my car. He starts walking towards his Denali and I head back towards the shop.

“Yo! Your nigga teachin’ you real good.” he say to my back.

“I ain’t got none,” I holla back. I bet you his mind is working overtime on that one! I go directly to my station, ‘cause the rest of my co-workers had shown up while I was handling business with Twan. Now I damn sure can’t fuck or victimize Talena’s man.

I might need him again.

Layers is the place to be if you're getting your hair done. Located in the heart of the city, you can't miss the shop. We have four stations, one for myself, Talena, Dahlia, and one for Kiana.

I've got two perms, one wash and wrap, and Ced's dreads to do for the day. I could work over today, but I'll pass on that. I have to check up on Beauty, too. Music is playing in the background, and everyone's talking and getting the latest news, when a flower delivery man comes through the door.

"Hello, ladies! I am looking for Corona," he says. Dead silence. Everybody in the place is looking at me.

"That's me," I say, knowing that I sound a little nervous. Damn, what the flying fuck is going on? This nigga 'bout to spray me right here. My fucking nina at home, damn!

"I have a delivery for you. I need you to sign here by the x," I did as he said, and he walked back out the door.

Conversation is almost back to normal when the door opens up again. My mouth flies wide open and my hands stop moving. Thank God I had just finished washing the perm out of my customers head, 'cause her shit would've been fucked up! The flower man is holding 24 pink roses with a small teddy bear attached to the vase with a pink balloon. See? This is the reason why I'll always ride Jay's bid out with him. He's the best. Since I surprised him, he had to surprise me back.

"Sir, can you put it on the desk, please? Thank you."

"You're very welcome! Have a great day, ladies."

Everyone says goodbye as he departs. I put conditioner in my client's hair and then move to the desk to check out my gift.

Damn! It has a card in a sealed envelope. I rip it open fast.

You are beautiful on the outside, but I am dying to know what the inside looks like. I think we should get to know each other better. P.S You better get on the Heat's team.

Cedrick

I feel like I'm gonna fall out. My head's spinning like crazy. I got to sit the fuck down. Talena must have caught the look on my face, 'cause she comes rushing over.

"Girl, you look like you seen a dead body," I hear her talking to me, but I can't even reply. I'm in a state of shock. No man had ever done something like this for me. And he isn't even my man. Get your shit together, girl, I tell myself silently.

I hand the card to Talena and watch for her reaction. She knows all about Jay, but she knows nothing of Ced, my new found friend.

"Somebody's got a secret admirer," she whispers in my ear.

"Our little secret," I whisper back before I return to my client.

I've got two heads done, one almost finished, and one left to come. I'm spraying oil sheen on my client's head when the phone begins to ring. It's A'dasia. "Girl, you ain't text me back," she complains as soon as I pick up.

"Damn, boo, I apologize. I'm at work," I say as I check my text messages.

"Look, I sent you the number for the bridal shop. Be careful with it."

"Thanks, girl. And I got you." Shawty has come through for me, I'm damn sure gonna come through for her. Business is good and looking better all the time! Today is turning into an amazing Monday with endless tomorrows. I see the information I need in my phone, and I smile. Hell yeah.

My last customer leaves, so I start cleaning up my station as I wait for Ced to show up. The clock on the wall shows the time as 12:55. I'm bent over with a dust pan in my hand and my ass in the air, sweeping up the last of the hair when I realize how quiet it seems to have gotten in here. There's nothing but music in the air until Kiana opens her big ass mouth.

"Damn! He's fine like a dime!"

I turn around to find Cedrick standing there looking at me like I am his first meal in a long time.

"We got an appointment at one, right?"

"Yeah, Cedrick. You know we do."

"How are you, beautiful?"

"I'm doin' good. How you doin'?"

"Fine now that I'm here." His eyes are scanning the place like an owls, like he can see in the dark and cover a 360 degree radius with his vision. I wonder what his eyes see.

"The roses are beautiful. Thank you so very much."

"Beautiful things for a beautiful lady."

I see that Kiana has to stop what she's doing. It's clear that Ced has already become an idol in her eyes. Kiana's a young twenty year old slut around town. The news is that she's already had over twenty abortions; that she'd slept with her mother's boyfriend and his brother too. The bitch just off the chain, but I promise on everything if this bitch ever touch mines, her ass gonna be history. So I give her that look that says, "Bitch, he's mines." Confuse that, ho!

Dahlia, on the other hand is the opposite. She's an older lady, but pussy ain't got no expiration date. She's got four kids and been married to the same man for 10 years, but as I say, not everything that looks good is good. Lord, is this a punishment? 'Cause this man is SEXY. Sexy from head to toe.

I wash, twist and dry his dreads. When I finish it's close to 3:00pm. He pays me, and even tips me very well.

"You know, you don't have to do that," I tell him.

"I am a grown ass man. I do what I want to do. I can take care of myself, and I can take care of you too."

"Thanks, but I got me covered."

Talena usually closes Layers at five, but today she's closing an hour early since Twan's got that weed to sell. Ced takes a seat, and starts playing with his phone. He watches me watch him, and shows me that beautiful smile.

I clean my station again, gather up my things and say my goodbyes to my co-workers. I nod at the flowers on the desk. "Would you please get those for me?" I ask Ced.

"Sure."

I hold the door open for him, and I notice that bitch Kiana's still got her eyes on him.

"Beautiful day isn't it?" he asks as we step out into the sunshine.

"It sure is, sir."

We walk to my car together. I push my alarm button, open the back door of the driver's side, and place my package on the floor with my bag.

"Thank you, Sweets. This is the best my dreads have ever looked. I see you put on in the shop the same way you put on in the club."

"Thank you." But you should see how I put on in the bedroom, I want to tell him, but I keep that little comment to myself.

I know he's thinking the same thing. This man is beautiful! Lord, give me strength.

"It's late. You gotta pick up your daughter, don't you?"

"Naw, her dad's got her."

"So you free?"

"Naw, not really. Probably later, though."

"You stay givin' a nigga the left turn. Why is that?"

"No, I'm not," I say and push him playfully.

He grabs my arm and pulls me into his. Now we're face to face.

I can feel my legs wanting to break down, so I school myself, RELAX! BREATHE!

"You are even more beautiful up close. How could any man allow you to labor?" He says it in such a sexy way that I can't even speak to respond. It's a good thing that I can't. He keeps going.

"Ever since Friday night I can't get you off my mind. Can't eat, can't really sleep, 'cause you seem to have all the qualities that I want in a woman. You remind me so much of my mother, that I will do anything to have you." I swear I see a tear fall from his eye. Am I trippin'? I can smell his Polo Blue cologne, and then it happens...He kisses my left cheek, let's go of me, and walks back to his all white Chevy Caprice. Lost in the moment, I watch as the old school drives away thumping Yo Gotti. It seems like I stand there for an hour or more. All of a sudden the sky opens up and rain drops begin to fall. It's the water hitting my face that brings me back to reality, and for a second I wonder how long his vehicle has been out of sight.

"You better get in the car before you get sick!" Talena yells at me from across the parking lot.

Damn, what just happened? Now I know I'm goin' crazy, 'cause I'm talkin' to myself. I get in my car and put my head on the steering wheel. Still dazed and unsure of what to do next, I just sit here until my phone starts ringing and forces me into action.

"Hello?"

"Let me know when you free, so I can take you out." His voice is driving me wild.

“Okay, Cedrick. I will.”

“Drive safe, and if you need any help with that package of yours, let me know.”

“Thanks, and you drive safe also. If I do need help, I’ll let you know, but you already know-” He cuts me off before I can finish.

“Let me guess, you’re a big girl, and you can handle it yourself,” he says with a little laugh. I have to smile at the sound of his laughter. Is there anything to dislike about this man?

“You’re learning,” I tell him as I start my car up. I’m ready to get back to the house. I can’t help but to ask...

“What would have happened if my man had seen you kiss me on my cheek?”

Then he better take it up with me instead of hurting you.”

“Oh yeah?”

“And if you had a man that you truly loved, then you would have set me straight from the get go, boo.”

The shit he’s saying makes mad sense. Do I really love Jay?

This nigga’s driving me crazy with my own damn thoughts. What the fuck?! We talk the whole way home. Truth be told, he is charming, full of jokes, and crazy as hell. I like it.

“I’ll call you later, ‘cause I gotta get this package into the house, and it’s still raining.”

"Cool, and be good."

"You too, Ced."

This whole conversation had a bitch wigging the fuck out. Where did this man come from?

Today's been a delightful day so far. How could I complain?

I call my daughter to see how her day's been, and as always, she puts the icing on the cake just by being herself. To my surprise, her daddy ain't even tripping. I bet you he feels like father of the year, but to me he is the sperm donor of the day. Sad but true.

I tidy up the house and then check my stash spot. Shit is looking good! As I sit at the table and think back to how far I've come, I have to mentally pat myself on the back, 'cause damn, it's been a long road. I also wonder if a day will come when Karma will hit me. How will it return to me? Will I die by the hands of my enemies? Will the system toss me in jail and throw away the key? My mind's racing all over the place.

My thoughts are rudely interrupted by Plies' song "Goons Lurkin'". It's Dimples' ringtone.

"I'll be over in an hour," she says, "I have to handle some business."

"Cool. I'm at the crib gettin' my mind right."

What's unsaid is always understood between me and my bitches.

It's already 5:00pm, and Jay still hasn't called. I want to call the damn prison to see what's up my damn self, 'cause truth be told, this nigga is acting totally abnormal. Now I see that I have to work as a spy to see what's really going on. I make sure he's right, nigga gets at least a stack a month, and that don't include phone calls and books. I always question myself where the money's going. Deep down I feel like I can never fully TRUST a nigga again thanks to my sperm donor. I feel like Jay is lying to me about some things, but I let him believe otherwise 'cause I really have no proof. Just doubts.

In due time if he's lying, then he'll betray himself. I just want to make sure that nigga isn't trying to play me. No one is safe around me but me, and that's how it's always gonna be!

"Yo, what's good, sis?" Black says as she enters the kitchen. "Damn, yo! You creepin'? I didn't even hear you come in."

"Look like you in Times Square, just standin', lookin' at a picture of Bin Laden."

"Naw, just thinkin'." I want to tell her what's up, how my mind keeps racing, but my mouth won't let me. Lately I find myself committed to myself.

"Damn, who died? These flowers are beautiful! Let me find out that you have that nigga Jay's nose wide open?"

"Bitch, think again," I snort. "Matter of fact, read the card. I want to know what's going on in her head as she reads, but she doesn't even have an expression on her face.

"They smell good," is all she has time to say before the house phone starts ringing. I already know who it is."

"You have a collect call from "your baby". Press zero to

accept."

"Hey, sexy girl."

"Hey, how you doin', stranger?"

"Shit, just chillin', thinkin' about you. Ready to come home.

You ready for your daddy?"

My mind's all over the place. Something about this conversation so far is weak.

"Yeah, you know I am, boy. What you been doin'?"

"Shit, just doin' this time, playin' cards. You know, same shit, different toilet, reused water."

Fuck what he's saying.

"So why haven't you been calling the way you used to?"

"Just busy."

"I hear you, and believe me, I am not worried."

I know he hears the attitude in my voice.

"What the fuck you mean by that shit?" Dimples has arrived, so I walk out, leaving her and Black to talk.

"Either way you take it, Jay. I ain't, and won't be losin' any sleep."

"You on some real shit. I ain't call you to argue, so chill the fuck out."

I just keep quiet.

"Shit, I just spoke to my ma. She and my aunt supposed to be coming this week or the next week, so you don't have to come."

I don t get along with his mother, 'cause she's grimey, but I still put up with her just for his sake.

"When you find out that she comin' to see you?"

"Friday that passed, she wrote me and sent a new number to call, but I ain't called yet."

Damn, and he's just now telling me.

"Well, I ain't tryin' to come up there and mess ya'll's visit up, so you just let me know when it's a good time to come see you."

"Now you tryin' to be funny."

"Nigga, how the fuck am I tryin' to be funny? You said what you had to say, and I said what I had to say. Conversation over, so let it go."

"The caller has hung up." It's that damn operator in my ear.

All I can do is look at the phone in my hand. This nigga had the nerve to hang up on me! I can't believe it.

I make my way back to the living room to see Black braiding Dimples' hair.

"Damn! That was 15 minutes already?" they both ask at the same time.

"You can say so. That was his 15 minutes. He hung up on me."

The phone rings again.

Oh.

Hell.

No.

He's trying to call back! He's got jokes for real, thinking he can hang up, call right back and I'll answer the phone. Nigga's got me fucked up! I turn the ringer off and put the phone back on its base.

"I damn sure have bigger fish to fry."

My bitches smile when I say that. We talk about our day, and our plans for the night, 'cause there's money to be made. Black braids my hair next, and after that I do hers, 'cause Dimples can't braid for shit. Damn! Now that I think about it, can't braid, can't cook, no wonder she's still kickin' it with Black Kong! She ain't gotta do shit! That's my bitch though, for real.

Time stays rollin' when I got shit to do. I glance at the television. It's 11:30. I check the caller ID on the house phone and see that I've got fifty-two missed calls, and they're all from Jay. Damn, I didn't get the chance to tell my princess good night, so I text her daddy's phone:

"Tell Regina thanks! Kiss Beauty for me. I'll pick her up from school tomorrow."

Chapter 18

Who Say What?

When we leave the crib at two in the morning to go to the spot, Dimples is driving, and Black is riding shotgun. I'm in the back seat, and we're on that all black party. Dimples drives around the building twice to make sure that we haven't been followed.

We park on Pierce Street, and I keep looking out the back to make sure we're the only ones out. We get out and travel the rest of the way on foot. As soon as we hit Buchanan Street we hear male voices, and stop dead in our tracks. I reach in the back of my tights and pull my baby out, one already in the head. I'd rather get caught by the police with it than get caught by a street nigga or a bitch without it. We listen hard, and we slide behind a blue house, where we see three figures in a car.

I keep my eyes on them, while Black keeps watch behind us, and Dimples scans the rest of the area. Six eyes are better than two, and that's a fact!

"Mane, fuck that bitch, Stacy. That bitch ain't shit, but she do give some good head. Her baby daddy touch down in thirty days, so now she tryin' to push me to the left after she had me all up in her."

"Damn, cuz! I know you ain't fell in love with that joint?"

"Yo, that bitches pussy is the truth, she got that snicker bar pussy. I just gotta have it."

These niggas are in our way 'cause they can see the storage place. We have to wait until they move before we can do anything.

"You smell that shit?" I whisper.

"Them nigga's smokin' some good ass dro," Black answers, keeping her voice as low as mine. Their car windows are down, and they're just smoking and talking away, not knowing who's listening.

"So look, yo! Tomorrow night we in that bitch. A nigga pockets hungry. Ain't even a crackhead out here, and that pluck is exactly what we need."

"Fuck that nigga Whyte and his crew."

The driver starts the car and drives away.

I'm surprised. Did I really just hear what the fuck I think I just heard? Me and my bitches look at each other, but Dimples speaks first.

"Only thing is, we gettin' it first"

We cross the street and look around to see if anyone else is out. One by one we clib over the fence. It isn't really very high, maybe five feet. The main entrance has a gate, but you need a code and a card to enter. Nina's still in my hand, ready to go to work. Black's got the bag, and Dimples has the tools. We get to unit 1426, and Dimples pops that lock in no time. We go slow sliding the door up and go inside. I'm surprised the shit actually looks clean. There's some construction supplies, a king sized bed leaning against one wall, an air conditioner and some toys thrown into a cardboard box that looks like it's ready to bust on one side.

Ain't this some shit!

"What the fuck, yo?!" Dimples sounds irate and Black is right behind her with it, saying, ""This shit can't be real."

"Calm down. Just think, yo. Where would you put money in here?"

Then it hit me the same way Traymon had busted my eye; quick and unexpected.

"In the damn mattress!"

The mattress has a zipper on it like it's a jacket. My heart is racing in my chest, and my hands are sweating a river inside these leather gloves. I hold my breath as I pull the zipper, and there it is.

"God bless America!" I'll be damned if I don't have some dead presidents looking right at me! I gotta give it to that nigga Whyte though, he is pretty smart. I just happen to be smarter. There's no drugs, just money, and I mean plenty of money! At first I think the duffle bag isn't big enough, but by the grace of God it's just perfect. The damn bag is so heavy that it takes two of us to lift it. We pull the door back down, arid Dimples puts the lock back on the latch while me and Black get the bag to the fence. Dimples catches up to us and climbs over first. Together we lift the bag to the top of the fence and Dimples pulls it over. Team work is always the best work, and there ain't no I in team. Once we get to the car I'm able to relax a little, but only for a second, 'cause driving with a gun and a bag full of money... mane, the Feds calling our names. If I'm going out, I'm going out with a couple of police officers under my belt. Fuck what you heard before. One thing for certain, two things for sure, I am laying one of them devils down. Fuck keeping my hands clean.

I have to drive, 'cause I know I want to see Beauty again, and that means the wheel's in my hands. We're about four blocks away when a police car gets behind us. I know for a fact I'm not speeding, but I check anyway. Exactly 35 mph. Tags are good, and all my lights are working. What the hell?

"Fuck."

The light at Bass School turns red. Now this motherfucker's directly behind us.

"Yo, if shit go sour, I am squeezin' this bitch," I say while touching the nina in my lap.

"Already! We in this together," Black reminds me.

Finally the light turns green, but for a second I swear I thought it wasn't going to change at all. As I take my foot off the brake and hit the gas, the motherfucker behind me hits the lights.

"Stop breathing so hard, Dimples." I can hear the air coming and going from her nose. I make the next right to get off the main street, 'cause I know what I'm about to do is beyond crazy.

This motherfucker does, a u-turn, and takes off in the opposite direction with the V-8 engine roaring. I guess he got a call.

Our hearts are pounding, minds are racing, and my finger is itching.

“I pissed on myself,” Dimples says out loud.

I look back just in time to see Black throwing up right there in the backseat.

“Bitch, I know you ain’t just throw up on the money?” I ask. “Hell naw, yo.”

Mane, these bitches weak! That’s all I can say. How’d they get so damn weak? Our trap car has to be replaced now.

We get home safe, I park the money maker on the side of the house, and we use the backdoor to go inside. Dimples goes straight to the bathroom to clean up while Black washes up in the sink.

“I know ya’ll bitches wasn’t scared?” I laugh as I ask them. “Bitch, you act like you wasn’t.” Black answers

“Hell fuckin’ naw! For what?” I lied. I had to, ‘cause truth be told, if I’d been by myself I would’ve shit myself.

I grab a blanket from the closet and spread it out on the floor. Then I open up the bag and dump the money out on top of it. This is gonna take forever to count.

Fuck getting a sheep, we got the sheperd himself! $100,000! Free money...

“That nigga gonna kill himself when he finds out,” Black says.

This is what the preacher's kid had to say, "Thank you, Lord for this blessing."

"Amen," we all agreed.

Shit is beautiful for us. Licks like these make me wanna quit my day job, but that I couldn't do… not yet anyway. We divide the bread up between us, but I don't ask for anything for A'Dasia. I'll pay her out of mines tomorrow.

Who say what? Who say bitches can't get money?

Dimples and Black call Allied, the cab service. They change their clothes, and we decide to make a toast to each other before they leave. Dimples grabs some glasses and I pour some Ciroc.

"To our friendship, to our bond, everything we do, we will take it to our graves..."

"Call or text me as soon as ya'll get home." I say after we drink and they're headed out the door.

Black's the first to call, then Dimples. It's 4:30 in the morning, my bitches are good, and I need to take a shower.

Then again, a bath sounds pretty damn good, whether it's late or not, especially after tonight. I run my bathwater and put some jasmine oil in the tub to help me relax. Then I undress and ease myself into the hot water. I reach for my phone once I get comfortable, and scroll through my contacts to find the number I want. I press send and wait, but there's no answer, so I end the call. I was just about to put the phone down so that I could dip under the water, when it rings in my hand.

“Hey, I hope I didn’t wake you up?” I say when I answer.

Silence.

“Hello?”

More silence.

I remember how it was when Regina answered my call. I know how bitches like to play. One more time and I’m ready to hang it up.

“Hello?” I say again.

“Hey, beautiful!” He sounds tired, but sexy. “Are you okay?”

“Yeah, I’m okay. Are you asleep?” I ask, knowing damn well he was.

“Yean, I was, but now I’m up. You must be planning a trip to come see me and put me back to sleep.”

“Is that what you want, Ced?”

“Hell yeah, that’s what I want, Sweets!”

“Well, give me the address. I’ll be there in an hour.”

“A’ite, let me text it to you. Call me when you get outside.”

“Okay.”

Damn! What have I gotten myself into? He’s winning me over. Life is a journey. Am I willing to travel?

I wash my hair, scrub my skin like never before, and lotion

myself from here to Africa. I put matching panties and bra on with my Victoria Secret sweat outfit with the lips on the ass. I grab the keys to my Lexxus, and off I go. I haven't been to sleep, and now it's a new day. I text Talena letting her know I'm taking the day off tomorrow, and that I'll call her later, 'cause something had come up.

Chapter 19 Certified

I call as soon as I pull up. He lives on the first floor, and he opens up the door as I'm getting out of the car. White tee, white shorts, white slippers, Damn! This nigga love white!

"Damn, you smell good." he says to me when I get to the door.

"I just got out the shower. May I come in?""

"Sure, my door's open for you."

He lives a one bedroom apartment. Not only is the place clean, but he has taste. Nice taste.

"I'm goin' back to bed. Join me if you like. Better yet, make yourself comfortable."

This nigga trust me already?

"Lead the way," I say to him. I follow him all the way to his bedroom. His bed's so damn big; it could hold at least four grown-ass adults! A 62-inch flat screen hangs from one wall. I have to find out: What's up with everything being white?

Music videos are playing on the TV. He climbs back into the bed like it's nothing. I lay my keys and Dior pocket bag beside the bed before I take my sweats off. I'm wearing pink boy shorts with a wife beater underneath my sweats. He watches as I undress myself and says, "You must be sleeping on the floor?"

"If you think that I came over here to sleep on the floor, then you need to get on some medication."

"You know I'm just playin' with you, girl."

I climbed on to the bed. It's so soft and cozy, with silk sheets. This nigga has taste and class! In need of some touch, I move my body towards his, placed my head on his arm, and we start talking. He tells me where he's from, about his parents and his kids.

His father is a Jamaican who had been a big time drug dealer, and met his American mother one day when he'd gone out of town to do business. He'd been born in Bronx, New York, but he'd moved to West Virginia when he was 17, and he is his parent's only child. His mother died when he turned 24, and two days later the system took his father. He lost both of his parents just like that, in the blink of an eye. He buried his mom and moved to Virginia. He's been here for six years now, blah, blah, blah, and I fell asleep while he was still talking. I remember him wrapping his feet around mines. I wake up on my side with his arms around me.

It's 10 am, and my stomach is talking. I go to the bathroom to release my bladder, wash my face, and I use my finger to brush my teeth. It's better than nothing. While I'm in there I notice there are no woman supplies in sight. He's still asleep, so I make my way to the kitchen, and since it's a one bedroom apartment, everything is easy to find. The refrigerator is well stocked, and I find everything I need. Bacon, eggs, sausage, cheese, grits, and pancake mix in the cupboard. I get to work, ‘cause you already know the kitchen is my favorite room in any house. I’m making the last pancake when his hands hit my waist.

“You got the dead walking, girl.”

I smile, but I don’t turn around.

“My stomach woke me up, so thought I’d help myself around, and surprise you.”

I feel his dick on my ass, so I push him back a little to let him know that he is way too close. Lord, give me strength! He let’s me go and goes into the living room.

“You look real sexy in my kitchen. Then again, you look sexy anywhere you are.”

I make him a plate and bring it to him with a Pepsi.

“Come sit in here with me and eat,” He says to me.

I make a plate for myself, and sit on the couch next to him. “Damn! Damn! You can cook, do hair, dress to kill, dance, I mean, damn! What else can you do?”

“You’ll figure it all out in due time.” I answer.

“I can’t wait either.”

I watch him eat and then watch as he plays the X Box Connect.

After I clear my plate, I clean the kitchen while I talk to my sperm donor on my cell.

“Can I keep Beauty for the week?”

“What?!” I ask. I know this nigga’s on drugs. This is not how he gets down. What the fuck is going on?

“Can Beauty stay for the rest of the week?

“Yeah, but only if she wants to though.”

“A’ite, I’ll call you when I pick her up from school.”

Just as I finish up in the kitchen, the door bell rings.

“Could you get that for me, Sweets?”

“Am I safe? I don’t need any weapons?”

“Just answer the door.”

It’s the same flower guy from the shop.

“Good day, I have a package for Corona.”

Twenty-four pink roses, no balloons or teddy bear this time.

I sign, say thank you, and close the door. I inhale their scent; they smell so good. I place them on the table, and read the card attached. Ced never takes his eyes off the TV.

“This morning when I opened my eyes and saw you next to me I saw an angel. You are beautiful, especially when you sleep.”

Ced

I know I’m cheesin’, but what else can I do? When did he even get the chance to do this? I push his leg off the sofa and grab the other controller.

"You think you're ready?"

"Don't hurt me too bad. Remember, I'm a girl." I say, knowing damn well he's about to trash me in this Madden.

"I will never, ever hurt you."

I know he means exactly what he says, too. Let's just say he whooped my ass bad in the game and left me for dead.

"You gave me a run at first, though. I gotta give you some respect for that."

That's when I move in real close.

"Thanks for the flowers, the balloon and the teddy bear at the shop. Thank you for the flowers today. They're beautiful."

"Naw! Thank you for keeping me safe last night, thank you for breakfast, and thank you for this..."

He closes the distance between us to lock his lips with mine and eases his tongue into my mouth. I couldn't take my lips from his even if I wanted to. Damn! I have been faithful to Jay until this very moment, this damn moment.

I find the strength in me to pull away from his embrace. I have to be real, 'cause that's all I know. I am Certified Real. "Look, I'm in a crazy ass relationship."

He gives me this blank look, so I know that I have to explain it to him.

"Home boy's doin' a bid, and I been ridin' with him for two

years now. He's got one left. I haven't even kissed another man, or even slept outside of my own house until I met you. No one's gotten my attention but him, until you came into my life."

"Okay." he replies.

"I can't say that I don't want you, if I did, Lightning would hit me right now."

I cut him off. I got to let him know.

"Just listen, please! I damn sure don't know what will happen a day from now, much less a year. Since you've come into my life a lot of things have changed, and it's only been a couple of days. I don't want to rush things, or start something that I can't finish, 'cause I do like you. Let's just take things slow, and see what happens."

"I'm cool with that. I respect you for tellin' me. It shows a lot about you, and that makes me want you more, but I gotta make one thing clear though."

"What's that?"

"Keep it a stack with me, and I'll keep it a stack with you."

"You got a deal, Ced. I'll respect you , and I hope you return the favor."

"Already, boo! Can I finish tasting your lips?"

"Naw," I say smiling, "I might not want to stop."

"Let me be the judge of that."

"I'll kiss you if you beat me to the bed!" I book it to the bedroom. Either way I am gonna kiss him. I make it to the bed first, and when I kiss him I make sure it's a healthy one. He doesn't let his hands roam my body or anything. Just our mouths move. Then we slide between the sheets again. With only a few hours of sleep and full bellies, we're out in no time, and sleeping like newborn babies. I sleep in his arms, just like last night.

The sound of his cell phone wakes me up, and I turn over to look at the time. 2:45 pm. My movements wake Ced up. He gets out of bed to get his phone, and I get up to get mines from the kitchen. Four missed calls! One from Black, one from Talena, one from Dimples, and one from a number that I don't recognize.

I call my bitches first, but I keep it super short. Then I call Talena back, and tell her that I have to take the rest of the week off, 'cause I have some business to handle. She asks me if everything is all right, and I assure her that it is. I call the number that I don't recognize next.

"Hello? Someone called me from this number?"

"Yeah." It's a female. I wonder who the fuck this bitch is, and why the fuck she's calling my phone.

"Who are you lookin' for?" I ask her.

"I'm looking for Corona. Is this her?"

This bitch knows my first name! What the hell?

"Yeah, this is her. How can I help you?"

Now Ced is looking at me, and he's all up in my space. Fuck it. I don't have anything to hide besides my business. He knows all about Jay.

"Um... your husband is locked up with my husband in Dillwyn, and he wants to know why you haven't been answering the phone."

"Tell your husband thank you for passing the message, and to let Jay know that he should call me. And thank you also."

"You're welcome."

This nigga has the nerve to get someone to call me 'cause I ain't answering the phone. A couple of days ago that motherfucker wasn't even calling, and he isn't my fucking husband! Ced is standing here looking at me like he can read me head to toe.

"Got something you'd like to say?" I ask. I can't help the attitude, I'm mad.

"One mistake can 'cause a nigga to lose you, and me to have you for a lifetime. Then I'm down to play, and win you forever."

"I hear you talkin'." I know what he means by that too.

"I got a couple plans I got to attend to, but I don't want you out of my sight for a minute," he tells me.

"I gotta see my daughter, but first I gotta take a shower, and pay my friend's storage bill. Since I didn't bring any clothes over here, that means I gotta go home."

"Well, I'm gonna take you to do all of that. Is that cool?"
"Yeah, that's fine."

"Let me get clean and fresh real quick, then we can be out, but first, can I get a hug?"

"Now you askin'?"

"You ain't mines yet, but believe me, once you are mines, I will not ask."

That word "yet" makes me smile. I give him a hug, a long one, and he leaves me there dazed.

While he takes a shower, I straighten the house up as I wait.

It isn't long before he's finished.

"You ready, babe?"

"Yeah, waitin' on you."

Let's just say this nigga looks like he's ready for an interview with GQ magazine. He must've read my mind easily, 'cause he says, "Even my socks Polo, baby."

I smile at him for the 20th time this morning.

We leavin' your car over here, okay?"

"Okay!" I'm down to ride.

He looks so damn good my pussy starts throbbing while I'm sitting in the passenger seat. A nigga who looks like this makes you want to smoke another bitch just for looking, real talk. I give him the address to my house, and it takes about twenty minutes to get there. Damn, 3:30 already!

Beauty's already with her dad. I open the front door, and show Ced into the living room.

"Would you like something to drink?" I ask him.

"Yeah."

"Pepsi, water, Red Bull, or Mountain Dew, which one?"

"Red Bull." He winks at me as he says it.

As soon as I give him the Red Bull and turn the TV on, the phone rings. The damn house phone!

"You have a collect call from "your baby"."

I can't even get a hello in there before Jay starts going slam the fuck off. The volume on the phone is up high, and I know Ced can hear him, but to be honest, right now I don't even care. "Where the fuck you been, yo?"

"Well, damn, hello to you too."

"Mane answer the fuckin' question, yo. I ain't even playin'."

"I never said you was playin', but you gonna calm down before you hear the dial tone."

I got to leave Ced, so I go to my room to get my clothes together so I can hit the shower and get fresh. I've got to get Jay off the phone before a shower can take place though. Fuck it, I can get my clothes together while we talk.

"Look, I ain't tryin' to fight with you, baby. I just been stressed and ready to come home to you. Shit is just crazy."

"And Jay?"

"I'm sorry for goin' off on you. I don't want to lose you, Sweets."

"I hear you."

"What you doin'?"

"Getting' ready to take a shower and go see Beauty. Her daddy's keepin' her for the week."

"What you got planned?"

"Shit, nothin'. Work." Hell naw, I ain't tellin' him I'm off work!

"I spoke to my ma today, and my baby ma was over there."

"You claiming that baby without a blood test, even when the little girl looks just like your friend Cambo?"

"Until a blood test say she ain't mines, then I'll stop, but for now, she's mines."

"What the fuck ever! Do you! I don't care."

"I mean damn, Sweets! I'm tellin' you, and you gettin' mad."

Now he's screaming, and that's when he gets the dial tone. I warned his ass, but he never listens. Some women mean what they say. I leave the phone in the bedroom while I hit the shower. I can hear the phone ringing again, but I pay it no mind. Shit, I busy. I get dressed and go to let Ced know I'm ready.

"Pack a bag, 'cause I want you to spend the rest of the weekend with me."

This nigga needs to see a doctor...but shit... okay. Maybe I do too. A few minutes later I've got a bag packed. I forward the house phone to my cell.

"You look amazing," Ced tells me.

"Thank you."

He takes my bag to put it in the car. I check my stash to make sure that shit is still the same, then I arm the alarm system and lock the door. It's time to roll.

Chapter 20

This Is How I Do...

Dressing is like a hobby. I take pride in it. I can dress any which way, and still look sexy, can't nae bitch see me. A fresh perm has my hair looking just right. Polo all the way down, I am so official, I should change my name to Horse! I'm wearing an all white short sleeved tee with a v-neck to show a little cleavage on top of a light blue skirt so short it shows a lot of thigh. With legs like mine I don't need heels. I'm rockin' some all white flip flops.

"On my momma, on my hood, I look fly, I look good."

Every boss nigga deserves a boss woman! Knowing that he wants me around makes me smile. When I get in the car he bites his bottom lip as he looks me up and down.

"Damn."

"Well, thank you for the unspoken compliment."

"Since you can read my mind, you must already know that you're very welcome."

How can a nigga so sexy and so well mannered be single? It's a mind blowing thought.

"You have to stop at the storage. Which one?"

"The one on Park Avenue by the train tracks."

"Then you gotta go see your little one, right?"

"Yeah! Let me text her dad and let him know I'm on my way."

When Traymon text me back I let him know I'll be at his crib in about twenty minutes.

Ced pulls into the storage facility, and I pull my skirt down before I get out, but my ass pulls it back up again. I know he's watching me as I climb the stairs to get to the office, so I let it ride up. I like the thought of giving him a little show.

"Hey, girl," A'Dasia greets me as I walk in. No one's around. I hand her a stack.

"Good lookin' out with them numbers."

"Girl, you know we family. You ain't never gotta do that!"

"Shit, I never know when I might need you again."

"A'ite, tell my cousin I love him."

"Sure will," and with that I leave. Ced's on the phone when I get back in the car.

"Hell yeah. I'll be through there in an hour, so make sure that shit correct. A'ite?"

He never stops his conversations when I am around. It seems that he trusts me.

"I gotta go to them apartments over there by Virginia Baptist Hospital," He says when he gets off the phone.

"The ones in the bottom?"

"Yeah."

"Today is a beautiful day. The sun is shining, and everything feels right," I say as I look out the window.

"Couldn't be better! I got the most beautiful woman in my car."

"Are you always this sweet?"

"Yeah, when it comes to you, but I do have an impure side."

"Hope I never see it."

He doesn't respond to my last statement. Instead, he let's Yo Gotti talk through the speakers. Now I'm putting it all together. Yo Gotti loves white, and Ced loves white.

I spot Beauty, Traymon, and Regina at the playground as we pull into the parking lot. Ced watches my face light up when I see Beauty.

"She looks just like you. Gonna make a nigga real happy one day." "One day." I answer.

I can't wait to get out of the car and hug my princess. Damn,

I've missed her! As soon as she sees me she runs in my

direction. “Mommy! Mommy!” She screams at the top of her lungs as she grabs my leg.

“Hey, baby! I miss you.”

“Mommy, I miss you more! Guess what?” Beauty tells me everything she knows or hears. I love our relationship. Why didn’t I have this with my mother?

“Daddy got me ice cream and some new games.”

Traymon and Regina are a few feet away. Ced stays in the car. You can’t see inside, ‘cause the windows are jet black. I want Traymon to see him so bad, ‘cause he’s never seen me with any nigga, but he knows I’ve been holding Jay down.

“He did? Do you like them?”

“Ma, I love them!”

It makes me feel good to know that Traymon has stepped his game up with being a father.

“Dag, you ridin’ clean,” Traymon’s paying attention to that white on white. I can’t blame him.

“Hell naw! Hey, girl,” I say to Regina.

“Hey, you look good,” she says, knowing she’s fake as fuck. “Thanks.”

That bitch recognize I am still the shit. She ain’t ugly, but she ain’t all that either, and she damn sure ain’t me. We’re about the same height, but my skin’s a little darker than hers, and my body leaves her wishing for a miracle.

“760, all white everything. Damn!” Traymon sounds jealous.

I turn around to look at Ced’s 760. Yeah, it’s beautiful inside and out. So is it’s owner, I want to say but don’t.

“Beauty, your daddy’s crazy.”

“Ma, you crazy, too.”

We all laugh. Can’t nobody help that little smart mouth of hers.

“Give me some sugar.” I wrap my arms around her and kiss her all over her face until she squirms and begs me to stop.

“Ma, can I stay with daddy?”

“Yeah, you can, but you better be good.”

“A’ite, ma, I will! I love you, but I’m goin’ back to play.”

And then she’s off, with Regina right behind her. As soon as she’s out of ear’s reach, Traymon turns to me.

“You look good. You eatin’ good?”

“Always. With or without you, nigga, I am always gonna look good, and without you, nigga, I am stuntin’.”

He shakes his head at my comment. He knows it’s the truth.

“Who with you?”

“A friend.”

“Oh, yeah? I told you a long time ago to let me hit that, but naw....” he lets his words trail off.

“Get the hell away from me. You the one with the wife from Mars, and Traymon real talk, we been over a long time ago.”

Why do I always have to tell him this? Is it ever gonna sink in? “Call me if you need anything for Beauty.”

“Corona, before you go, let me tell you somethin’ funny.”

I see something move from the corner of my eye. It’s Ced cracking his window. I can actually see the top of his fitted hat. Traymon hasn’t noticed, or he wouldn’t have kept talking. “Beauty’s teacher said some little girl pushed Beauty, so Beauty two pieced the little girl in the mouth and nose. I told Beauty to tell the little girl sorry, but she said, “Naw, daddy. So I asked her why not, and she said,” She snitched on me, so naw, I ain’t tellin’ her sorry.”

“That’s our child. She got that temper from you, damn sure not from me,” I reminded him.

“Hell yeah! She looks like you, but acts just like me.”

I shake my head and start walking back to the car. I know Traymon is watching, so I do my stunt walk. As I open the car door, Ced speaks.

“Can you drive me?”

“Now?”

“Yeah. Right now.”

This nigga wants my baby daddy to see him.

“Okay.”

Ced gets out of the car and walks around the front of it. I see how he keeps his head facing Traymon, and I smile at him.

If looks could kill, I swear I'd be a dead bitch right now.

I adjust my seat, and put my seat belt on. When Ced gets in on the passenger side he pushes his seat all the way back, and props his right foot up on the dashboard. As I pull out I let the window down to speak to Traymon one more time.

"Call me later, before Beauty goes to sleep."

He's silent. He just throws a peace sign my way. I blow the horn at Beauty and Regina, and they both wave at me.

Ced breaks the silence first.

"You know them apartments on Ward's Road?" He asks.

"No."

"Drive to Target, and I'll show you how to get where we goin'."

I know what apartments he's talking about, but I play dumb. You just gotta play the game right. You never know when the card up your sleeve can turn into an ace in the hole.

"He still wants you," he says next.

"What?"

"You can tell by the way he looks at you."

My eyes are on the road, but I hear him loud and clear.

“Why you say that?” I’m curious to know what he sees.

“He’d be a fool if he didn’t want you back.”

“Not interested.”

“I had to let him know that you are in good hands. I’ll protect you with my life.”

“So that’s why you wanted me to drive? So he could see you?”

“You think you know me, don’t you?”

“I’m tryin’ to know you, Ced. Every part of you.” I take my eyes off the road for a moment to meet his eyes and let him know that I am serious. Dead ass serious.

“Don’t worry, you will. You just make sure you’re ready.”

He doesn’t give me a chance to reply this time. He just turns the music up. We listen to rap all the way to Ward’s road. I sing along while he bounces his head. If he only knew I’m ‘bout that life! I have an idea what he’s about, but I want to know every detail.

We get to Ward’s Road in no time. He directs me to the apartments by moving his hands, gesturing left or right...

Chapter 21

He Da Boss

"Yo, I'm outside," Ced's on his cell.

"I know damn well you ain't gonna leave me out here by myself?" I had to ask him.

"I told you once, but I see I gotta tell you again: I want you in my sight forever."

"A'ite, I'm just sayin…" He cuts me off with a kiss.

"Let's go. I have business to handle."

The door is already open. He steps in first, and I close the door behind us. Damn! Nigga's every fuckin' where, like fifteen of them. Ced leans close and whispers in my ear, "Stay here."

"Okay."

I stay standing at the door. Weed smoke fills the air, and I can smell alcohol, too. I mean, this shit right here is crazy.

Ced walks in front of the TV, and I hear him tell two niggas to pause the game they're playing. As I watch Ced, I have to say that his demeanor is priceless. This right here is a boss nigga. Young Jeezy's blazing through the system, "Posted up chilling, stacking to the ceiling, trying to figure out the fastest way to grind a million."

Someone turns the music off, and everyone gets quiet. I swear, I can damn near hear hearts beating. Then Ced speak up. "Yo, Butter! You got that paperwork ready?"

This nigga who's leaning on the counter is the shade of butter for real, so it doesn't surprise me when he's the one who answers.

"Yeah! I gave that shit to Slim last night."

"Oh, A'ite. So what the fuck's goin' on with Clap now?"

"That nigga holdin' on, but he got four holes in him. His shawty down there with him as we speak." It's the nigga by the radio who relays this message. I count the nigga's while they talk; there's twelve, not fifteen. I don't count Ced.

When Ced speaks the room goes dead silent again.

"I want ya'll to lay low for the rest of the week. Today's Wednesday. I want shit back to normal by Monday."

A'ite's, okay's and yup's erupt throughout the room.

"So what we gonna do about the situation with Clap?" the nigga by the window asks.

"You know who's responsible for that fuckery?" Ced asks, sounding mad as hell.

“Word on the street, they say some nigga name BU did that shit,” Butter says.

“Make sure for a fact before you handle that shit, Trigger,”

Ced tells this one skinny ass nigga.

“You already know, my nigga,” Trigger responds.

“Ya’ll stay out the way, lay low, relax and chill. Don’t get caught slippin’. Be here Monday at 10 am.”

“Who that?” The only white boy in the room asks, referring to me. Everyone turns around to look at me, but I keep my eyes focused on Ced, and wait to see what he says. He motions with his head for me to come over. Damn. I got this short ass skirt on, and all eyes on me. I hear someone say, “Hel-lo!” and laughter explodes. When I get to where Ced stands, he puts his arms around my waist.

“She off limits. Way off limits.”

He flicks a military salute at the men, and they return it.

I keep my arm looped through his, and we exit the way that we came.

“I’ll drive, boo.” He opens the passenger door for me, and I adjust my seat back to its original position when I get in. “Girl, you look so good, I could tear you to pieces right here right now.”

“Believe me, the feeling is mutual.” I can’t even lie.

“You think you ready?”

“I was born ready, and I stay ready.”

“I’ll see if you ready in due time.”

I change the subject fast, before it can get any hotter in this 760.

“Where we goin’ now?”

“Don’t worry, Sweets. I won’t hurt you.”

Deep inside of me I’m glowing. How does he always know when to say all the right things?

“I take you at your word, just let me think on it. You know I got that nigga, and I’ve always kept it real with myself, so give me time.”

“Have as much time as you need, boo. I ain’t goin’ nowhere, and you ain’t goin’ nowhere either. So think, and plan it all out for our future.”

Damn! How can this nigga possibly say all of this to me?

“Oh, don’t worry, Ced. I got us. As you say: as long as we keep it real with each other then we good right?”

He just smiles that perfect smile at me and turns the music up. This is his way of letting me know that he agrees. Damn! So do I want to do this nigga in, or cherish him to the fullest? Fuck! I’m stuck.

I close my eyes, picturing us together, and the shit is so good that I dozed the fuck off! After a while I wake up ‘cause my phone keeps vibrating. Six missed calls! What the fuck? Where the fuck am I at?

"You know you look so beautiful when you're asleep, and even more beautifuller when you're awake."

"Thank you, but is beautifuller even a word?"

"In my book to describe you, it sure is." This nigga has the sexiest sweet talk ever.

"I know you thinkin' I'm crazy. Strength, Stability, Power, Loyalty, and Respect are all hard to find things, but I have all of these things in me."

I don't even give him time to say anything else.

"Let me tell you something, Mr. Williams. I've got all those things and more, you just haven't seen them yourself yet. So don't ever put me on the back burner 'cause I go just as hard as a real nigga, and if you ask me, I go harder than any nigga!"

"I can dig that all the way, boo. The chemistry we have is off the meter. It feels like I can show and tell you anything. I've never felt this way. Ever since I laid my eyes on you, I knew we were meant to be." This nigga's getting deep.

"We gonna give time time, and see what happens. Even if it's us against da world, then I'm down. Right after I close up this other problem I got goin' on."

We finally reach where the hell we're headed.

We pull up a long straight driveway to a two storey brick house that's really too big to be called a house to begin with. This is MTV Cribs worthy, for real! This nigga's got a mansion! "Damn!" I say. "Who lives all the way out here?" I don't mean to sound so excited, but damn!

“This my other spot. Besides my kids, no one else knows it exists but you.” This nigga’s taste equals money. He opens up the door, and my eyes ‘bout jump the fuck out of my head. This shit is laid. Green and white are the main colors of the decor. This shit is beautiful, better yet, enchanting! He tells me that the house has seven bedrooms, and seven bathrooms, two kitchens, and two game rooms: one for children, one for adults. There’s one dining room, and a living room that could each fit one hundred people easily, a gym in the basement, a recording studio and a backyard the size of a football field, let’s not forget to mention the four car garage. Me and this nigga = GREATNESS, or me by myself = ONE LUCKY BITCH! I’m in such deep thought, that I don’t even hear him ask me if I want something to drink the first time.

“Girl, I’ve asked you twice already if you want something to drink!”

“No. Yes! Yes, please.” Get it together, I tell myself.

Damn! There goes my phone. This fucking thing will not stop ringing for shit! It’s my sperm donor. Nigga trying to be funny, so I answer.

“Yo.”

“Damn, yo, I called you three times,” He sounds mad.

“Beauty okay?” I ask him, knowing damn well she’s good.

“Yeah, she good! So you fuckin’ with that nigga now?”

“Damn, last time I checked I’m a grown ass woman! I don’t question you about how you live your life, do I?”

This nigga is losing his mind.

"You can give that nigga Jay a chance, and now this other nigga, but you refuse to give me a chance again so we can raise our daughter and be a family." I know he ain't copping a plea, for real now.

"Look, T, I don't know how many times I'm gonna have to tell you this, but please, let this time stick in your head: what we had is dead. The only blessing that came out of it was Beauty! I can't go back, and I will NOT go back." With that being said, I end the call. I know that Ced has heard the entire conversation, and to be honest, I don't give a fuck. He hands me my drink.

"I got you some fruit punch, didn't know if you wanted a real drink so early in the day."

"Thanks! This is just fine! I love your house, and I admire your style. You have a lot of skills. Did you come up with all this on your own?"

"You might think I'm lyin', but yeah, I did. Green was my mother's favorite color, and since she's no longer around I thought I'd hold her extra close to me by putting green all around me."

Awww, he loves his mother!

"I also love white, as you can tell."

"Well, you did a wonderful job. And yeah, I figured white was your favorite color."

The question won't leave my head: why is this nigga single?! What the fuck is wrong with him? I wish I could read his side effects! Damn! This nigga's got me speechless!

"I wanna know this though, why did you pick me out of all the other women to share this moment with?"

"As I said before, there's something about you that pulls me to you. I've never felt this before in my life. Ever!"

My mind ain't working no more. My pussy wants to do the thinking so I let it take the lead. It's been a minute since I felt anything sexual towards anyone besides Jay. I push my lips against his and then whisper, "I think I might be ready."

"Naw, you gotta be fully ready. I mean all the way ready, Sweets."

"Well, I am!" To show him I'm ready I push my tongue into his mouth as I bring my body closer to his. I can feel his dick getting hard. I take his hat off, and then I let my hands roam through his dreads. My lips never leave his, but after I take my hands from his head, I use them to unbuckle his pants. I want to see what he's working with. This nigga is not 99.9, but 100% ALL wood. It feels like he's got a 45 and a 9 down there, so I take my eyes off his face to make sure I'm not tripping out.

"God blessed me, baby."

I drop to my knees and glance up at him. I look at it, and then I smell it. Dimples taught me that. She said, " Bitch if it looks funny that's okay, but if it SMELLS bad hit the door."

I grab half of it, 'cause truth be told, how the fuck am I gonna put 10 1/2 inches all the way in my mouth at one time?

Fuck it! I am willing to try!

I suck the head real slow, as I use my right hand to beat the rest of it and my left hand to massage his balls. Call me a masseuse if you want to, I'm about to show this nigga I'm ready. I hear a moan escape from his mouth. I lick his dick carefully, and then I suck it like I have nothing but gums, section by section until he puts his hand at the base of my neck, guiding me up and down. I feel like I'm almost swallowing the whole damn thing. I gag, but I keep going. He's already taken his shirt off when he lifts my head up and I release the wood from my mouth. I kiss him from his dick all the way up his body until I'm face to face with him again.

"You got some freak inside of you," he says with a smile.

"Naw, you just bring it out in me."

He carries me up the stairs and into one of the bedrooms.

He lays me on the bed and undresses me until I'm butter ball naked.

"Sweets, you better than a full course meal."

"Oh yeah?"

"Hell yeah."

"Once you eat some of this you gonna be straight."

I don't know how he turns on the music, 'cause he doesn't leave me, but Usher's 'Trading Places' comes on loud and clear.

I ain't never had my toes sucked before, and I don't expect it to make me come, but it does. When he finishes with my toes he makes his way up my legs and thighs where he stops. I'm trying to get my breathing together. I hear him say, "beautiful." And I know he's talking about my pussy, 'cause I think it's beautiful too.

He digs his whole face between my legs. He licks me wet, and practically licks me dry, but when he turns me over and tells me to put my ass in the air I swear I go to heaven. My pussy aches to be fucked so bad I want to cry, but he continues to punish me with his tongue. "Please! Please, just fuck me." I beg him, but he's not listening to a word I say. He licks my pussy, then my ass, then my pussy. I swear his tongue is wiping both places at the same damn time. His head game is better than a wash cloth! I come twice, without him even using his fingers. His face does all the work.

Finally, he kisses my pussy like he kisses my lips, and then he licks my navel. He pulls each of my nipples into his mouth, like a baby sucking milk. I can feel his dick on my pussy, and I need it inside of me so bad.

"Don't move," he commands me.

I lay still and watch him. Well, I watch the dick between his thighs as he walks to what seems to be a closet. He returns with a condom in his hand. He rips it open, and puts it on without ever taking his eyes off mine. He eases his body on top of mines as we keep our eyes locked on one another. His eyes hold a story that I want to know more about.

He gently pushes my legs apart, and then he slides his dick into me. It's a tight fit, and it hurts enough that I bite my lip and try to move away, but he doesn't let me. He takes his time, nice and slow, and it starts to feel so good I hope he never stops. Once he's in, the rest is history. I'm seeing stars, two moons, the sun all put together and some more shit.

He knocks my walls like he's laying bricks. Stroke for stroke he gives it to me, and I match his rhythm. I take it like a champ, close my eyes, dig my nails into his back, thank God, and even holler Amen!

"I ain't think you ready?" he asks.

"My turn," I tell him. He's already had the first two quarters. "Let me finish the game."

"Do you," he responds.

"Lay on your back. Grab a pillow while you're at it, and put it behind your head. Like Wacka Flocka said, 'no hands so you can't touch me in any way."

A smile comes across his face. Damn, this nigga is sexy!

I get on top of him, but from the back, with my ass facing him.

I ride him like I'm drivin' a five speed. He tries to hold on to me, but I turn my upper body to smile at him, and then I shake my head no. I grab his ankles, arch my back and ride my dick... Yeah, I said it... MY dick.

"Damn, yo! What the fuck?" I hear him say just as I am about to come. I do a 180 on that dick to face him.

"Can I please touch you?"

"No."

I bounce up and down, and rock side to side until I feel his legs shaking. I watch him close his eyes, and I know he's near to climaxing, so I lean down, kiss his lips and whisper, "Let me see you come all up in this pussy." My words push him over the edge. He grabs my ass, digs real deep in my guts, and stares into my eyes. I can't take it anymore, and neither can he. We orgasm; together to the sound of Rick Ross and Nicki Minaj singing 'You The Boss'. We lay together, chests heaving, and try to catch our breath.

"Damn, you can cook, you can do hair, you can dance, you can dress, and you can fuck. Damn, boo. Where you been at all my life?"

"You got jokes, as always, but I've just been waitin' on you to find me."

"Really?"

"Hell yeah."

We lay in bed, just listening to the music, and holding each other.

"I'm hungry, and I'm pretty sure I just heard your stomach talkin' to your back," I say after I hear his belly growl.

"Let's take a shower, and you make us some dinner. Then we'll watch a movie and catch up with each other," he says in a Bossy Way.

"Okay."

"I'm gonna go get your bag from the car."

"Okay."

He gets dressed and leaves the room. I get up and look around in the closet to make sure he ain't trying to be someone else in their shit. The closet is big as hell, and his clothes and shoes are all in order. Damn, this nigga is the nigga for real.

I carry my ass to the bathroom, where I notice just as I had in his apartment that there are no lady items anywhere. Damn, I wonder how much he paid for this house? I step into the shower, press the hot water button, and let it relax me. I close my eyes to enjoy the heat of the water on my body.

When I open my eyes Ced is standing there watching me.

Join me, I offer, and he does. He washes me from head to toe, ass crack and all. I can't help but wonder again, why is this nigga single? He's perfect in every way. I guess I am just one lucky bitch. I wash him from head to toe also, but I leave his ass alone, 'cause I damn sure ain't trying to make him uncomfortable or disrespect him in any way.

"I'm diggin' everything about you, Sweets. I want you in my life forever," He confesses.

The dick is splendid, he's sexy, perfect in every way, plus he's paid. The two of us together might equal Greatness for real!

"God knows I am feelin' you too, Ced. I don't know what it is, and I'm willing to give it a try, but-"

"There goes that word that I hate."

"You know I gotta end this other thing I got goin' on anyway."

"I know you do, and I'm waitin' on you, real talk."

We get out of the shower; he wraps me up in a towel and sends me to get dressed. He had left my bag on the bed when he brought it in, but instead of putting my clothes on I slide into his closet and grab me a t-shirt and a pair of boxers. No need for bra and panties. I pull my hair into a neat ponytail and head to search for my phone.

This house is so damn big, the shit is crazy. I almost get lost, but I eventually find my phone exactly where I left it with my glass of fruit punch.

Thirteen missed calls. Dimples and Black had each called once, but the rest are from Jay. I make my way into the kitchen as I call Dimples back.

“Damn, bitch! Where you at?” She asks me as soon as she answers. “I’m with Ced.”

“Let me find out you creepin’ now?”

“Shut the hell up! What you doin?”

“Shit, nothin’ really. Black says she’s got some jobs lined up.”

“Well, call her on three -way then!” I hear Dimples comply, and soon the phone is ringing in my ear as the call goes through. I’m so amazed at this house. The man who owns it has got me thinking. I’m lost in a world by myself with Ced, and it’s got me speechless for real.

“Dimples, you heard from Sweets?” Black asks immediately, no hello, no nothing.

“Yeah, she’s on the phone too.”

“Damn, where you at?” Black wants to know.

"Shit, I'm at home. Sweets with Ced. Where you at?"

"Oh, I'm at the crib."

"Anyway, what's up with these jobs you got lined up?" I ask.

"Yo, girl, this shit is super sweet! This nigga who goes by Swoll, he's got one eye, so that's a plus, 'cause he'll never see us comin'. I heard he's got stupid cheddar, no kids, main bitch stay out of town, but the best part is that he only lives blocks from Dimples!"

I almost drop the damn phone! That's my sperm donor's cousin!

What a small fuckin' world, full of nothing but money to be gained.

"I hear he just got back in town too, so you know the nigga is straight," Black tells us.

"How the fuck you know for a fact?" I ask.

"Cause his right hand man told me."

"And you actually believe this nigga, yo?" inquires Dimples.

"Have I ever led us wrong?"

"Naw, so run it down by us then," I say. I really can't talk how I want to 'cause I don't know what Ced may have planted in his house. I just listen as she runs it down, and it makes sense, so as far as I'm concerned it's a go.

"A'ite, see ya'll tomorrow." We disconnect.

Damn, this refrigerator is stacked! And since the kitchen is my favorite place to be, I'm 'bout to put on in here. Oh yeah! Thyme seared steak with sautéed onions, green peppers and mushrooms, paired with mashed potatoes and some string beans sounds great. You know what they say, the way to a man s heart is through his stomach. This man's about to love me for real! I get to work.

I text T's phone telling him to tell my princess goodnight for me, and as soon as the text goes through my phone rings. "Hello?" I answer.

"You have a collect call from "your baby"."

What a night this is shaping up to be!

I press 0.

"Damn, yo! 'Bout fuckin' time you answer my phone calls!"

This nigga's been showing his ass off lately, like I'm the one behind bars.

"Let me know when you're gonna stop cussin' at me, 'cause I am not in the mood for this shit today."

"And bitch, you think I'm in the mood?"

"Call me another bitch, and I swear on your momma I'm gonna show you a bitch for real. You done lost your mind talkin' to me like that!"

"Sweets, you actin' like I don't even matter to you any fuckin' more."

"Every time you call, you stay goin' off. You act like you the only one doin' time! Nigga, I been doin' this time with you! When you call, I fuckin' answer. Visit comes, guess what? I'm fuckin' there! The money you get, I send it! The mail you get, I fuckin' write it! Tell me when's the last time you I actually wrote me a letter tellin' me thank you? How the fuck you think I feel, Jay? Nigga I try my best to make your time go by easy, and look how you treat me. Come the fuck on now, yo! I got feelings too, and I don't think you give a fuck about how I feel, or how I'm doin', but you know what? I'm good, ALWAYS good, remember that, 'cause a bitch like me is meant to last forever."

He's silent. Not even am I'm sorry or nothin'!

"You ain't gotta come see me this weekend. My mother and them coming, so come next week or whenever," he says instead.

Yeah, I was born at night, but not last night.

"Cool, I can do that." I press the end button, and stop wasting my time. My life is a book, and it's pages just won't stop turning.

I'm still at the stove when Ced comes up and grabs me from behind.

"Damn, you got this joint smellin' good, like you," he says.

"I know you hungry, so you better leave me alone before I don't finish, and we start somethin' else," I tell him as I arch my back and push my ass up on his dick.

"You right, I'm hungry, but I wouldn't mind gettin' some more of this," he says, reaching around to grab my pussy.

“Don’t worry, you will. Anytime you want some, all you gotta do is find me.”

“Didn’t I tell you I wanted you in my sight all the time?”

“You crazy.”

“Crazy over you? Yes, I am!”

Dinner’s off the chain. He cleans his plate, and helps clean mines to. We clean the kitchen up together, with not a word to be said between the two of us, but the chemistry is like electricity Eventually, he asks, “Shottas or Love and Basketball?”

“Oh, since I’m the guest here, you want me to pick?”

“Please!”

“Shottas.” Shottas is the shit! No matter how many times I see it! Mad Max is amazing and crazy beyond explaining. That nigga don’t take shit from anyone.

After a while he pulls out a bottle of Patron, and we drink it straight, shot after shot. I squeeze my little body under his on the sofa, and let the liquor work it’s magic. My body is aching for his touch, and as soon as his hands touch my pussy I rock my hips forward to let him know that I am ready for round two. It’s goin’ down, and I mean ALL the way down. This is ridiculous. He’s a beast in bed! Got me screamin’ Jesus and amen like I think it’s a revival.

Chapter 22

Back 2 Grindin'

It's the light through the blinds that wakes me up. It's 7:30 in the morning, and Ced ain't in the bed with me. My head's bouncing and my body definitely feels the workout from last night. Damn, I'm sore! I find his shirt, pull it over my head, and run to the bathroom to release the pressure from my bladder. As I wash and dry my hands, I hear Ced's voice.

"Bout time you wake up, Sleeping Beauty."

"Why?"

"I made you breakfast. I can't cook like you, but I tried my best."

"You are an amazing man."

"Naw, you are amazingly better."

"You and your words! Let me guess, that's in your dictionary, too?"

"You know it!" he laughs.

Breakfast is pretty good. He made some pancakes with scrambled eggs and grits. I ask myself for the million time, WHY is this man single?

"Look Ced, on Saturday I gotta go see this nigga, 'cause I gotta set things straight. I am gonna tell him that I'm seeing someone else."

Ced nods his head, but doesn't say anything.

"I'm not gonna say who you are, 'cause that's none of his business, and I don't want no drama comin' to you."

"I respect your gangsta all the way, but I don't give a fuck if you tell him who I am 'cause at the end of the day, no nigga puts fear in my heart. I only fear God!"

"I understand, and I hear you loud and clear. I also told Dimples that I d help her pack, 'cause she's goin' out of town with her parents. I'm drivin' her to the airport on Friday." That's a straight up lie, but what am I supposed to do? Tell him I gotta go hit a lick? It ain't time for all that. I continue what I was sayin, "So, I got Dimples Friday, that nigga on Saturday, so I won't be back until that evening."

"That's cool. I'll grab my kids and take them out somewhere. What time I gotta take you back home?"

"Later! Are you mad?"

"Naw, never! When you give me a reason to be mad at you, then I will be, but for now, I'm good."

"Will you always agree to everything I say?"

"Only if it helps the both of us. Then it's whatever you want and like, baby."

Our day is beautiful. I retwist his dreads and braid them back. We play a few games, clean the house, talk, and just enjoy each other's company in general. Leaving him for two days is gonna be hard; super hard.

When we pull up in front of his apartment to get my car, we kiss like the end of the world is on its way. When I finally pull away from him he looks into my eyes and says, "I'm gonna check up on you, but if you ever need me for anything I'm just a button away. Call me!"

As soon as I get home I text his phone:

"Crossing paths with you has been a blessing. You have everything that I want in a man, there is no word to describe you, but you are perfect for me in every way! I had so much fun with you, and I can't wait to get back to you. :)"

I forward the calls back to my house phone and text my bitches to let them know that I'm back at the house. Then I call Beauty to see how she's doing.

"Mommy! Daddy got me so many toys, plus he's takin' me shopping later!" she practically shout into my ear.

"Oh yeah? So you havin' fun?"

"Lots of fun, ma. I love you! Daddy wants you now! Bye ma!"

"I love you more, Beauty! Bye!"

"Yo, what's up?"

"What's up with you, T?"

"I'm just checkin' on you, yo. That's all," he said.

"I'm good. Later, then!"

"A'ite."

As I end the call Ced texts me back: "I am gonna make you carry my last name as soon as you give me the green light! Can't wait to have you back in my presence."

He's got to have a Webster's response book memorized, 'cause he's got all the right answers.

I check my stash. I can't complain at all. Shit is lookin' sugary. Free money always needs an owner, and I am happy that owner is me! I'd forgotten about giving T that work that I got from the last lick. Even though I'm not hungry, I know that T may as well be starving 'cause he's trying to be a boss, and at the end of the day, he's still my sperm donor.

I texted him to see if we can handle this work.

"Yo, what you doing, nigga?"

"Shit. Bout to make a run real quick."

"Meet me on Memorial Ave in ten minutes, and you better not bring our child or that bitch."

"A'ite."

I pull the work from my stash, and drive to Memorial. I park in the Family Dollar parking lot and text him again, so he knows where I'm at.

Thirty seconds later his car pulls up with Joey driving. He one of our friends, a cool ass white boy who goes super hard when he's high. He loves smoking crack, so we call him The Tester. Even though that nigga weighs a good four hundred pounds, he stays fly, and all that crack don't take any of his weight off. He thinks he's the next Eminem, and I can't lie. White boy's got skills with the beat. As soon as I see him I ask him how his wife's doing, and he says she's good. I pass the work to T and drive off. Two minutes later my phone is ringing off the hook.

"Yo."

"Damn, nigga, the snow that heavy?"

"Maybe today. You ain't gotta pay to get that shit shoveled either, just enjoy the weather," I say.

"Nice lookin' out, yo."

Sometimes I think I miss him. That nigga showed me everything about life, and for that I respect him to the fullest, but he ain't for me. Him and Regina deserve each other. Two pieces of shit equals one pile. I am one cold hearted bitch.

I get back home just in time, 'cause Black and Dimples pull up right behind me.

"So tonight's the night, huh?" I ask Black.

Hell yeah! Me and Swoll's cousin, Cuzzn been kickin' it hard.

Cuzzn say that Swoll ain't breakin' bread like he suppose to, and he treats his workers like they ain't shit."

Damn family ain't shit either, nigga hating on his own blood ain't cool. Even family out to get you. This is a fucked up world, I keep telling myself.

"Cuzzn baby ma's brother got on Swoll's team. Long story short, the little nigga got picked up and Swoll turned his back on him. The little nigga so loyal that he didn't even tell."

"Damn, now that's fucked up, yo! The game changes every minute," Dimples says with dismay.

"Anyway, what else is new?" I want to know.

"Look, I know this shit might sound crazy, but I got a job lined up for us."

Me and Black just look at each other. Dimples lined something up.

"So what's up, Dimples?" Black asks.

"I met this bitch named D'Wonda at the strip club the other night. We talked the whole night about me joining, but she said that I didn't look like the stripper type. I should be the one collecting all the money, she says. Let's just say the bitch got extra mustard. She's pushing weight for somebody, 'cause the whole club was rollin' like a motherfucker thanks to her."

"Well, I'm gettin' real impatient with this story already," I say.

"She invited me back to her crib, and we was chillin'. Shawty kept talkin' like a parrot, tellin me how many pills she's pushin' a week."

"How many?" Black's getting real impatient too.

"Five thousand pills a week, hittin' the streets at $20 a pop, so if you do the math, that bitch makin' forty stacks a month, easy, and let's not forget she bad on a pole, too. So you know she's paid the fuck up."

This shit is crazy! I'm thinking so hard, I can actually hear my mind talking to me, but the look on Black's face said something else: Something's up! I know it.

"What you think, Black?" I ask her, trying to get up inside her head.

"That bitch is a target, and I'm ready to hit her."

"So tonight we hit Swoll, and then tomorrow we smack D'Wonda," I tell them. It sounds good, but is it really?

I get my shit together, and we leave my crib to go to Dimple's spot. Something's up. If it wasn't clear before, it's clear now. The ride is so quiet, that it kinda scares me. What's going on with my bitches? No one sings along to Young Jeezy's "Focus". Could they just be nervous? When we get to Dimple's house, we get dressed and wait. It's 12:30 in the morning when Black finally gets the text from Cuzzn.

We walk through the bushes and other people's backyards all the way to the nigga's house. A light is on in the bathroom. "They all in the basement and the door's open," Black tells us.

I pull my mask over my face, adjust my mouth piece, and make it my business to have one in the head of my P89. If I have to empty that bitch, then I will.

I try the knob, and it turns. These nigga's can't even hear us 'cause they too busy watching Kevin Durant dunk on LeBron James. "Lay the fuck down, bitch!" I yell at the nigga closest to me. Dimples and Black lay the other two niggas down.

"I ain't gonna say this shit too many times, 'cause I hate sounding like a scratched up CD, so where the fuck the money at?" My words are met with silence. No one says shit, so I fly into action like a Tasmanian Devil. I shoot the nigga to my left in the leg. The P89 barks like a pit bull on steroids. The nigga starts to holla like a bitch.

"Shut the fuck up! If you don't, I'm gonna shoot the other leg, and make my way up."

"Swoll, just give them the money, yo." I hear the nigga beside Swoll say.

"I agree," Black says, putting her two cents in. The nigga Swoll really has one eye. I wonder how he lost it. Since the nigga ain't talking or giving shit up, I feel like he needs a little incentive. I shoot the nigga in his other leg, and then I shoot him in his right hand. This nigga's gonna have some trouble wiping his ass for a little while, 'cause I'm gonna get that other hand of his if he ain't careful. No money, more blood to let loose. Dimples and Black keep looking at me like I'm crazy. Maybe I am. Maybe I am losing my fucking mind all the way.

"A'ite, A'ite, yo! It's in the sofa, in the middle seat. There's a button on the right arm rest. The middle seat will lift up." Dimples follows Swoll's directions, and BAM! There it is: free money. I pull the three trash bags that I brought along out of my pocket.

"Cuff them up, my nigga," I tell Black. I keep my P89 on these niggas. Dimples loads up the trash bags, and we leave the same way we came in. I am so glad when we see Dimples' house light come into view, 'cause this damn trash bag's got some weight to it!

Once we get inside the house, the questions come at me direct. “Damn, what the fuck was that all about, Sweets?” Black asks. “What the fuck you talkin’ ‘bout?”

“You hit that nigga up three times! For what?”

I don’t know what my friend is thinking, but I gotta let her ass know.

“Them nigga’s wasn’t movin’ until that P89 got to talkin’.”

“I had to show them that we meant business and not games. We didn’t go over there for a slumber party!” To my surprise, Dimples doesn’t say a word, it’s like she isn’t even there. “Damn, Dimples! Do you have something to say?” I ask her, surprised by her silence.

“Yeah, we safe, but ya’ll goin’ at each other’s throats like sharks!”

“Fuck that. Let’s count this bitch up and split it, then I am out, I tell them. We can hear sirens flying up the street.

That nigga Swoll almost got his homeboy bodied.

“Pussy ass nigga! I should’ve shot his ass in the other eye!” I exclaim.

Dimples takes a long deep breath like she can’t breathe, Black just rolls her eyes at me. Something is up with these bitches,

I swear!

It’s six in the morning, and we’re still counting money. I feel like Jeezy for real! I should change my name to Lil Mizz Jeezy! $180,000, damn! This shit is magical! I feel like I deserve more, 'cause I sure put in the work, but fuck it! I ain't trippin'. We split the shit three ways, $60,000 each. I give Black $10,000 to give to Cuzzn for lookin' out, call a cab, and leave as soon as it gets to the house.

I text Ced as soon as I walk through my front door, letting him know that I'm thinking about him. Tomorrow that bitch D'Wonda's gonna get smoked if she don't give it up. I swear on everything I love.

Black's acting funny, so I text Dimples to let her know that I made it home. Actually, they both acting funny. I fall asleep counting my stash, and wake up looking for my phone. It's under the money. I can hear it ringing.

"Hello?" I answer.

"Babyma, you sleep?"

"Naw, what's up?"

"Mane, Swoll and them niggas got hit up last night!"

"Are you askin' me or tellin' me?"

"I'm tellin' you, fuckin' E got shot!"

"Damn, yo! He still livin'?"

"They say he holdin' on, but he lost so much blood that they don't know yet."

"You good though?" I ask.

“Yeah, but that shit fucked me up.”

“Where the shit happen at?”

“At Swoll’s spot!”

“They get anything?” I want to hear how the news has spread already.

“Swoll’s sayin’ they got fifteen bricks, $200,000, and two hammers.”

“Damn! Somebody sure is heavy today, then! Real heavy.”

“I know, yo, but damn! Be careful, babyma.”

“I will, and you too, nigga.”

Crazy how shit hits close to home, and niggas get all soft and shit. T sounded like he wanted to break down. Bitch ass nigga. Now you tell me, what the fuck can I do with him after he made my heart cold? Nigga’s nowadays ain’t built to last. They forget that Eve made Adam eat the fruit. This is a woman’s world.

I got me a new stash spot for all this money I got now. I want to change my locks, but I’m not going to, ‘cause that would let them know that I am aware of their antics. I’m one step ahead of them bitches, and I want to keep it that way.

Can't Be!!

That bitch D'Wonda gave the shit up easy! Now that's how business is supposed to operate! 10,000 pills, and $50,000 in cash! Yea, for a single black woman nowadays, that bitch was living large, waiting on someone like me to come take it, and that's exactly what I did.

"Just give me $15,000 and 2,000 pills, Dimples." Shit, it's free, plus it's Dimples lick.

"Sweets, you sure that's all you want?"

"Yea! I'm good with that!" Once I get my share I dip from them.

I give the pills to T.

"Christmas in summer, yo?"

"Get your bank roll up, playa, and don't let that bitch know shit."

"You a real ass bitch, Sweets. No disrespect, but I swear the nigga that gets you is gonna be a lucky motherfucker.

It's Saturday morning, and I got things to do. I get dressed, and I know from head to toe I am the shit. These skin tight apple bottoms show my ass perfect. When I wear them with this white fitted T that says "You can't touch this" across the chest it makes my waist look crazy small, they say dope man's are for trappers but shit I am a motherfuckin' killer in these all white air force ones. When I leave the crib I go to Payday to send a money gram to Jay for $2,000. Crazy right?

I jam all the way to Dillwyn listening to Jeezy and Lil Boosie "Better Believe It" and some other song of theirs. When I finally arrive I see his mother's car in the parking lot, but I don't see anyone which means they're already inside. When I get inside I still don't see them, which means they're in the back with Jay already. The officer processes and searchs me. Then someone comes to escort me to the visiting room.

When Jay sees me he looks like he's seen a ghost. His mouth drops open, but what I see has my hands sweating. His mother is holding his so-called little' girl. Damn!

"Hello everyone." I say.

"How you doing?" his mother asks me.

"Great, and you?"

She doesn't get the chance to respond 'cause Jay jumps in.

"Yo, I know I told you not to come this weekend!" I know this bitch ass nigga didn't have the nerve to say that. My feelings are hurt! I want to cry, but I laughed it off instead.

"Yea, you did tell me not to come, but for real, I've been coming up here for two years, and this is what you say to me?"

My brother always told me to use logic over emotions. Damn, I miss King, but when the little girl's mother came out the rest room, I knew what time it was.

Now all eyes on us...

"Nigga, you done fucked the church's money all the way up! How could you actually play me like a lotto? How could you take my mind and fuck it crazy? I motivated you, I dedicated my time, fuck that, my life to you, and this is what you give me?"

Now the bitch is sitting down and I'm in his face.

"Nigga, you so funny, Kevin Hart ain't have shit on you at all.

With that being said I walk off to take a picture.

"Yo Slim, how you doing?"

"Good."

Slim is the picture dude, old but sexy! Been down for like sixteen years, got four left. Don't have no family, been knowing him since Jay got moved here.

"That's what's up! Do me a favor, 'cause I know Jay got picture tickets."

"What's up?"

"Can you take a picture of me?"

“Yea, on his joint!”

I mean everyone’s looking at me, but I don’t give a fuck. They’re lucky I don’t turn the fuck up. I flash my middle finger in the picture. That’s something he’ll never get ‘cause no inappropriate pictures are allowed. Only thing he’ll be getting is a letter from staff. “Thanks Slim! Keep your head up!”

“You too, shawty!”

I walk my fine ass back over to Jay’s table to say something but head to the exit instead. His nasty ass so called baby ma felt like she had to speak up.

“Thanks for all your hard earned money!”

I stop dead in my tracks and look back to smile, I swear all thirty-two of my pearly whites are showing.

By the time I get to my car tears are flooding my shirt. Why does this even bother me? I was gonna break it off anyway! Damn, he’s been giving that bitch my money! Damn, another nigga just made my heart even colder. I want to flatten every fucking tire on his mother’s car, but prisons got cameras every damn where!

I get in my car to drive away but my nerves got me paralyzed, so I call Ced.

“Hello.”

“Can you please come get me?”

“Where are you? What’s wrong?”

“Dillwyn.”

"Don't move."

I hear him telling someone they have to drive him 'cause he had to drive another car back. I hung the phone up and hold my head down while I cry my heart out. Once again, I'm hurt by a man.

I turn the music on and listen to Lil Boosie's "Betrayed" 'cause that's exactly how I feel, but the conclusion that I come up with has me smiling like nothing even happened.

When a bitch is real, ain't nothing you can do about it. You can either be down with her, hate on her, or you can sit back and give that bitch the utmost respect. Some niggas and bitches are haters, while others would do anything to have a real ass bitch on their team. Real ass people salute realness, but some snakes claim they real till they show their heads. I am a real ass bitch with what's getting to be a cold ass heart.

Ced finally shows up with that white boy. He gets in my car and his people drive off.

"Damn, you got here quick" I tell him.

"If I could've flown I would've been here faster. Now tell me what's wrong." I give him the story start to finish.

"Sweets, I apologize for dude, but I'm glad that's over with 'cause you mine now."

"Really?!"

"Really! And I don't want you doing nothing; just take care of your daughter, yourself, and me with my help!"

“Thanks, but no thanks. To be honest I was taught to depend on no one, especially a man!”

“You just got caught up with the wrong niggas!”

“Let me think about it.”

“Cool! Let me drive, ‘cause you ain’t stable.”

“Funny! Since I’m not stable, can you make me stable?”

He grabs my face in both hands and we let our mouths dance. My pussy was already wet just from looking at him, so I told him between kisses, “We can do it now, right here in the prison parking lot and go to jail for havin’ sex in public, or we can do it when we touch the front door.”

“Jail will keep us apart, and that I don’t want, so I’d rather wait.”

The ride back home seems long, my body here, but my mind far away.

“You know I just sent that nigga two stacks before I got there, and for that dusty bird brain bitch to tell me thank you means he’s sending my money home to her”

“Well not anymore. Everything he got in his account you can get back.”

“How can I do that?” Now my mind’s coming back. Money’s involved.

“My people’s girlfriend, Lex, works up there as an accountant.

I can get her to wipe his account clean. She can send you a

check and put purpose of it as a gift."

"Could you please?"

"Hell yea! No problem, you know that any nigga in his right mind should be savin' if he got a rider dropping bread like that in his account."

Nowadays it's not what you know, it's who you know. Ced gets on his phone, and handles that for me.

"Lex says first thing Monday morning and it's on her to do list."

That nigga Jay just went from stunting to being dead ass broke and don't even know it yet. I hope he's got that bitch saving some, but knowing that bitch, she probably spent it. At the end of the day I'm still good, but having Ced, I'm gravy...

If I want to become warrior I have to maintain a peaceful mind, use intelligence over emotions and stay strong, or this world's gonna eat me alive.

We don't go back to the mansion; we go to his other spot. As the door opens we attack each other like vampires. From the living room to the kitchen, I grab some ice from the freezer and hit to my knees to suck his dick like a mad woman. I rub ice on his balls as I attempt to drain him of everything he's got inside his body. "Baby, I'm 'bout to bust!" I don't say anything; I just let my mouth do the talking. I pull his dick into my mouth with my lips and lock my tongue around it. When he releases inside my mouth. I think for a second that I'm drinking Redbull! I lick up every drop. What's the point in wasting good juices? I try to find the words to say, but all I come up with is, "You have the potential to hold a huge piece of my heart forever."

Shit! What am I doing? I ask myself. He smiles at me as he lifts me up, and puts me on the counter. He reaches inside the freezer and grabs a jolly rancher Popsicle. He pulls the stick out and inserted the whole Popsicle in my pussy.

"Oh my!" I gasp.

He put his face between my legs, and sucks the whole thing out before pushing it in again and repeating the process until it was all gone. When he finishes he carries me to the shower, where he straight fucks my brains out. I bend over holding onto the toilet as I let him man handle me, but I started throwing that shit back at him like a pitcher out for revenge. We make it to the shower where he lets the wall hold me while he fucks me some more. I don't want to stop. I hit the shower button and as the water hits our bodies he slides his dick out of me, to then use his face to suck my pussy some more.

"I can't take.." I come so hard I slide straight down the wall, my knees buckling under my weight.

"My turn" I tell him. I push him against the wall and I suck; the whole ten-and-a-half. I grab his hand and put it behind my head. I let him fuck my mouth like an open pussy, and I didn't even gag.

I feel his legs shaking like he's warming up for a track meet, and I know I've got more red bull coming. He lets loose in my mouth and all I can think is "Redbull; it gives you wings."

"Damn!" he pants.

We wash each other from head to toe; I could fall in love with his dick, him, or maybe both. We laid up all weekend. Pillow talk is a motherfucker!

Chapter 24

Come Clean

"You may or may not know what I do for a livin', but I am a hustler. More like a money maker!" He says. I give him a look like, keep talking.

"I push almost everything, but my choice is cocaine and crack." They forgot to say that pussy makes a man confess. It's true. It's happening right now.

"I get it right off the boat myself, because I got a Mexican plug that loves me like family. My father turned me on to them. Since my dad was so loyal to them, they cherish me and treat me like their own. I push everything in this city; and in two others also. Nothin' little; all major. In a week, I average almost a million, so do the math."

Damn. This nigga could write a book about money if he wanted to. "I treat my crew like I would want to be treated. When something happens to them, it happens to me also, but at the same time, I don't sleep on none of them 'cause this is a crazy world. Everyone wants to be a boss. I respect them, I treat them well, and I pray that they never try to cross me in any way, 'cause if I live to see the next day, they will not be so lucky, and I make that clear as day to them."

Sometimes silence is the best! Why interrupt him? He's on a roll!

"Yeah, I have competition everywhere, 'cause everyone needs to eat, but I keep the peace," he says.

What can I actually say to him that he hasn't heard before? I question myself, but before I even finish that thought, the words fly out of my mouth on their own.

"We could be a hell of a team together." I watch his face, but he's playing poker. His reply says he's interested anyway. "How?"

"Since you came clean with me, I'm gonna come clean with you.

The only people who know the truth are my girls... I'm a STICK UP BITCH."

This nigga's still wearing that poker face, so I can't read him. "Yeah, I work at the salon, but that's to throw everyone off! I go out and see who's doin' what, my bitches get in good with the victim, and then we go from there. Does that mean that I am watchin' you? No!!' At first, I didn't know we was gonna be close, but as I said, my GIRLS get in good with the niggas, and then we go from there. You're not a target. You've never been a target"

"So how can we be a great team?"

"You show me your competitors, and I take them out."

“And?”

“And I’ll split everything with you straight down the middle.” “Sweets, I am astounded! I never would’ve thought you had that in you. In the bed, you a beast; so I can only imagine you with a strap in your hand!”

“Don’t worry, you’ll see for yourself if we become a team. As you say, don’t no nigga put fear in your heart. Well, not one person puts fear in me, and I mean no nigga or bitch at all! If we do become a team, I will have the final say so on how the missions should be completed.’”

“And why is that?” He asks.

I hate it when a motherfucker questions my gangsta.

“Because this is my hustle, this is what I do. I truly enjoy this, it’s something I’m blessed to know, and I know you understand so I don’t have to explain myself.”

“I respect that. The less I know the better it is, so let me give you a rundown,” he says.

“I’m all ears.”

“Corona, don’t get it fucked up though. I got your back 103%, and that will never change unless you cross me in any way. Then I gotta handle my end to the fullest, ‘cause you damn sure ain’t no average woman to be played with.” This nigga will not be sleeping on me, and for some reason that turned me on even more.

“We both on a different level, but at the end of the day we want the same thing from each other.”

"And what would that be, Miss Lady?"

I finally tell him what I know he wants to hear.

"Each other. We want each other forever." As soon as I let those words leave my mouth, I realize that I mean it. I know that we're perfect for one another. Me + him = Greatness!

"I can dig that. So here's what you need to know; I got six niggas in my way. I don't care how you handle your business, as long as you come back to me in one piece, 'cause then life will still be worth livin'."

"Don't worry. I'm gonna be good, 'cause I got a little girl to live for. Now that I have you I'm comin' back home to you untouched, and if I don't, you better clean the entire city until you're satisfied."

"On my mother's grave, I can promise you that!"

We seal our conversation with a kiss, and then I encourage him to get my pussy wet by telling me about this money we're gonna share together.

"Ain't no words to describe you girl, I swear!"

"Anything is good, but Bad Bitch says it better."

CHAPTER 25

Count Down: Number 6

"The first nigga go by Milk. He's pushin' heavy weight. We ain't beefin' or nothin', but he dropped his prices, so he's got way more people than me. He tried stuntin' on me one night, hard. Had too many witnesses, so I couldn't really do anything but walk away. My nigga Trappa's girlfriend, Lex, got a baby by him. He don't even claim her kid, don't do shit for lil man, my nigga Trappa raisin' his kid."

I see the hurt in his eyes for that little boy.

"I'm gonna make you proud, so don't worry, baby."

He gives me the rundown on where Milk lives and everything he thought that I need to know. I was born ready and real, so yeah, I put my bitches on the lick with me. Ced's cool with that.

Milk is a straight up bitch ass nigga. I catch this nigga slippin' super hard. He's livin' large, I mean dumb large. The shit has me zoned the fuck out. I keep thinking this nigga is Tony Montana, but Tony could get his ass touched if he was around too. I get in his crib through the back door, and post up in the niggas tub waiting on him to come home from the bar. As soon as he comes in the house the first thing he does is head to the bathroom to release that liquor.

When I hear his piss hitting the water, I pop up like a jack in the box and put the burner on his ass. His piss dries up quick.

"You know you should always check your home when you get in, no matter what," I tell his dumb ass.

"If it's money you want, you can get it. You can get the work, too."

I laugh at him.

"Let me tell you off the top, my people's already searched the house, they found the drugs, but no money, so yeah, I want it all, baby!"

Dimples' and Black's masks are down, but mine's not. I wonder why they're being sloppy, but I guess it doesn't matter. I've already got the feeling this nigga won't be telling any stories anytime soon. I escort him to the kitchen. Dimples and Black are talking like nothing's going on. I bark my orders.

"Somebody give this nigga a chair, and cuff his feet! Cuff his hands behind his back too!" As they comply I go to the sink. I wet the sponge so it's soft, and I stuff it in his mouth.

Then I tell him exactly what I expect to happen.

"When I ask you a question I'll take it out of your mouth. Tell the truth, and don't lie about anything! Agree?"

He nods his head yes like he thinks he has a choice. He doesn't. "First question. Where's the money at?" I remove the sponge. "Bitch, fuck you!" Oh hell no! This is not a good time for him to get balls.

"What did you say? Let me ask you that again. Where is the money?" 'Cause I know this nigga didn't say what I think he said.

I said, "Bitch, fuck, I stuff the sponge back in his mouth."

"Yo! One of ya'll bring me a knife."

Dimples puts a knife in my hand. I cut this nigga's pants straight the fuck off of him. He's wearing some bugs bunny boxers! I pull his dick out, spit on my leather glove, and beat it to get it hard. Once it firms up I slice the very tip off. Oh mane, this nigga's screaming like he's giving birth! Blood spurts, but it's not as bad as I thought it would be. I take the sponge out of his mouth so I can get an answer. I put it on top of his dick so it can soak up some of the blood.

"It's a 32 inch old school TV in the closet of my bedroom. The money's in there!"

""Go get that!" I tell my bitches as I stuff his mouth back up with the bloody sponge. That's right, I'm a cold bitch!

When they leave, I get to talking to him again.

''How old is your son?"

"I don't have a son!"

"Yes, you do, Milk! He's seven years old, you don't do shit for him or his mom, another nigga's playin' daddy to your seed, and you have the nerve to say that you don't have a son? Nigga, you don't deserve to have a dick!" I solve that problem by taking it off for him. He's screaming, screaming, screaming, and fighting cuffs that won't give.

When Dimples and Black come back they are in shock to see his dick laying on the floor beside him.

"Bitch, you done lost your mind?!" Black yells.

Why is this bitch always questioning my gangsta?

"Yeah, I done lost it. Take that shit apart, and see if the money is in there."

They bust it open, and there ain't one wire in that thing.

With all that money, who needs wires?

"Put that shit up, grab the drugs, and load the car up. I'll be out in a few." Milk's losing enough blood that he keeps fading in and out. I'm glad that he isn't screaming anymore. That was getting on my nerves. I lean in real close to ask him my next question.

"Do you know Ced?" He hears me. His eyes fly open and he nods his head yes.

"Well, this nigga's raisin' the son you have with Lex, takin' real good care of him too. You tried to stunt on Ced one night. Then you dropped your prices so low that it started fuckin' up his bread. I don't give a fuck 'bout none of that though. What I DO care about is that you lied to me about your only seed, so you shall not live!" I pull the sponge out of his mouth so that I can hear his plea.

“I gave you everything that you asked for!” This nigga can’t even say that he has a son that he needs to live for.

“Do me a favor, when you get to hell tell all the other fake ass niggas I’m sorry I didn’t get to meet them.” I let my P89 speak for exactly how I feel. Brains splatter, and blood runs. I even shot his dick once, just for good measure.

Dimples and Black are waiting in the car when I come out of the house. Black drives, and no one says a word until we’re about five minutes from my place.

“You killed him didn’t you?” Black asks.

I give her a look like, Bitch don’t ask me no questions. I can say that Milk had it going on. 25,000 grams! That’s twenty-five bricks flat, plus $80,000... Damn!

“I’m keepin’ all the work, and the money’s gotta be split four ways.” I wait for someone to say something, but no one speaks up. They get their bread and dip. I call Ced as soon as they’re gone. We keep it short and sweet.

“Come see me.”

“I’ll be there.”

His voice alone lets me know that he’s glad to hear from me.

It isn’t long before he pulls up outside.

“There’s 25 bricks, plus $20,000 for you. I sliced the bread four ways. I didn’t touch the work, ‘cause that’s not me.”

"Yo, I swear you somethin' else," he tells me with a smile. "Don't judge me, just get this shit out of my house."

His homeboy had driven him, so Ced speaks to dude in the living room, and dude loads up the bricks and leaves.

"Let's go, I'm gonna stay at your house with you, 'cause I don't want to go to sleep here."

"Cool."

We get into my car and leave. No words had to be spoken.

When we get to his mansion he turns my face towards his and finally tells me the truth.

"I've been worried sick about you."

"I told you not to be, 'cause I would return in one piece, right?"

"Right! You did that Miss Lady."

"Can we take a shower and make love until morning," I ask.

When two people understand each other, words are extra.

We make love into the early morning until just before dawn, when my body gives out and gives up, and I finally sleep the sleep of a working woman.

I wake up to the sound of a newscaster. Ced's watching the flat screen.

"This is Helen Short reporting to you live from Forest Road. Around 6:30 this morning Devone Shaw was found dead by his brother, Marcus Shaw. Reporting officers say that Devone suffered a cruel and painful death. The deceased's genitals were not only removed from his body, but also suffered a gunshot wound. As you can see family and friends are arriving here now at the scene. At 12 noon there will be more details. As of now there are no suspects in this horrifying tragedy. Back to you Oswald."

I look at Ced.

"I couldn't let him live, 'cause for one he lied, for two he disrespected you, for three he seen my face, and four , most of all, he didn't deserve to live, 'cause he wasn't doin' nothin' for his son." The words all tumble out of my mouth faster than I would've thought possible.

"Baby, you ain't ever gotta explain yourself to me! You got this under control."

"You kept your word with me about the money I sent Jay, and your people put herself in danger to send me that check. All I can do is help her live in peace now."

Jay had had almost 10 stacks on his books. When Ced had that money returned to me, I'd given every dime of it to Lex.

"That's my thank you gift," I'd told her. It's been weeks since I'd heard from Jay. He had tried calling me at first, but I hadn't answered. I'd also told Traymon that he had to keep Beauty for the next two months. He was cool with that, 'cause I kept blessing the nigga. Sad you gotta pay a father to keep his child, but fuck it!

Number 5

"The next nigga comes from New York, so you know he's

about that Big Apple money. This nigga Sham stays strapped even when he's fuckin'. It's hard to catch him slippin', and he's trigger happy."

"There's always a way to get a nigga with money," I say. "Nigga's with mad money always think they can't be touched, but they fail to realize that's just a saying and not a fact. Pussy is a powerful thing. They say this is a man's world, but pussy runs this shit. If they only knew... and if you don't believe me, let me show you. '

Two bad bitches at the same time is something that no sane nigga would pass up. I watched this nigga's Sham for a week nonstop. Every bar he went to, Dimples and Black was there. Every sale he made, I seen it, every bitch he fucked, I seen them. I'm his GPS.

I could have been the Alphabet Boys. He wouldn't even have a clue, but soon, and very soon, I'm gonna be his worst nightmare.

On Saturday nights Big Licks stays packed 'cause drinks are super cheap. Bitches out match the niggas four to one, so you already know shit going smooth as ever.

I watch as Dimples and Black work on Sham. They're acting gay, like they're a couple. Only thing missing is that solid dick of Sham's. If I didn't know them bitches I would've thought that they were gay for real. They could get a Grammy for the best acting ever, 'cause them bitches are definitely putting on for the team. Pussy is a powerful thing. If pussy tells the hard dick that it needs to be touched, that hard dick gonna try to be superman. Two pussies at one time is heaven sent, that's what that nigga's thinking. I watch them getting into his car. They all pile into the backseat. As I wonder who the fuck's driving I see big ass Trill come out of Big Licks. Damn he is hit too; my question is why the fuck are they together? The nigga Big Trill gets into the driver's seat of Sham's car. Mane, what the fuck is going on?

The car starts and then pulls out of the parking lot. I follow them for a few minutes, and they pull into the first hotel they see, The Lodge. It's an okay joint, niggas and bitches go there to get their freak on,'cause they can pay by the hour. Trill gets out and goes to the hotel's office. Sham's charger is moving like they're already fucking. Trill gets back in the car, and drives around to park in front of room 123. The back seat door opens and Dimples comes out first, then Sham and Black follow. Together they head to 123, but Trill stays in the car. Tell me this nigga's leavin', I think to myself.

Yup! When 123's door closes behind Sham Trill drives away. I watch and wait just to see if the nigga's coming back. Twenty minutes later, still a no show.

Krystal, this girl from around the way working in the office. When I go in she doesn't recognize me 'cause I have six braids in my head, covered by a fitted hat with my breasts taped down, and I'm wearing some black Dickie's with black Timberlands. I m looking like a pretty nigga. I put some bass in my voice and say. "Yo, shawty, I just lost the key to my room"

"What room is that?"

"123"

"I just gave Mr. Flex a key to that room about thirty minutes ago," she says.

"Well, I left to go to the store while my nigga took a shower. I ain't on no homo shit," I answer as she laughs.

"Ok, that'll be $5 for an extra card."

I hand her a twenty and tell her to keep the change and she gives me the new card. I walked away and just as I'm about to step outside the door Krystal hollers, "Have, a good night!" after me.

I didn't turn around, but I did toss a say, "You too shawty" over my shoulder on my way out. I pull the fitted hat down over my eyes a little more. Ready to get this shit crackin'.

I slide the card into the slot slowly, trying not to be heard. The lights are off, but the TV is up loud. I can't hear shit except Dimples hollering like a mother fucker, at least I think it's her...

***

When I flip the light switch on I 'bout run the fuck back through the door. Sham's getting his dick sucked by Dimples, and Black's eating Dimples pussy from the back.

What the fuck? So who the fuck hollering? Is it this bitch ass nigga?

"Nigga if you as much as blink, I swear, tomorrow you'll be the guest of honor at your own wake." His dick goes soft immediately. "Cuff this nigga to the bed, and put some fucking clothes on 'cause ya'll bitches on another cloud." Black laughs, and Dimples cracks a smile. Had to give it to them though they got it going on. Even had my pussy itching for a minute and missing Ced's touch for real.

“What’s good, nigga?” I ask Sham.

“This gotta be a fuckin’ freak show! Ya’ll bitches done lost your minds! Ya’ll got me cuffed to this damn bed, ya’ll got me fucked up.”

“And how is that, sir?” I ask him ‘cause I really want to hear what the fuck he’s got to say.

“Do you know who the fuck I am?” he screams.

“Ya’ll take the sheets off the bed, tie one around each ankle and pull his legs apart.” This nigga has way too much mouth, and I’m about to shut him up. I get his pants off the chair, and search his pockets.

A wad of dead Presidents, cell phone, a bag of X pills and a 9mm. So that’s what’s going on..

“Text Trill, and let that nigga know you gonna take a cab home.”

“How the fuck am I going to do that if I’m cuffed up like this bitch!”

“The next time you call me a bitch make sure you say Miss Bitch, you bitch ass nigga!”

“Pull his legs apart some more” I tell Dimples and Black.

He hollering like a bitch now for real.

“Nigga, I told you to shut the fuck up.”

I put the head of my P89 at his ass and told him, “You scream again, and I swear this baby going inside your ass nigga.” I see tears in this nigga's eyes.

"A hard dick can always get you in trouble, and that's for real. You got greedy trying to have two instead of one, but in the end, look at who got their legs apart; your bitch ass!"

Niggas like this make me sick!

"She gonna uncuff one hand so you can text Trill. If you try anything funny, you can do me a favor and tell Milk when you get to hell that as long as I'm alive his son gonna be good without his bitch ass." Black uncuffed his hand so he could text Trill. Trill text back, "Ok"

This gotta be the biggest bitch ass nigga ever, 'cause as soon as I asked him a question he would answer. I had to do this nigga in 'cause no nigga or bitch in their right mind would not be out to get revenge. I had the keys to his stash spot. He told me where the money, X pills and guns were. I know the nigga isn't lying 'cause I've been watchin' him like a hawk.

"I've got two 9mm in the car. If anyone gets in ya'll's way, don't wait. Smoke their ass!" I tell them.

"You already know we comin' back in one piece to get you!" Black says.

"That means a lot to me," They leave and I re-tie the sheets, one to the vent, and the other to the bathroom door. I know the nigga wants to scream, and I am surprised that he doesn't. He must have remembered what I told him about putting my baby in his ass, and I mean all the way up in that shit.

I take a seat on top of the dresser, and just look at him.

"How do you know Trill?" I ask him.

"We have the same baby mother!"

"Damn, she's one lucky bitch! She's got the best of the same world with the both of ya'll."

"Instead of us beefing, I thought we could be parents and partners."

Damn! Thank God this nigga hasn't gotten picked up by the Feds, 'cause God only knows his ass would be singing Amazing Grace like no tomorrow. Ugh! He made me sick just looking at him.

"How much bread you sittin' on?"

"500,000." His voice cracks as he says this.

"How many pills?"

"Probably 250,000."

"How many guns?"

"Thirty!"

"Damn, you a one stop shop'!"

"Why you asking me all these questions, since you gonna have it all?"

"You want me to keep it a stack with you, Sham?"

"Yea."

“For one, I don’t trust my bitches like I use to. They acting too funny. Second, I wanna see for myself how loyal they are not only to themselves, but to me, and truth be told nigga I can’t let you live!”

I watch this nigga swallow the lump in his throat. Damn! Knowing that he’s about to die is mind fuckin’ blowing.

“If a nigga or a bitch did this to me and let me live, I know in my heart I would kill everyone close to them until I get them.”

“Ma, on some real gangsta shit, I respect you ‘cause you a gangsta mother fucker! You super real, brave as hell, and sexy as ever!”

“Well, thank you but I’ve been told all that before. The only way I’ll let you live is if you let me fuck you in the ass with my P89.

“And you’ll let me live?”

“Yes.”

“Well, come on then.”

My phone rings. It’s Black saying shit’s straight, so I tell her to meet me at my place in an hour. I hang up the phone and return my attention to Sham.

I ram my gun straight up in his ass and this nigga doesn’t flinch, move or scream. It’s like he’s enjoying it, and I know for a fact that I’ve gotta smoke his ass.

“I’ll be right back,” I tell him. I go to the bathroom, ran the sink water. Damn this mother fuckin’ P89 smell like straight shit! I attach my silencer to my gun, and then flush the toilet.

“You know, I wish you had told me to fuck myself, then I could’ve respected your gangsta, but instead, you told me to fuck you with a damn gun a P89 as that. How can I let you live after I done took your pride like that?” Before he can even answer, I ram my gun up in his ass again. As he starts screaming, I put six bullets in him and they rip his belly open. I can smell his shit and see pieces of his intestines on the blood soaked sheets. I put two more in his head, just for GP...

I get to my house, clean up, take a shower, and wait for my bitches. As usual, I text Ced to let him know I’m safe, and at home. Dimples and Black pull up just as Ced’s text comes through to me, letting me know he’s on his way. They carry everything into the house.

“That’s all that was there?” I ask.

Black answers “Yea!”

$400,000. 150,000 pills and thirty guns... The numbers don’t match, so I ask them again. “Was that everything in the house?” These treacherous ass bitches.

“I told you, yea. You keep askin’ the same question, like we lyin’.”

“We gonna split the money four ways; pills and guns goin’ to the other person.” Once again, Black speaks up, “Cool, we can live with that.”

We? Who the fuck is we? And why the fuck she say it like that?

Dimples ain't said shit. What the fuck is going on?

They leave when they get their cut. What to do but shake my damn head, 'cause the president of America can't pay me enough to believe that they're actually stealing and betraying me like I ain't nobody. It's taking everything in me not to smoke both their asses.

Finally Ced shows up in his car with Snow driving. I watch Snow park the car in the drive way through my kitchen window, as I wonder how he ended up with name Snow 'cause ain't nothing on him white, not even his teeth. Snow stays in the car when Ced comes in the house. I explain everything to him except for how I killed Sham.

"Damn, your home girls are dangerous."

"Them bitches don't scare me. I help them bitches eat; I put them on. When did money and drugs become such a big problem between us?! I always had their back no matter what." Tears are in my eyes, but I swear to God I refuse to let that shit drop, fuck that!

"It's all good though. I'm gonna use them to get the rest of these niggas, and then I got a surprise for them both."

"The ball in your court, play with it baby, but always remember I got your back Sweets. You ain't never alone!"

"Tomorrow's Sunday. How about we get your kids and I get Beauty, we go out and have some fun ?" I ask him.

"Yea, we can do that! Grab some of your shit, 'cause you damn, sure ain't gonna sleep here no more."

I give him his share.

"Let me put Snow up on what's goin' on Ced tells me.

As I am getting my things together, Snow loading Ced's share of the profit into the car.

"Snow's gonna take my car, so we're taking yours to the mansion 'cause he's gotta take the shit back to the trap."

"Ok" I say as I nod at him.

I text T as soon as we get to the mansion, "I'm coming to get Beauty in the morning, so please have her dressed around eight for me."

All I want to do is go to sleep, but Ced had something planned for me. He runs my bath water, places candles all around the tub, and tells me to relax, before leaving me alone in the bathroom.

My mind is working overtime. Dimples and Black are fucking around, gotta be, but I just don't understand why they lied to me about the money and the pills, but not the guns. That shit doesn't make any sense at all to me. No matter how hard try to figure the shit out, it still isn't coming to me. All this thinking got me so tired. I can feel myself drifting off to sleep in the heat.

Ced returns," Damn, you wanna drown yourself, baby?"

"Naw, just tired."

He washes me and dries my body before carrying me to the bed.

Once there he lotions me down, he grabs one of his t-shirt and puts it on me. Then he carries me downstairs. He's got candles on the table, plus roses, and dinner. Well, not dinner, but a snack. Chicken fingers with fries!

"You have such a soft side to you, and I love everything about this. Thank you for taking care of me. I love it Ced! You're the best baby! Everyday just brings me closer and closer to you."

"The night just started."

We eat and discuss how tomorrow's gonna go down. Then he carries me back up the stairs.

No panties, no bra, or nothing, so I know it's going down for real! He lays me on the bed and walks away. What is he doing I'm confused. He walks back over to me and hands me a small gift box.

I open it and gasp!

"Four-and-a-half karat green diamond stud earrings" he tells me as my mouth hangs open.

"They're beautiful! I love them, and thank you so very much" I put them on and look at myself in the mirror. "Even sexier! Come let Daddy put you to sleep now."

I hit the stereo remote and wait until I heard Ace Hood's "Body to Body" playing. Tonight I am going every angle in bed, but first, I want to tease him. I dance a little.

"Damn, pop that ass on this dick like that."

"Don't worry; I plan on doing that too!"

The sex was off the chain, no condoms, just body to body.

I came three times, and he came twice. Just as I began to doze off I heard him say, "I love you. You're the best thing that s ever happened to me beside my kids." What the fuck he want me to say?

***

We wake to the sound of my phone ringing. I mean, the shit won't stop ringing. I look at the alarm clock and it says 6:45am. I answer my phone, not even looking to see who's calling.

"Damn, you had to kill the nigga like that? What the fuck is 'wrong with you, Sweets?"

I don't say shit, I just hang up on Black's crazy ass. That bitch will not hear me say I did anything. I didn't do shit. That's my story and I'm fuckin' stickin to it!

Breaking News

"Early this morning, police were called to The Lodge Hotel on Main Street. Dispatch received the call around 5:00am saying a dead body was discovered in one of the rooms. No names have been released as yet to the public. Coverage and updates will continue throughout the day..."

"You plan on taking them all out, don't you?" he asks me.

"Stay tuned, and don't turn the channel."

I'd be stupid if I let these mother fuckers live. Damn right every one of them that I touch gonna pay...

“We have kids we gotta get today.”

“Get ready then, soon-to-be-Mrs. Williams.”

I stop dead in my tracks and look at him.

“Did I say something wrong, Sweets?”

“Naw, but we got a long day ahead though”

***

Beauty is dressed and ready to go. We pull up in the all white Expedition and all T can do is shake his head. I get out of the truck, to talk to him for a minute.

“I’m bringin’ her back later, ‘cause I still got shit to do.”

“Cool.”

“And make sure you stay sucka duckin’ nigga.” I tell him once I close Beauty’s door. That nigga is not on my level, ‘cause he looks lost as fuck when I say that.

“Ma, who with you?” her little smart ass mouth had to say.

“My friend, Cedrick. Say hello.”

“Hi Cedrick.”

“Hey pretty girl, you gonna play with my girls?” He asks her.

“You have kids too?”

All I can do is smile.

"Yea, I do. Two girls and one boy."

"Ma, you gonna give me a brother?"

"You want a brother?"

"Yea, ma."

"Ok, let mommie think about it and I'll let you know, ok?"

"Ok!" I can hear the excitement in her voice.

Her ass too damn smart for me. Ced can't stop smiling. He looks at me and winks.

4+2=6

We pull up in front of a green house on Taylor Street. 2736 to be exact. He calls to say he's outside. The front door flies open, and the kids come running out with a woman behind them. She's pretty, with a lot of ass. I can see it from the front. I try not to stare but it's hard. Ced's already out of the truck and talking to her.

"You act like every time I come 'round here I gotta give you money! I just gave you eight stacks last week!"

"You did, but damn! You act like you ain't got three kids with me. You have kids somewhere else?"

"Look, Tarsha, I ain't goin' there with you. Ya'll get in the truck."

"And whatever bitch you have ain't got shit on me!"

He left her standing there and got in the truck. The passenger side of the truck is facing her. He rolls the window down, ‘cause they’re black as tar and you can’t see through them at all. When she sees my face all she can do is look and shut up.

“A’ite, Tarsha. I’ll bring them back later.”

She turns around and walks away. She’s mad and I mean heated. Soon after we pull off his phone gets the ringing. He doesn’t answer.

Must be her. Christina, Cobra, and Ced Jr. are all three the spitting image of their father. Cobra and Beauty stuck to each other like glue already like old best friends.

We have a ball. We shop, go the fair in Danville and get some pictures made.

“You’re great with kids,” Ced tells me.

“How you figure?”

“‘Cause you just are!”

We drop Beauty off first. It’s around 11pm when we get her back to T’s place. He doesn’t say shit to me out the way, but says “Be careful yo! Niggas droppin’ like flies out there!”

“You should already know me.” I answer on the way out.

Cobra gets up as soon as we get in front of her house.

“When can Beauty come see me again?” She asks.

“Whenever you want to see her you tell your daddy, and he’ll let me know, ok darling?”

"Ok!"

Tarsha opens up the door and Ced carries them inside one-by-one.

Christina and Ced Jr. are both fast asleep. I get the bags out of the truck, and wait for him. Now this bitch Tarsha has the nerve to start talking shit.

"Nigga, I know you ain't bringing this bitch back here?"

I am glad she remembers my face.

"I don't say shit with you having fifty different niggas around my kids, do I?"

I've already had enough of this big ass bitch.

"You know what? If you weren't his babyma I'd drag your ass from here to Africa and back! Bitch, you better recognize real when you see real! We can get along, or we can get this shit crackin' right now, so you let me know."

Ced looks at her and laughs. "Come on, Sweets. She ain't worth it."

The bitch ain't say shit. She walks her fat ass back in the house and we get back in the truck and drive off.

"You know something funny? Her ass didn't know what to say or do, she thinks she's crazy, but you brainsick, got her beat ten times over!"

"Well, Ced, you crazy twenty times over for fuckin' with me to begin with." He turns the music up and let's Young Jeezy's "Everything" blast.

I can't help but think about Dimples and Black, so I decide to text them. "The store still open up tomorrow? We gotta go shopping."

Black text back, saying, "Yea, meet you at the laundry mat on Campbell Avenue at 6pm."

Dimples text back "Ok." and I let her know where to meet up at.

Me and Ced chill for the rest of the night. We talk and fuck, fuck and talk. I meet up with Dimples and Black and give them the run down about our next mission. Truth be told, I want to do the shit by my damn self, but fuck it, they're in it and I can use the hands.

Number 4

Jimmy is our next target, a Haitian nigga who lives in Atlanta but pushes his weight in Virginia. He's a real black ass nigga, too. He looks like a jet black statue, but money makes him look like a sexy chocolate bar. That's the power of paper.

At first I was kinda scared to do this one, 'cause you know them Haitians are some crazy ass fucks, and they're on that voodoo shit. Plus, I don't really know for a fact if my bitches have my back or what. I'm ready for anything.

This nigga lives on a dead end street called Federal, the last house on the left. Why's a big time drug dealer living on a street called Federal? Ain't no alphabet boys here, though. It's just me and my bitches.

The nigga isn't even home when we get there, but his bitch is. She doesn't hear us come into the house, but when she sees us on the stairs the dumb bitch screams.

“Scream again, and you won’t even remember it, I promise.” I tell her.

“Please don’t hurt me!” she whimpers.

We’re masked the fuck up like the DEA. Them Haitians can put a root on you from the grave from what I hear, so I ain’t letting no one see my face.

“Please, please, just don’t hurt me!”

“Bitch, I heard you the first time,” I say.

“Where’s the money?” Dimples asks her. “Black’s tearing shit up already.”

“I don’t know where anything is at.”

“I kind of believe her, but you can’t put shit past a bitch.

“Where’s that nigga at?” Black asks her.

“He went to make a run; should be back any minute now.”

I hear a car door slam.

“That’s him outside,” the bitch says.

“Take that bitch in the closet, B, and if she screams, tell her goodnight.”

Black does as she’s told. I’m halfway surprised she doesn’t question my gangsta.

“D, get in the bed, cover your head, and lay there. I’m gonna be behind the door.”

‘Baby! Baby, I’m back!” Jimmy yells as he comes into the house. “Tammy, wake the fuck up! I swear you pregnant, all you been doin’ is sleepin’!”

As soon as he comes through the bedroom door. I put my Glock to his head. “Bring that bitch out!” I yell.

The closet door opens, and Black’s got the bitch in hand. She’s got her nine shoved into Tammy’s mouth.

Dimples comes out from under the covers.

“I know what you’re thinkin’, but please don’t try it, ‘cause you will not make it! Jimmy, all I want is the money and drugs, and you can live with your Tammy forever in peace. Just give me what I ask for.”

“Mane, I don’t have shit here.”

“Lie to me again and I’ll show you that I mean business, nigga.” “How the fuck you gonna tell me I’m lyin’?”

“Cause your bitch told me already, so I’m gonna ask one more time: where’s the money and drugs at?”

“It’s not here.”

“Oh, really? Since you wanna play games, let me show you that I am not in the mood for games.” I walk over to where Black is holding Tammy, and shoot that bitch in the head twice. She falls from Black’s hands like hot fries. Brains, blood, and pieces of her skull fly every fuckin’ where. Dimples has her hands over her mouth, Black's stuck, and Jimmy's on his knees begging Tammy not to leave him, but she's already gone. It's too late for all that.

"If you would've listened to me she would still be here! Now that you know that I ain't playin', tell me where the money and drugs are at, nigga, or you gonna meet her on the other side."
"Under my doghouse outside."

"What the fuck we waitin' for then? Let's go!"

Thank God this nigga's shit had a fence around his house. Black and Dimples better be inside searching that motherfucker down. "Rocky! Rocky!" He calls his dog. I do know one thing about dogs: they don't like anyone but their owner. Rocky's a big ass red and black pit bull. What the fuck is he feeding this dog?

"Get that shit, 'cause I don't have all day, nigga."

He moves the doghouse to the left, and pulls up two big ass suitcases from under that shit.

"There you go," he says.

"Nigga, if you don't carry that shit in the house you and Rocky both gonna see Tammy." He grabs the suitcases and carries them into the den as I follow.

"Open the motherfucker! you act like my life in danger and not yours nigga!"

When he opens them both up, all I can do is plan my dream for tomorrow. I don't know how long it took him to make all this, but I know it ain't gonna take me long to claim it.

Six seconds, that's how long! I shoot his ass six times, close both of the suit cases, and leave him where he lies. Black sees me smoke him so I know Dimples is only two seconds off her ass.

"Ya'll ready?" I ask them.

Neither one of them speaks.

"Ya'll follow me, it's time to go."

I can't be nothing other than what I am, and I am one cold hearted bitch on a mission!

Back at the spot I open up the suit cases and smile. Thank God I had invested in a money counting machine, 'cause I don't know how long it would've taken me to count a million dollars.

I split the shit into four shares.

"Keep ya'll's phones on. The next job ain't far," I tell them.

Our relationship sure has changed. It just ain't the same. I can feel it in the air when we're together. They must have sensed that I was feeling a bad vibe, 'cause Black calls the cab service and five minutes later they're gone.

As always, I call Ced. "Dinner's ready, baby."

"A'ite, boo. I'll be home in a minute."

A minute is sixty seconds, and sixty seconds later he's standing in front of me.

"Damn, yo. Nigga's is really eatin' in this small ass town," he says with surprise in his voice.

‘I m glad they eatin’, ‘cause that means we’re eatin’ too.”

I give him his share, and tell him, “I need some work, it doesn’t matter how much. That nigga Jimmy had had fifty bricks, so gives me twenty-five.”

“That’s all you want?” he asks.

“Yeah, ‘cause that’s all that nigga T gettin’!”

“Yo, you are a real ass bitch! Don’t ever forget that!”

“Don’t worry, I won’t!”

I text T and tell him to meet me at the Family Dollar in twenty minutes. Ced’s worker, Snow gets the money and work, and leaves right before we do. Ced drives, and on the way we see like twenty police cars flying towards downtown. I tell T to drive to Park Lane Street instead.

T’s car pulls up, and I see that Joey’s driving. That means Beauty’s with shawty. I can dig that. T gets out and comes to the passenger side of my Lexus thinking that I’m alone. I let the window down and give him the bag.

“Call me, nigga!” I say to him as he’s looking at Ced. Mane, oh mane; that look he’s giving Ced, I know right then that I have to check this nigga myself, or there’s gonna be problems.

T calls me in less than thirty minutes, just as we walk through the door of Ced’s little apartment.

“Damn, you must still love me?”

“Naw, nigga! Don’t get it fucked up. I eat, you eat, so get that shit straight. I don’t disrespect ol’ girl, so don’t cross that line on my end."

"I'm listening, Sweets."

"Traymon, you can listen, but I want you to understand me. I am not playing."

"I understand." He sounds mad, but I'm glad he checked his temper, 'cause sperm donor or not, he can get it too.

"Good! Enjoy your gift, kiss my princess for me when you touch the door, and be careful, nigga"

"I got you babyma."

Ced don't waste any time. He undresses me right then and there in the living room. We fuck like friends, no feelings at all. Ain't nothin' better than some good hard core fuckin'.

***

Lynchburg's on lockdown and people are scared to even open the door to get the mail. The city's on fire and probably hotter than hell. Satan ain't got shit on me. I am stuntin' on that nigga, and only God can intervene, but there's a developing situation: Nigga's had made my heart cold, but my bitches are making it colder. So on this next mission I've decided to leave them out of it. I gotta do it by myself. Ced is worried, and he wants to come with me, but I can't let him do that.

Number 3

Big Trill, ain't no average size nigga. They call him big for a reason. At 5'9" and three hundred pounds, can't no one call this nigga little! I know I've got to catch this nigga slippin', and eventually I do. I catch him coming back from his baby mother's house, but not that same bitch that him and Sham both had a kid by. This is a different female. That dirty dick motherfucker.

This piece of shit had left the doors of his truck unlocked. That's good. Sometimes other people's stupidity comes in handy.

I open the back door, and climb in. I search the truck, looking for anything and everything that might interest me, but all I really find is a .38 under the driver's seat. Okay. I got this nigga. I kick back in the back seat for around two hours, just waiting on him to come back. The element of surprise is priceless. Especially when a dumb motherfucker thinks he's safe.

When he finally gets in the truck and starts driving I speak up.

"You know, I can't stand a dirty dick nigga. I can't stand a nigga that lies and cheats. A nigga like that don't deserve to breathe." I say as I put my baby to his head.

"And how you figure that out?"

"Well, for 1, you have a main bitch, but you choose to keep fuckin each and every babyma of yours. Ain't you scared of gettin' an STD or AIDS?"

"Huh?"

"Nigga, I know you don't think that you the only nigga they fuckin'!"

Silence. I can see the thought never crossed his mind.

"Cat got your tongue?" I ask.

"What the fuck you want?"

"Talk to me without respect, and watch this motherfuckin' .45 knock the waves out your fuckin' head."

"I got you."

"Good, now that we have that clear, let's handle business."

"What business is that?"

I hate it when people ain't on the same page as me.

"Nigga, don't act slow, or try to lose your memory all of a sudden, 'cause that shit ain't gonna work with me. I hate repeating myself, so listen closely if you wanna live. Understand?"

No reaction. I take that to mean that he's listening. Not that he's got a choice or anything.

"Where's the money at?" I ask.

"My nigga got killed the other day. He had everything."

"Nigga if you think I'm gonna believe you, then you're stupid. You and I both know that you've got something put up somewhere for a rainy day."

"I mean…"

I cut him off, fuck what he's got to say.

"You lie to me, and you'll see who else is in hell when you get there."

I am not a woman to be played with. Games are for kids. If I wanted to play a game, I know Beauty would've been happy to play with me, but I'm not with her, I'm sitting here with ol' dirty dick. Ain't no games in me for this nigga.

He drives to Beford Avenue. I can smell the fear coming off of him. He turns right onto Boston Avenue, where he parks on the left hand side in front of the very first house, 1927.

"Let me tell you something! You listening?" I ask.

"Yea."

"Your babyma's don't know about this spot. I know this is where you keep everything. None of your niggas know about this place either, except Sham, and since he's gone, that leaves you and me. So let's handle business. This is how this is gonna work. I'm gonna climb over this seat, and when I get out, you're gonna climb over here and exit through this door. Act stupid or froggy, and I swear on Sham that you will be left right here!"

This nigga must be a bitch. He doesn't try to tackle me or nothing, but maybe he's just smart. He keeps a little of his dignity by keeping his mouth shut. Not that it matters. If I want it I'll take that, too.

When we get into the house the first thing I notice is that it's clean, like a bitch is living here.

"I don't have all night, so let's get goin'. Give me what I ask for, and I'll leave." All of a sudden it seems like this nigga done lost his mind, 'cause he starts talking cash money shit.

“Bitch, I ain’t givin’ you shit! Go fuck yourself!”

“Oh, yeah? I like that.”

He pulls the .38 from his pocket and points it at me. He must’ve grabbed it on his way out the truck. I just keep my Glock on his ass.

“Now you lookin’ like a real bitch ‘posed to look,” he says with a dumb fuckin smile on his face.”

“Nigga, I’m lookin’ like this ‘cause I wasn’t gonna kill you.

“You got kids that need you.”

He pulls the hammer, but a good weapon ain’t shit without ammo. When he realizes it’s empty he rushes at me, and this is a big ass nigga, but he ain’t big enough to run through these bullets.

I light his ass up like the Fourth of July!

I text Ced and tell him to be at the end of the block.

He texts back one word: “Done.”

I search the whole crib, and find NOTHING! I’m SO mad! All this for nothing?! I kick this big dead motherfucker as hard as I can; expecting his ass to be like Jello, but it’s not.

He feels firm against my foot, and it almost sounds like I’m kicking a wall.

“What the fuck?” I say out loud. I kick him again, knowing that this motherfucker ain’t got muscle like that. I pull his shirt up and see stack strapped to his belly. This nigga is wrapped up like a mummy, and I can't stop laughing about it.

***

"Ced, you ain't gonna believe what I'm about to tell you, but it's the God's honest truth."

"Tell me."

"Trill had the money strapped to his big ass with plastic wrapped all around his chest and waist. I couldn't believe the shit my damn self, so I rolled his ass over and cut the plastic off."

"No need to explain. I believe you, baby."

We go to his apartment and count the bread up. Some of the bills have holes on them, looking like New York pot holes. All together the nigga had fifty stacks on him! We split that shit down the middle. He tries to push forty on me, but I tell him no.

"Why don't we just put the whole fifty towards our future?" he suggests after I refuse the extra money.

"Meaning, until death do us part?"

"Yeah, actually. That sounds better than what I was gonna say."

"So what are you sayin', Ced."

I want you to be my wife, Sweets. You're perfect for me. You make me happy! You go harder than any nigga I've ever known, my kids already dig you, and I can't live without you, my Black Diamond."

"Is that really how you feel, Mr. Williams?"

"Yes, Mrs. Williams, that is exactly how I feel. I'm in love with you. From the very first night, I knew that I had to have you."

"I hear you loud and clear, but let's not rush things. Ask me again when you beatin' my pussy up. Then I'll give you an answer."

***

He fucks me on top of the money, which is something I've never done before, and won't soon forget. Then he makes love to me from the front.

"You gonna be my wife?"

He's looking dead into my eyes. I can feel his love, and I'd heard those words before, but when I feel him enter me again I know my answer.

"Yes, I'll be your wife, Ced"

Tears dripped from his eyes and onto my face when I spoke my answer to him. His emotion moves me.

"Yes, I'll be your wife forever!"

The first thing we do as a man and woman engaged is come together.

Number 2

Lip is sexy, and he's gotta be one of the sexiest men alive,

I swear. He looks like an angel from heaven, but that's too bad, 'cause that nigga's headed to hell, and I'm the one sending him. The nigga's a cornball, a straight up pussy, and sexy or not, his mama should've swallowed the batch that made him. Nigga's so terrified he can't stop shaking. Even his damn lips are shaking. No wonder they call him Lip! He's a yellow bone nigga with hazel eyes. He's about 5'7", 165 pounds; I mean a real pretty sexy nigga. He's got Ced beat; I hate to say it, but it's true.

I catch this pretty boy nigga sitting in the trap on fifth.

He's waiting on the fiends to come through, but the only one who's coming through is me. I knock on the door and wait. I know where he's at, 'cause I've been following him for the past five hours.

"Who dat?!" He yells when he comes to the door.

"It's Cupcake! I need a twenty rock!" I'm hoping he just opens the door.

"Cupcake?"

"Yea, Cupcake. Lala sent me up here." Lala is the pipe head I met a few minutes ago.

"Oh, okay!" I hear him throw the dead bolt back and I get ready to move. As he cracks the door, I rush his ass. This nigga ain't even strapped!

"Rule #l, always stay strapped!"

"Who is you?" He asks me.

"Fuck questioning me, nigga! This is my house now! I ask all the questions and you answer!"

"A'ite, ma," he says, shaking like a leaf.

"Where the bread at?"

"Shawty, I don't have none."

"You don't have none? So how the fuck you hustlin'?"

"I'm just makin' a little somethin', nothin' major."

He starts running off at the mouth, just telling everything, his connect, and this, and that, blah, blah, blah. Niggas and bitches kill me nowadays. Just 'cause they getting a little money, they wanna act and put on like they got shit. Where they do that at? He's just a flunky trying to pretend that he's balling. Altogether this nigga ain't got but five stacks. Yes, you heard me correctly; five fucking thousand dollars to his damn name. After I collect the money, I give him something in exchange for his cooperation. I give him four shots to the head. I'm taking head shots all day. A nigga or a bitch who can't hold water in their mouth when they're under pressure don't need to live. It's sad, but true, 'cause they be the same ones screaming Death before Dishonor, or Snitchin' Ain't for Me. That's why I say move your lips, get your soul transported.

Number 1

This last lick has to be done proper, 'cause the shit that I hear is that this nigga plays no games. Since I'm going for him, I'm going correct. I didn't start doing this shit yesterday, and I feel like I was born with this gift, so that means that I am READY!

This nigga lives out in Boons Borough, I mean all the way out in the cut, on some hide and seek shit. How the fuck does Ced know where this nigga lives? When you in the game, you ain't never safe!

This money paid drug dealer nigga's got it going on. His place looks like a single spot of civilization out in the middle of nowhere. There are two Suburbans, two old-school Chevy's, an all black 745, and an all white Mayback. This nigga ain't just balling. This nigga's the plug himself.

I park about a mile away from his place. I have a surprise for the king of this castle, and I can't wait to show him either.

The only light in the house looks like it's coming from a TV somewhere upstairs. I walk around the whole house looking for an open window or a door, but my luck ain't hitting on shit and everything's locked. Good thing I'm always prepared. I pull out my glass cutter and cut a whole fucking window out. I hold my breath as I do so, knowing I can't afford any sound. I lean the glass against the side of the house, and enter into what looks like a playroom. There's a pool table, stripper poles, a dice area, I mean this nigga has every fucking thing!

I keep my P89 in front of me at all times. I search the entire ground floor and find nothing. Next step, second floor! I make my way up the stairs, and half way up I see a woman's shadow. The bitch looks like she's got some curves. I back up against the wall, and breathe through my mouth. Whoever she is she's in the wrong place at the wrong time, but that's how life goes. You win some and you lose some, but fuck that! I have a daughter I gotta get back to, and a nigga who claims to love me. A nigga I believe.' I can't afford to lose.

I can hear three different voices, but the TV's on so loud that it's hard to tell. It could be more. Fuck it.

"I was born for this," I tell myself under my breath. The bedroom door is open, so I can hear more clearly as I creep closer.

'So you sayin' you never had a threesome before?" A woman asks.

"Naw, never! I swear!" The nigga said, his voice deep. That's gotta be Rell, unless there's another nigga in there.

"You tellin' me that tonight was your first time ever?"

That's a different female's voice. So far the future body count's at three.

"Yeah, I ain't lyin' to ya'll."

"How long you think we can last for?" the first female voice asks.

"Shit, if we keep on rollin', we can last till next week!" he answers with a laugh.

"I got us some water," the female says.

"I'm poppin' four this time," This nigga must really be tryin' to last till next week!

"Well, we gonna take two a piece then." One of the females says.

I peek into the cracked door just in time to see them pop the pills. All three of them are in the bed together. Damn, they're slipping hard! This is why I am drug fucking free! I pull my flashlight from my Dickies pants and exhale slowly. It's time.

Ready...

Set...

Go!

***

I've got my flashlight hand stacked on top of my P89. Niggas and bitches don't know nothing about tactics these days. The first thing I do is shoot the light out of the TV. The bitches start screaming under the covers. Rell tries to make a run for it, but he doesn't know who he's fucking with. Running from me is like trying to run from your mama when she's trying to whip your ass. It's only gonna piss me off, and I'm not using my hand, a shoe, or a switch.

POW!

I got him in the right calf.

"And if you so much as breathe, your ass will not remember it!

Ya'll bitches shut the fuck up!" I use my flashlight to find the light switch, and I turn the light on. Rell is holding his leg, and blood is everywhere. I know I hit a vessel for sure.

"Ya'll bitches come out from under the covers, 'cause only Jesus himself can save you now, and I ain't seen him lately."

My eyes gotta be playing tricks on me...

"What the fuck?!" It's Dimples and Black...

“Nigga, get your ass up and get between them bitches on the bed.” “Bitch, you got me fucked up!” He don’t know that I’m Satan himself.

“She ain’t playin’, yo. Just come over here!” Black tells him.

It’s nice to hear her doing something other than questioning my gangsta for a change.

“You better listen to her, ‘cause I know for a fact YOU got ME fucked up. All the way up, nigga.”

I watch him drag himself to the bed, and I follow him with my P89.

“Ya’ll bitches better start thinkin’ about the explanation ya’ll ‘bout to give me, ‘cause I want to know what’s goin’ on. Where the money at Rell? You know, money over everything is my motto.”

These bitches is in here naked. They gotta be fucking each other, for real. One of the Suburbans out front must belong to Dimples. My mind is racing as I watch Black help Rell into the bed. I hear Dimples start praying.

“You think I’m gonna hustle my ass off for you to come in here and demand my shit after I done survived the game this long?”

“You can’t knock a bitch for tryin’, can you?”

“I mean, to each their own, but if you want it, you’re damn sure gonna have to kill me before I give it up.”

“How sure are you about that?” I ask him.

"150% sure, shawty. You think 'cause you shot me already I should just get to talkin'?"

"I mean, you are a grown ass man. This your shit, so do and say as you please, but remember I am the one in charge."

Dimples is crying, but Black's just holding her head. They already know I'm not one to be played with. I'm giving this nigga six seconds to tell me what I want to hear. I start counting him down. "One... two... three... Fuck you, nigga! Six!" and just like that I stopped his heart. What they say is true, real gangstas don't live to see thirty 'cause they're either dead or doing life. Dimples is crying so hard she's shaking. It's starting to get on my nerves.

"Why the fuck you had to kill him?" Black asks.

"Why the fuck you had to steal from the team like that?! Ya'll took an extra cut of everything but the guns! Ya'll think I'm stupid?! And while we're on "why the fucks", why the fuck ya'll on drugs?! And when the hell ya'll start fuckin'? Ya'll gay now?" I'm yelling at them and can't help it. Good thing we're out in the cut. Dimples is crying even harder now, but Black seems calm, cool , and collect.

"Ever since you got with that nigga, Ced, you been brand new." Blacks says with disgust.

"How you figure?"

"You don't have time for us anymore!"

"I have time for ya'll. We gettin' money, and livin' good. All them licks we did, Ced put me on, and guess what? I put Ya'll on, but look at ya'll! I put ya'll on everything; I taught ya'll how to do this shit. All I ever showed ya'll was love, and loyalty, but look at what ya'll showin' me."

"Sweets, I hated you from the moment I opened my eyes. I wanted to kill you then, but Dimples talked me out of it."

"What?" I'm shocked, hurt and confused for a split second before the coldness begins to sink back into my heart where it seems to belong.

"I knew about you before you even knew me. I knew your life from start till now. When you helped me in Hardees's that day, it was all planned out. Dimples been gay. This ain't nothin' new. She didn't know how to bring me around you, so we came up with a story and a plan-" She's still talking, but I'm done listening.

Fuck what she's saying. One to the head will keep her speechless forever. I wonder if she hears the bark of my P89 before her body hits the floor. I'll be sure to ask her when I see her in hell, but that's gonna be a long time from now.

Dimples brings her knees up to her chest. "I know you hate me, and you have good reasons to, but please, know that I am truly sorry."

"What did I do to you, Dimples?"

"Nothing. It's what happened to me."

"What happened?"

"I've been hurt by the ones who were supposed to love and protect me. My parents ain't even my parents, Sweets. I know you think that you know them, but you don't. Not really. I hate the ground they walk on. My so called father, the pastor, he's ..." her words trailed off for a second as a brief flash of pain crosses her face before she continues. "They adopted me when I was six, and used me to get where they're at now. Every deacon you see on the list at church has had their way with me, and not only them, but my fake ass parents, too. They would offer me to people of high standing, people of influence, people with money and power who were willing to help them get the things that they wanted. Anytime somebody wanted me, they could have me. I hate men, I hate them!" She practically spits the words when she says them.

This is some heavy shit. What the fuck is going on here?

"They buy me everything to cover their dirt up, Sweets. They even wanted me and you to sleep together so they could watch, but I think they were really just setting it up so they could ask to join."

"Naw, Dimples! You lyin' to me!"

"I swear; I put it on Beauty's life!"

This shit is crazy!

"I met Black years ago. Her boyfriend tried to kill her when he found out that she was gay, but I helped her out. She was the only person that I was ever with who didn't use me or abuse me. Her love for me was real love, but she hated how close me and you got. She was so jealous of you that we came up with the Hardees's situation to have her closer to me, and it worked, but I never meant for things to happen this way."

A part of me feels sorry for Dimples. We've been friends for years, and she is as close to a sister as I've ever had. Cold hearted or not, I can't kill her. I decide not to pull the trigger. Instead, I leave her where she stands until I find what I came for to begin with. This place is huge, and it takes me almost an hour to find it, but when I do I can hardly believe my eyes. Jackpot! I get on the phone immediately 'cause I know I m gonna need help. I tell Ced to get up here. Ain't no way I'd be able to load up all this shit by myself. I head back up the stairs to check on Dimples, but to my surprise she's gone, and what's left of the woman formerly known as Black is gone too.

Now she's only known as that Dead Bitch I used to know.

***

I run down the stairs two at a time, and make it out the door just in time to see her struggling to get that dead bitch into the truck.

"Bitch, I tried to give you a break, but I can see you don't want one!" I'm starting to think they make a pretty good couple, Dumb Bitch and Dead Bitch, but if she's gonna test me, Dumb Bitch will be a Dead Bitch too.

She drops Black, and when she hits the ground I notice that she's still breathing. Dead Bitch ain't dead after all. That's okay, I can fix that. I put two more in her. Can't nobody live with that much lead in their head. Dimples covers her eyes, but doesn't scream. Good. I'm sick of hearing that kind of shit.

"Carry your ass! You get in that truck, and carry yourself somewhere far from here, Dimples. Move away, and don't ever come back, 'cause the end result won't be pretty."

Tears flood her face, but she heeds my words. She gets in her truck and drives away. A few minutes later Ced pulls up "Who the fuck is that?" he asks, tilting his head towards the body on the ground.

"A bitch that was in my way." Something in my voice must have given me away, 'cause Ced pulls me to him.

"It's gonna be alright. Real gangsta bitches like yourself don't cry."

We get to work loading everything up, and then we leave.

I left one of my best friends hack there. Dimples is gone forever, and there ain't no coming back, but that fake ass bitch deserves it. Fuck it. That's just one less fake bitch to worry about.

I can't drive, so Ced takes the driver's seat and drives to Snow's house, where we count the money and drugs. In the end, we've got two million cash, a thousand pounds of hydro, and five hundred bricks of pure white cocaine, just like my name.

"I need to get out of these clothes," I tell Ced. I'm exhausted. "A'ite, let's go to my crib. Snow, handle this shit, and I'll holla at you later!"

The ride to his place is silent, and I face the window to hide my tears. I can't believe how this night has turned out. Both my bitches are gone. One's dead, and the other's gone with the wind.

I can't stop asking myself what the fuck is really wrong with me?

I always lose everyone to disloyalty.

As soon as we get into Ced's crib I head to the bathroom, removing my clothes as I go. I get in the shower and scrub myself from head to toe. It doesn't matter if my eyes are open or closed, all I can see is Dimples face streaked with tears. I hear every word she said again and again, echoing in my head, but it seems like I don't hear the right words. How can this be real?

I know Black's in hell already, probably waiting on me so we can go ham on each other, but for right now, I'm holding the Realest Bitch down...

My Damn Self

All of a sudden I feel Ced's hand on my hip. I know he's got to be thinking some crazy shit. I turn around so I can read his eyes, and when I look into them they just look cold and calculating.

"Do you regret anything you ever did?" he asks.

"No! I don't regret shit! Everything that happened was meant to happen so that life can go on." I answer.

"I have been through so much, I have seen a lot, and I've heard it all before, but I swear on my mother I ain't never met a woman like you before."

"And you wanna know why? 'Cause I am one of a fuckin' kind, baby. Not too many bitches can say they've done or seen the shit that I have done and seen. Don't get me wrong though, I know I can be touched. I'm not invincible, but for right now I am just livin' and doin' all the touchin'."

"You are the realest bitch ever."

“Real Recognize Real As Always, ‘cause I know you are the realest nigga ever.”

Ced uses his mouth to wash me all over again, and then he makes me come with that beautiful dick of his, but I’m so tired I don’t even let him get his in. He doesn’t trip either. Nigga better not! Shit! I needed that to the fullest.

Chapter 26

4 Real?

I hear the front door coming off the hinges! "FBI! Lynchburg Police Department! Don't move!"

I try to move anyway, but the police are already holding me down. They have Ced down on the floor.

"Ms. Corona Cocaine Cash, AKA Sweets, you are under arrest for 7 murders," the man who's holding me down says to me.

"I ain't kill nobody, motherfucker!"

"Not only did you kill them, but you took their drugs and money also."

"Fuck you, you stupid motherfucker!" Deny, Deny, Deny! That's the only way to deal with this, and I know it. All of a sudden I realize that Ced's down there talking, and his words are making sense to me. He's telling them how I killed everyone!

"That motherfucker's lyin'!" I scream as I struggle against the hands that hold me down. "You lyin' piece of shit!"

"Ms. Cash, don't plead your case to me, plead it to the judge." "Suck my pussy when I'm red from the back you ugly cracker motherfucker!"

"Baby! Baby, wake up! You havin' a bad dream!" Ced's shaking me awake. "You're talkin' in your sleep and everything."

"That was a dream straight from the pits of hell." I get up from the bed, grab his shirt, and pull it over my head as I walk to the kitchen to get something to drink. I know he's on my ass, I can feel his presence. This nigga told on my in my dream! I take two shots of Ciroc back to back. Damn.

"I gotta make sure my daughter's okay."

"So call her daddy."

My cell phone's plugged into a charger on the kitchen counter.

I pick it up and press two. Speed dial.

"Sweets, It's five in the morning and you callin' me?" Traymon sounds sleepy and irritated.

I've got the phone on speaker, and I m looking Ced dead in his eyes.

"Yeah, I know what time it is. Ya'll good?"

Yeah, we good. You callin' 'cause you want me to come put you to sleep?"

Ced's eyes get bloodshot red in an instant. I'm tired of putting Traymon in his place! He just won't give up!

"I have a man to do that already, so stop disrespecting him!"

T hangs up on me.

Ced smiles, and then picks me up. He carries me to the sofa in the living room, and seats himself without letting me go. I'm comfortable in his lap, wrapped in his arms.

"Whenever you wanna talk, Sweets, I am all ears."

We sit in silence for a few minutes before I finally say something. "I don't think I can ever love you like you say you love me."

"Why…"

I cut him off. "I've been hurt by so many, it's crazy. It's hard for me to trust anyone. When love comes to me I try to push it away, or run away from it, 'cause it always ends up no good for me. You've seen my good side and my bad side. You know my secrets. They say fear God, love no nigga, and trust no bitch, but for me, I fear God, I trust no bitch, but I love and trust you, and I put that on everything. You are the man of my dreams, and I'm sorry that it took me so long to find you..."

We make love like tomorrow is never going to show up. We fuck each other from the living room, to the bedroom, and when the sun comes up we still aren't finished. Finally, we end up falling asleep. When I wake it's 1:00pm; Ced's nowhere in sight but there's a note on the dresser with some green and yellow flowers in a crystal vase.

> "I searched everywhere to find you, but I wasn't searching hard enough. Then, just like magic, you pop up, and look where you at now.

I love you, Sweets,"
Ced.

"My baby daddy used to cheat, beat on me and dog me out back then, but now look at me. I have a real live trill ass nigga who's down for me no matter what. How could I go wrong?"

The phone interrupts my thoughts. It's Jay. Shit. I press 0. "Hello?"

"You got some nerve to say hello, bitch, when you left me high and dry."

"Naw, nigga, you mean low and dry! You played me like a sucka, a real pussy sucka! I feel like you gave me a stupid pill, and I took it."

"It wasn't even like that! You came up here and started thinking crazy. You ain't even hear me explain it to you."

"Jay, do us both a favor and delete this number. I am no longer yours. Change the address on your release papers, 'cause you will not be there. Don't waste your stamps, pens, paper or envelopes on me, 'cause it will be returned to you, and when you get home, please don't start no shit, 'cause I will not even spare your momma!"

"Bitch, fuck you!"

"You better be careful, 'cause I might get you fucked for real!" I hang the phone up on that note. This dumb nigga tries calling back again and again, but I ignore him. Fuck that nigga.

***

When Ced gets back he asks me to move into his house with him.

“Is that what you really want?”

“Sweets, I know what I am askin’ you. Just give me an answer.”

“Yes.”

“Well, we got a lot to do then, so let’s get goin’.”

We rent a U-Haul truck, and pack up my house. When it’s time to go, I head to the back yard and dig up my flower-garden.

“Baby, what are you doin’?” Ced asks, coming up behind me while my hands are still in the dirt.

“Pay attention,” I say, without stopping.

I dig all the flowers up, and a few inches beneath them until I see a wooden box. It’s heavy, so he helps me lift it out of the ground, and take it to the truck. He never asks what’s in it, and we never say a word to each other about it. I look back at my house as we drive away, and a tear falls from my right eye, but a smile comes across my face. One chapter ends as another begins. I turn the music up just in time to hear Jeezy’s new hit, “I Do”. Ced and I smile at each other as we listen to the words.

“Remember the night we first met,
I caught a contact,
now she my ride or die.
It’s us against the world,

You know we both hustlin',
so hustlin' is our world..."

When we finally arrive at my new home, we unload the truck, and unpack everything in Ced's mansion. I even put Beauty's room together, and I know that she's gonna love this! After we finish, Ced pulls me into his arms.

"Let's relax and take the truck back tomorrow," he says.

"Do you really think you can let me live with you after everything you've seen?"

"Yes. If you seen half the shit that I've done, you might not want to be here either. What can I say? We both have the same hustle, just on different levels, and we not here to judge each other. We're here to love each other through the good and the bad, right?"

"You right, Ced!" Why is this man still single? It's the ever present question that I keep asking myself. There doesn't seem to be an answer for it. "Ced, let me show you something!"

I open the wooden box and smile up at him.

Ced's eyes don't budge from the box when he speaks to me.

"How long you been doin' this?"

"For a hot minute. I only spend what I have to, 'cause when I leave this life I want my daughter to be stable more than anything in the world. She's the only reason why I do this shit like this. I kill because I don't want to have to watch my back everywhere I go. If they're dead, they can only haunt me in my dreams."

I've got a wooden box worth five million. Three from all the random jobs I've pulled over time, and the two we got from Rell. Shit is looking damn good. I change the subject. "I'm ready for a vacation."

"How 'bout we and the crew take a trip?" he suggests.

"Yeah? To where?"

"New York City!"

"Cool. I was thinkin' the same thing, 'cause I have some unfinished business to handle."

"On a vacation you're supposed to be relaxing, not working, Sweets. That's why it's called a vacation; you're supposed to rest and have fun."

"I will. As soon as I finish what they started with me."

"Huh?"

"I'll relax, baby!" No need to explain.

"You better, 'cause this is our world , baby girl."

For real, I know it is.

"So when we leavin'?" I ask him.

"How 'bout tomorrow?"

"What? Ced, you had this planned already?"

"Naw, I just got it like that, and money talks, so everyone except you gotta move when I speak. Boss niggas do boss things, so enjoy life, baby. I'm gonna show you nothin' but the best!"

"You are somethin' else, boy, I swear!"

"Trappa, Snow, and Clap comin' with us. They'll probably have their ladies."

"So?"

"I'm just lettin' you know. I don't leave town without them."

As long as they ain't in my way, I'm good. I have a lot on my agenda, even if no one knows it yet.

"Where am I gonna put this money at?" I ask him, changing the subject again.

"You have a whole house and ten acres of land at your disposal! Pick a spot, and do you!"

"Where is yours safe at?"

"Sweets, is that a safe question to answer?"

"Well, you have a choice. You can tell me, or I can find it myself. Pick one."

"Since you have such a smart mouth and a cold heart, I'll just show you. Come on."

Let's just say my shit ain't got shit on his money. His money can count itself. I am dead ass serious. This nigga is PAID!

"I'm not gonna ask how much is there."

"Good. When you become Mrs. Corona Williams, it's all yours. Until then, no more questions."

"I'm gonna put mines in there with yours."

'Cause when I come to take it, I am taking all of it. This devil on my shoulder is a greedy little motherfucker.

"Fine with me," he says.

"How did you come up with an idea like this to hide your money?"

"No questions!"

He walks away and leaves me standing there still looking at all this money. There's got to be at least 20 million in here!

Damn...

***

I call Traymon, and tell him he's got to keep Beauty for a minute, 'cause I'm stepping out of town. He doesn't trip. He handles the situation better than I expected he would and I'm impressed. Wow! Maybe this nigga is really working on changing. For real though, I don't give a fuck. He didn't change for me, and I ain't gonna hold it over his head, 'cause Karma's gonna catch up to him in due time. Until then, the life that I am living only gets better, thanks to me.

Chapter 27

New York

Instead of driving, we fly. There's eight of us since everybody brought their women. Trappa and his girl, Lex. Snow, and his wife Jade. Clap and his down-ass bitch, Jasmine. The plane is okay; not as bad as I thought it would be, and since it is my first time flying, Ced holds me the entire ride. He's perfect. When we arrive in New York a limo is waiting on us.

"Where are we staying?" I ask Ced.

"Bronx, baby."

"Bronx?"

"You seem worried. Are you okay with that?"

"I'm fine with that."

"My peoples have a four-bedroom house in the Bronx, on Eastchester Road. It has enough space for all of us. The shit is mad big."

"How much space we talkin' 'bout, baby?"

"Four bedrooms, two bathrooms, a big ass kitchen that can hold at least twelve people comfortably at one time. It's carpet all the way from the living room to the front of the house, then the porch is hard wood... you'll see. It's real open. Nothin' like the mansion we got though."

"Okay, sounds good!"

New York City is beautiful to me, but I hate this state. I know that I'll come to love it again before I leave.

Ced's Uncle Shevan is so glad to see him.

"Boy, luk pon yuh," his uncle says with a heavy Jamaican accent, as a wide smile covers his face. Shevan looks just like a real damn Jamaican. He's got dreads down past his ass, with a Jamaican flag printed wrap used to tie his hair back out of his face. He's got a goatee that covers his chin, but no mustache to go with it. I know they say that Jamaicans are black, but this motherfucker's so black he looks purple.

This is amazing, but I swear, when Ced starts speaking, I come in my panties.

"Yuh know seh me can't stay little fi eva."

Next time we fuck he's gonna talk to me like that! Hell yeah! Damn it, that's sexy.

It seems like a family reunion. I meet so many people that can't even remember their names. We do a little running around and shopping. We're just enjoying New York in general. Each couple splits up to do their own thing for a while. Jasmine tries to get friendly with me, but I let her know that I'm not in need of any friends. She says she understands, and gives me my space. Fuck letting another bitch into my life! All I need is my man and my child!

“Ced, I need to take a trip into Brooklyn,” I tell him over dinner at the 40/40 Club.

“By yourself?”

“Yes, by myself.”

“Do you need anything?”

“Yeah, a .45 and a silencer.”

“Sweets, can you promise me that you’ll come back.”

“I promise you I am coming back!”

“Can I come with you?”

“No. I have to clean this up by myself, but don’t worry. You are always with me, ‘cause I am carrying you in my heart.”

“I’ll take your word.”

“You better do, ‘cause my word is my life.”

***

I’m dressed all in black, so you already know what kind of mission I’m on. I’d done a little research on the man who had turned my life upside down before we left for New York. God bless the internet!

This fool ain’t changed for nothing, except to get even uglier. I follow him from his job all the way to his house.

He lives in the back of an apartment complex on President Street. It's taken me a long time to get around to this, but I've always known this day was coming. When he parks I pull up right beside him and get out of my rental car to face the man who raped me when I was a little girl. I don't even give him time to get out of his car, much less turn the engine off.

In my head all I can see is me in my room that night when that ugly motherfucker took my pride. Now I feel no pain. Matter of fact, I'm not even thinking. What's there to think about? The motherfucker didn't think about me back then, but I am glad to show him that he should have. He may not have changed, but I have. I'm no longer defenseless. There's no words, just the sound of me emptying the .45 on his ass. I get back in the rental and drive away. I've got one more stop to make.

It's 1:30 in the morning, and I'm on a mission. My father, Richie, lives by himself. I guess he ran out of women to fuck. His address is 1038 Nostrand Avenue, which is an apartment on top of an old printing shop that appears to be out of business. I need a key to get in, but I'm lucky today, 'cause the side door is unlocked. I climb the stairs as quietly as possible, but for real, I don't give a fuck if he hears me or not, 'cause tonight is the night he meets his maker. This is his home, something that I never had. I ring the bell, and put my back to the door so that I face the stairs.

"Who is it?" I hear his voice muffled by the door that separates us .

"Sir!" I say loudly in response.

As he opens the door, I rush my way in with my .45 aimed at his head.

"Corona!" he exclaims like he's surprised to see me.

Yeah, me too.

"Oh what a surprise! You know my fuckin' name!"

"You are my child. Why wouldn't I know your name?"

"Shit, you tell me."

This is the same man who didn't do nothing for me when his bitch's son raped me.

"You have grown."

"Spare me the bullshit, Rickie! You ain't my father! What the fuck did you do for me as a child besides providing a roof over me head? The government could've done that!" I can't keep the tears from falling, and that pisses me off. My soul has a hole in it from the hurt, all the hate and pain that I suffered as a child.

"I hate you!" I shout at him. "Everything about you makes me sick! I am so sick I can't even stand myself, but you know what? I have a child to live for, or else I would've killed myself thanks to you. My grandmother should've pushed you out in the toilet!"

"Corona, I know I was the worst father ever, but I've changed. I'm sorry for all the pain that you went through, but your mother should have aborted you!"

My heart stops in my chest for a second. I know this mother fucker didn't just say that!

"FUCK YOU!"

Those are the last words that he hears from my lips, or from anyone else's for that matter. Father or no father, I have shown this nigga that I am one bitch who deserves to live.

Now when I visit New York, I'll love it to the fullest.

***

A whole week has flown by, just like that! I miss Beauty so much it hurts! I have to get back home to my princess.

Ced's holding a family meeting on our last night in New York. "I'm glad to have all of ya'll here today. We started at the bottom, but now we stand at the top. We have on hell of a team. Untouchable!" Ced announces. Clap had finally gotten out of the hospital just in time for- this vacation. He had a sideways stance, and you could tell that something bad had happened to him. He's one of Ced best and most trusted workers, been on the team since day 1. He got shot four times, but he's made it through. Now that he's standing, I wonder what he's got to say. "This year so far has been crazy, but I'm blessed to have my freedom, blessed to be alive, and I'm blessed to have a family like ya'll who care, who would lay down their life for me. I don't know where we would be if it wasn't for the love that we have for each other."

Mane, this is some real deep shit. Ced keeps his eyes on him, and so does everyone else, but we can tell that he ain't finished. "Jasmine, I love you! Don't ever think different! You are the bullets to my Glock, and for that I am very thankful. Ced, my nigga, even through rain, we still stangin'. I love you, no homo..."

At those last words, everyone bursts into laughter. When the happy sounds die down, he finishes what he has to say.

"Blood doesn't make us related, but LOYALTY makes us family." Everyone cheers for the sentiment that he's shared. This team is loving and trustful, but most of all loving. Damn, I actually miss my bitches. Ced must be a mind reader, 'cause he leans over and says, "We gonna have us some fun, so cheer up." He hits the music as he leads the way, and we start dancing to some old school jams in the living room. Just like that, everyone else follows.

"You are the most beautiful woman ever, and I am super blessed to have such a diamond in my life! I really do love you."

"I love you too, Ced."

"Yo, Snow! Hit the button to the system for a minute! I have something else to say," Ced tells Snow and walks away from me towards Clap.

"I hope everyone is enjoying themselves. I love and cherish each and every one of ya'll, so I didn't want ya'll to hear this from someone else. I'd rather ya'll witness it for yourselves. Corona..."

Now I'm holding my breath. Is he really...

"You are the most beautiful woman I have ever seen. You are the definition of real. You go just as hard as a real nigga, and even harder. I don't ever have to worry about my back, 'cause I know you got me all the way. I never knew I would find someone like you, but God proved me wrong, since you're here now. I'd like to keep you in my life forever, so with that said, will you be my wife?"

He's standing right in front of me now, all the ladies are crying.

I can hardly breathe, and I felt like I have to keep one hand over my heart to make sure that it doesn't jump out of my chest.

"Yes, I would love to be your wife, Ced."

He gets down on one knee and pulls a black box from his pocket. "They say diamonds are a girl's best friend, right?" After he slips it on my finger, everyone goes wild with applause, and I have a feeling it's as much because of how big my ring is as how happy they are for us.

"That's a seven-carat marquis-cut diamond set in white gold, baby." Ced tells me as I look at it. My left ring finger has to cost at least 200 stacks, 'cause it's sure shining. This is a night I'll never forget. We get twisted and head to the bedroom to tear it up.

Ced pushes me gently to the bed and slowly removes my clothing piece by piece. He kisses me from my mouth to my breasts, and trails down my stomach, between my legs and down to my toes.

My pussy is so wet and ready for him. I want him to touch me, at least breathe on it, shit, but he doesn't. He just covers me with kisses, every part of me, back to front.

Please, Ced, stop teasing me."

"Yuh sure, yuh whan dis?"

Oh, hell yeah! That Jamaican talk!

"Whatever you say, I say yes to! Please, Ced!"

"How's it feel," he asks me.

"Good, baby, but can you make it great?"

It feels as if he puts his whole tongue inside my pussy. It feels so good I can't take it. I try to back up, but Ced won't let me.

He hooks his arms around my upper thighs and pulls me closer so he can eat my pussy and ass at the same time until I beg him to fuck me. "Please. Baby, just fuck me!"

"In every hole, Mrs. Williams?"

"I ain't never been fucked back there, but since I am about to be Mrs. Williams, Mr. Williams, do as you please."

He fucks my pussy so good from the back that it makes me cry. He got me over the side of the bed, and hammers away. He nuts right on my asshole. It's warm and it feels so good. Damn! I can't wait for him to fuck me in my ass now. His dick is hard and ready to go again in like thirty seconds. He's a beast.

"Just relax and breathe. It's gonna hurt at first, but once it's in, it's gonna be great."

He ain't never lied! That shit hurt like a motherfucker! My ass expanded so far his whole dick fit inside of me. My pussy gets so wet that it feels like I pissed myself. As he's fucking me in my ass, I'm playing with my pussy. He grabs my hair, and I throw my ass back. He fucks me so damn good I get to shaking.

"A fi mi pum des?"

"Yes, daddy."

“Yuh whan mi feh buss in den?”

“Yes!”

When I hear his breathing speeding up I know he isn’t far behind. He fucks me harder. The strokes get longer, and we come together. I come so good I cry like a baby wanting a bottle.

***

On the way to the airport Ced stops at the store to get a newspaper. He reads part of it before he passes it to me. I read where it’s opened to.

“32, Damien Fuller was found dead in his car in the quiet part of Brooklyn. He was shot at least seven times.”

And “Richie Cash was found in his apartment by a friend. He was killed by a gunshot wound.”

I love the way things turned out! I know Ced’s looking at me, so I look back at him and wink.

“New York will be better next time, boo,” I tell him with a smile on my face. This little vacation has been amazing. I got engaged and I cleaned up my dirty laundry.

Chapter 28

Back N Da Burg...

Life is hell here in Lynchburg, Virginia. So much has been discovered while we were gone. Traymon fills me in immediately.

He tells me about how the police are looking for me. Black's body had been found, but Dimples is missing. In an effort to remove myself from the light the first people I call are Dimples' parents.

"Hello?"

"Can I speak with Mrs. Marshall, please?"

"Who is calling?" she asks.

I hold my breath for about five seconds. "This is Sweets."

"I am not going to ask you how you are doing, 'cause you didn't have the nerve to come to say goodbye to your so called sister.' Mane, this bitch is crazy, all the shit that she did to Dimples.

"First of all, I didn't even know anything until I came back last night, and that's when I heard the news."

"Oh yeah?" she says, sounding like she's got an attitude. This bitch really has some nerve.

"I am sorry that I didn't make it to the funeral, but I am much more worried about finding Dimples."

"Funny how Black is dead, Dimples can't be found, and you just getting back in town."

"What you want me to say, Mrs. Marshall?"

She got quiet, I mean dead silence on the other end on the line.

"Mrs. Marshall, I apologize. Black can't come back, but I'll try my best to find out where Dimples is at."

"If you need to make a call, please hang up and try again. If you need help press 0," the operator tells me.

I know this Chester the Molester ass bitch didn't hang up on me!

Pastor or no pastor, that bitch ain't invincible. I run the whole thing down to Ced.

"Just relax, baby," he says in a soothing tone.

"Oh, I am relaxed! Don't question that."

Call the police station, and see if they have a warrant for your arrest. If they do, go down there and hear what they have to say. If they don't have anything for you, then good. Fuck the world."

I know this nigga's going crazy! "Go down there? Them motherfuckers gotta come get me they damn self!"

"Look, baby. If you go to them, then they'll know you're innocent, but if you run from them, they'll hold you as suspect, so you gotta think and act smart. Whatever you do, I got your back all the way."

"So I may as well call and see if they want me, right?"

"Yeah, and don't worry, you'll have the best lawyer ever."

"What the fuck you mean, best lawyer ever, Ced?! You know something I don't know?!"

"Naw, but just in case."

"Just in case my ass! Listen to how that shit sounds! You want me to go to jail, Ced?"

"Calm the fuck down, baby. You makin' yourself scared! You gonna be alright, yo! And no, I don't want you to go to jail Mrs. Williams."

I feel so sick to my stomach; I have to run to the bathroom to throw up. I feel so weak, so tired. Thank God Ced is with me, 'cause he helps me clean up, and then puts me to bed. My nerves are all in pieces.

"First thing in the morning I'm gonna call those people and see what they want," I say to him as he pulls the blankets up over me.

"Okay."

I know I've got all my tracks covered, so why am I worried? I call T and put him on to game.

"Damn, babyma, I got your back. Me and Shawty gonna keep Beauty 'til this shit is clear, so you don't have to worry about her."

"Yeah, do that, and make sure shawty don't do shit to my daughter, 'cause on everything I love she will not be able to fix it!"

"Come the fuck on, yo! Don't carry me, Beauty's mines too!"

"A'ite then." I end the call. I will smoke that bitch's ass in a heartbeat, and not even think about it.

***

I call the police station. They tell me to hold on, and just when I'm ready to hang up the phone the lady picks up and says, "yes, Mrs. Cash, Detective Harris would like to speak with you in person."

"Is today a good time?"

"Hold on a second, let me check the calendar... Yes, you can come down here to the West building at 2pm this afternoon."

Damn. It's already noon.

"Okay, I'll be there at two."

"I'll let him know that you are coming."

"Thank you."

Ced wants to drive me, but I'd rather drive myself. I've got to get my thoughts together, and I don't want us to be seen together by these motherfucking devils. Police stations make me sick. Why the hell they make places like this? When I arrive I text Ced to let him know I've made it safely.

Mr. Harris, or must I say, Detective Harris, is already waiting for me.

"You must be Ms. Cash?"

Motherfucker knows good and damn well he's already looked me up, so he knows exactly who I am. I can play games too.

"Yes, and who are you?"

"I am Detective Harris."

"Well, nice to meet you."

"Likewise."

I can tell that he's blown away by my looks, 'cause he just can' stop staring. Aside from a desk, two chairs and a map of Lynchburg on the wall, the room is empty. I take a seat and wait. After about five minutes, he returns.

"Sorry about that. I had to get myself a cup of coffee. I didn't know if you would want any, so just to be on the safe side I brought a cup for you also."

"Thank you, but I don't drink coffee."

"Would you like me to get you something else?"

"No, thank you. I'm not trying to be rude, but my daughter gets out of school at three and I have to pick her up."

“I understand. Well, your name has come up in an investigation, and I would like to ask you a few questions. I know you, Black, and Dimples go way back...”

I don’t know why these motherfuckers always wanna seem like they down with us and they know damn well we and them ain’t cool. My thoughts are killing me! Play the game, Sweets! Play the game!

“Yes, we’re friends. More like sisters.” I ain’t giving no more information than I have to. He’s gonna have to work for it.

“So I know this has to be hard for you and their families?”

“Yes, it sure is!”

“Where were you on the night of Black’s death?”

I don t even know what night she was killed!” I guess he thinks I’m stuck on stupid.

“Well, the autopsy says between Sunday night and Tuesday morning, so I need to know where you were on those days.

Easy, I think to myself.

“Sunday night I was at Buffalo Wild Wings on Ward’s Road. Monday I was packing for my trip to New York, and Tuesday I was in New York.” These detectives nowadays look like some shit out of the movies, and they all say the exact same thing. This dumbfounded, retarded, pussy looking motherfucker thinks I’m gonna tell on myself. He’s got me fucked up, I mean all the way up, and he needs to HURRY the fuck up!

“And do you have proof for those nights, Sweets?”

“Yes, I do, and that’s Ms. Cash to you.”

Motherfucker, me and you ain’t friends. Just ‘cause I don’t say it doesn’t mean that I ain’t thinking it. I know he knows it. “You can get the video from BBW, and check with the airline that we flew on. No need to be rude, but you already know I have to get my daughter from school.”

“Yes, I know you do, but I have one more question for you.”

“Why did you move, and where are you living at now?” Motherfucker, that’s two questions.

“I moved because I wanted to, and I am living where I want to. You can take my phone number. Call me anytime, and I’ll show up, but aside from that, if I’m not under arrest for anything, my life is my own, and I am allowed privacy. Is that correct?” Don’t get it fucked up. I know my rights.

“Yes, Ms. Cash, you are correct.”

“Here is my number. Feel free to contact me if you need me.

“Would you be willing to escort me out of the building, please?”

“Sure, and thank you Ms. Cash, but I must warn you... the next time we meet probably won’t be this lovely,” he tells me as he shows me the door. I want to smile, ‘cause I know that I’ve won this go round, but I keep it to myself. As soon as I get to the car I let out a sigh of relief. I refuse to let them see me sweat. Something is up. I just have to put my finger on it, and once I do that, I know I’ll be able to fix it. This shit is getting out of hand, fast.

I text Ced to let him know I'll be home soon. He text back saying he's in a meeting. Next, I call Traymon. "I'm gonna pick Beauty up from school." I say as soon as he answers his phone.

"A'ite, you good?"

"Nigga, I am always good, like your nuts!"

I miss my daughter. I want and need her with me. She is my only peace of mind. She keeps me sane and on track. I don't know where I would be if it wasn't for her. I want her to know just how much I love her, to show her just how much she means to me.

At the end of the day, she's the only person that I have to be loyal to.

I pull up at her school, and wait for her to come out.

Chapter 29

Family

She looks just like me, my image for sure.

“Beauty!” I squat down so she can jump in my arms.

“Ma, you come to get me?”

“Yes, baby!”

I want to break down and cry just holding my daughter, thinking about why I didn’t have a mom. Fuck it! My heart is soft only for Beauty.

“We gonna go chill and have some fun, just you and me ok?”

“Ok, ma, I’m ready!”

We go to Chucky Cheese and the mall where we get our nails and toes done, before we do some shopping. Just me and my Lil nigga having fun while blowing money. On the way home she says “Ma, put that Lil Boosie song on.”

“Which one, Beauty?”

“Wipe me down.”

I had to laugh ‘cause she had to brush her chest off telling me that. I put it on for her, and she goes ham singing Lil Boosie’s verse “B-O-O-S-I-E-B-A-D-A-Z-Z, that’s me” She says pointing to herself. When I say this is a little monster in the making, I ain’t never lied! By the time we get home, her ass is out like a light. Ced carries her into the house, and takes her into her room, where he puts her to bed.

“Hey, baby.” I greet him when he comes back down stairs.

“I miss you girl, how did things go today?”

“Just as planned, did you tell your peoples to handle that?”

“Yea, they changed the date and time on the video. You should already know I’m on top of that! I ain’t no slouch ass nigga. I’m a warrior, boo” he says as he pulls me into his arms for a kiss.

“I got you a gift, Mr. Warrior!”

“Oh yea? Let me find out you had a nigga on your mind?”

Nigga? You know about my life, damn right I have you on my mind all the time. Is what I think to myself but “Oh, believe me, you stay on it!” is what I actually say out loud.

I got him a bracelet for his arm, yea, he have a watch, but you could tell how jealous his right hand is, so I had to balance it out for him. That shit cost me twenty stacks! I ain’t ballin’ for nothing!

“Baby, it goes perfect. Thank you!”

"No problem at all! Every Boss deserves to shine, and as long as we together I'm gonna make sure you glow all the time."

"Already!"

He knows I mean every word I say.

"Tomorrow's Friday. How about you get your kids after school and bring them back here so we can enjoy the weekend together?" I asked.

"Yea! I can do that, Mrs. Williams."

***

I kept Beauty home from school today and let her roam the whole house. She loves her room so much she doesn't want to leave it. "Cobra coming over later" I tell her.

"For real, Ma?"

"Yes, baby."

Beauty is so excited about seeing Cobra later, so we cook dinner and wait for them to come running through the doors.

Can you say one happy family? We play every game you can think of. By 12:30am they are fast asleep, Ced included, so I decide this is my time to go. Just as I'm closing the door behind me I hear Ced's voice, "Make sure you come back to me in one piece, Sweets."

I m dressed in all black, so he knows the devil in me is ready to come out "Don't worry. I will!"

Chapter 30

I'm Judging You!

As I travel up Timberlake Road, I realize I know what has to be done. There's just no way around it. I notice all the lights in the house are off. I don't know why rich people who live around rich people hate locking their doors, but they do. I guess they figure no one needs to steal or kill, 'cause they have it all among themselves.

The house is quiet. I know my way around this house like I know the back of my hand. This is not my first visit, but it will be my last. As I climb the stairs, I can hear someone snoring. They're sleeping! Either way, they're gonna stay asleep so it doesn't matter. They're just gonna have a little red sauce to go with it.

I've got my silencer on, and one's already in the head.

My finger's just itching to pull the trigger. I can tell who's who by the way that they lay together. She's got her head tucked under his chin. I figure I'll do him first. My itchy finger pulls the trigger twice. She must have felt the blood as it began to drip down the side of his head, 'cause she opens her eyes. She doesn't scream or anything, but her eyes tell it all. She's scared, and maybe she even knows why I'm here. I tell her any way. I'd hate for her to die confused.

"I'm here to judge ya'll! She was only a child! She did what she was told, and that killed her, she just ain't laying down." I don't give her a chance to say a word. Instead, I put her back to sleep, and let myself out of the house.

On my drive back home, I feel better knowing those motherfuckers ain't breathing no more. I had to kill Dimples' so called parents, based on principle alone. They had cost Dimples so much. I know I did her a favor, but now I need her to resurface so I can finish what I started.

Ced's asleep on the sofa when I get back to the house. I go upstairs to check on the kids, and then I hit the shower. By the time I get out of the bathroom, Ced's in the bed.

"I hope I didn't take too long to get back to you."

"Naw, never! I'm glad you're back in one piece, 'cause if one piece of this family is missing then we ain't complete at all."
"Well, let me show you that I ain't goin' nowhere, baby."

We make love; sweet, sexy, juicy love, all the way into the early morning. By the time we get up, Christina's got the other three kids at the table eating cereal. As the oldest child, she's definitely the most responsible. She's a good big sister, and they love her. After breakfast, Ced cuts the grass, while the kids spend the day riding their bikes and playing outside. We fire the grill up for dinner, and after the kids eat and get their baths, I do every body's hair, Ced's included. Afterwards we eat popcorn, while we watch "Fast and Furious". Around 11:30 I tuck them all into bed. Christina and lil Ced have their own rooms, but Beauty and Cobra sleep together. Those two are attached at the hip.

I go back downstairs to clean up. Ced is on his phone, doing what he does best, #Handling Business#. I clean the kitchen while he plays the X BOX 360 Connect.

“You know I ain’t tryin’ to leave, but I have something that I really need to handle,” I finally tell him.

“Do you ever get tired?”

“No. Not when it come to my freedom. I’ll never get tired.”

“I understand, don’t explain yourself, just-”

I cut him off, ‘cause I know what he’s going to say.

“Make sure I come back in one piece.”

“Yeah, you got it!” he says as a smile breaks across his face.

Chapter 31

Affiliate! Wrong Choice...

I need to pay a visit to Park Avenue. I have to see this nigga named Alphonso. He was Black's side meat, and since I now know that Black and Dimples was sleeping together, I figure he may have been hitting them both off at the same time. Nasty bitches.

This nigga's on some late night shit, too. He doesn't wanna go to sleep, 'cause he's always thinking about those boys in blue, but he should be thinking about the stick up boys. The police he can't beat, but those ski mask nigga's? He'll try his luck.

This must be my lucky day, 'cause this nigga's sleeping on the sofa with a blunt hanging out of his mouth. This right here is the reason why I don't do drugs. That shit just ain't for me I gotta stay on point at all times, so drugs are out of the question for me.

He must have been cooking up, 'cause the kitchen window's wide open. Thank goodness he lives in the cut too, that's even better. I climb through the window while I keep my .45 on his ass, 'cause if he moves, I am touching him.

Yup! I was right. He just finished cooking up. Paper towels with crack are lined up all around the table. I walk over to the sofa, and just look at him. Has to be 5'7" and around three hundred pounds; solid. He's got waves in his hair, and he's sharp from head to toe. He's so black he's purple like Barney. How can weed make a nigga not hear shit? I know he's gonna feel this steel on his head.

"Sleep is for the weak, Nigga!" I yell at him, expecting him to jump, but he doesn't even open up his eyes, he just speaks."

"You better kill me, 'cause I ain't givin' up shit."

"How you figure?"

He recognizes my voice, so he opens his eyes to see my face.

"Damn, Sweets! That's how we playin' now?"

I've run into him on the streets before, spoke and kept it moving, "you my lotto ticket, and I'm gonna cash you in for a little change!" I tell him.

"This is a cold world, but I do wanna know why?"

"'Cause loyalty is a must! If I let you live, I know for a fact that you'll never let me live, nigga." He tries to reach for the gun, but I rock his ass to wonderland. I search his place, and find the money. I grab a trash bag, to put it in and bag it up.

Next, I throw the dope all over the house, so it would look like a drug deal gone wrong. I shoot his ass one more time just 'cause he didn't want me to go back to my daughter.

It's crazy how you know people, and just 'cause you know

them you have to suffer like them. Crazy fucking world.

Chapter 32

Questions?

Sixty-four thousand dollars and five bricks! Shit, a nice little change. I give the money to Ced, and the dope to Traymon. T is so happy he doesn't even question me, but Ced does.

"What did I do to deserve this?"

"It's your world, baby," I say, using the same line on him that he used on me. My body count is getting off the chain, my pockets are looking beautiful, and my heart is growing colder by the second.

Lynchburg is off the fucking map right now. Bodies are coming up like flies from a pile of fresh shit. The city counselor Joseph Duff has the nerve to get on TV with his cock-sucking co-worker, Wayne Woody, and say, "We need to come together and find out who is responsible for all this blood. I promise you, when they are caught, they will never see the light of day again." Original Dick-licking Cocksuckers!

Aww, mane, I am so fucking scared. Ha, ha, that cracker truly thinks his ass is the boss, huh? Imagine me being scared! As long as the sky is blue, my pockets are right, and my child is living, fuck the rest! At the end of the day, I am Sweets!

You know what they say: Hell hath no fury as a woman scorned. My heart has been scorned, so anyone who had anything to do with it has to pay. And I mean anyone. I'd rather die by the streets than live in a 6' x 9'. What the fuck I look like?

Months go by, and not one case is solved. That just goes to show how much this world cares about them. When you're dead and gone, that's it! Motherfuckers move on with their lives, and the dead gotta fight their case on judgment day.

Chapter 33

Normal...

I go back to being a full time mom again. Not to 1, but to four . Shit is crazy, but I enjoy these kids like they actually mines. I would want Regina to treat Beauty like her own. My relationship with Ced is perfect! We don't fight, and we don't argue. We just keep it trill with one another to the fullest. When he goes out to chill with his boys, I'm cool with it 'cause I trust him. Like tonight, I wait up for him until 4:00am, but then I dozed the fuck off.

Eight a.m. and Ced's still a no show. Eight-forty-five, and he's pulling up in the driveway. The kids are upstairs playing, and I'm cleaning the kitchen when he walks through the door.

"Good morning, beautiful."

"Good morning, Ced! How was your night?"

He'd gone out with Clap to handle business.

"Great, but I have to run something by you."

"Go ahead, I'm all ears."

"So, I'm at the bar with Clap, me and him just choppin' shit up. I see Regina and her friend. We pay them no mind, but next thing we know, they're walkin' in our direction. I keep talkin' to Clap. Regina and her friend come over to where we're at."

"And?" I'm mad already.

"Baby, hold on. I'm gonna tell you the rest, just relax!"

"Oh, I am relaxed." But I'm also super pissed.

"She's like, how ya'll doin'? I ain't answer, so Clap speaks, sayin' we good, and ya'll? She says she's good but Ced, I'm talkin' to you. I look at the bitch, then I turn my head back to the bar, ignoring her ass. Then she says, you need a real hood bitch in your life."

Now I'm so hot steam's coming off my feet, 'cause I'm about to stomp this bitch wet.

"I wanted to smack the bitch, but I knew I wouldn't have made it home to you, so I got up and walked away. This joint has the nerve to grab me by my pants and say I can be your side bitch!"

"Yeah," I'm mad to the tenth power with a degree of 360.

"I told her, bitch you got me fucked up! I wouldn't fuck you with someone else's dick! I have a real ass bitch, and don't ever touch me again, and then I walked off."

Before Ced can finish talking, I'm on my way out the door. He doesn't try to stop me. He knows better, and I'm glad he does. Thank God I don't get pulled over, 'cause I know for a fact I was doing at least 100 mph in some places. I call T.

"Yo, I'm on my way over."

"Okay."

Six minutes later, I walk straight past Traymon at the door.

No hello, no nothing! This bitch is in the kitchen, T is on my neck. When she sees my face, she already knows what time it is.

Bop! Bop! Bop!

I rock that bitch with a fresh three-piece, and when she falls, I start kicking her ass.

"Bitch you got me fucked up! You took my baby daddy, but I refuse to let you take this one! I will smoke your ass!" Traymon's in the middle of us now.

"What the fuck is goin' on, yo?" T asks as he faces me.

"That bitch right there ain't shit, and she better be thankful that it's your dick that's slidin' in her, 'cause you already know how I get down!"

1 walk out, hearing Traymon asking what the fuck was that about. Let her explain that shit to him, 'cause I don't have the time, or the patience, but I know that bitch has got me fucked all the way up.

Ced doesn't say shit when I walk through the door, but he makes the mistake of laughing.

"You think this is a joke, Ced?"

"Naw, it ain't no jokes, but who do you fear, Corona?"

“I fear God, but no humans, ‘cause they bleed just like me. I promise you that bitch will never look at you again, much less speak, and if she decides to be superwoman ‘cause she thinks she’s brave enough, her ass won’t live to tell about it.”

“Thank you.”

“Ced, ain’t no need to thank me. That’s my place and my job. A bitch-or a nigga gets out of line, you should always run it by me, ‘cause at the end of the day, it will be handled!”

Chapter 34

Watch! Ride! Show!

Ced asks me to be his partner in business. At first I feel a little hesitant. Me being the only female there is gonna be crazy. Some nigga's don't like to take orders from bitches at all, and I don't want to be the one to break this shit up, 'cause I have my own shit going on, but he wants me at his side so bad that I tell him that I'll be happy to be his backbone.

He tries to school me on a few things, but I'm already schooled. He puts an ounce of cocaine in front of me and tells me to cook it up. I do, and I get three extra grams back.

"Make that into fifty-two grams," he tells me. I do that like it's nothing. Now he's amazed.

"Bring the thirty-one grams back."

I do that too.

"Where you learn to do that?"

"Ask no questions, Ced, 'cause I will tell you nothing but the truth! Traymon! I used to watch him, then I did it myself. If you want some fire ass crack, some shit that will have your phone jumpin' off the hook, I can do it! Say you know a nigga that you don't fuck with, but he needs some work like ASAP, I can bake his ass up too, in two different ways!"

We both laugh.

"Damn, girl! What the fuck can you not do?"

"It's nothin' that I've tried that I can't do." I smile at him. Now it's my turn to school his ass for a minute.

"First of all, there is always a snitch in a crew. You'll never know until shit hits the fan, then the shit gets to stinking, so be on the lookout. I know you know your niggas, but pay close attention to them, they'll rotate..."

His ears are taking in everything that I'm saying, and he hasn't even blinked. I have his FULL attention.

"Then there's always one nigga who wants to take your place. Loyalty don't last forever unless they were born with it. That one hater can put a bug on you to the others. Next thing you know, it's them against you. I am here with you and for you. Four eyes are always better than two. Your crew probably thinks don't know shit, so we gonna keep it like that."

"Damn," he says. He's blown away.

I've got him stuck, but I need him alert.

"Ced, always expect the unexpected, 'cause no one is to be slept on!"

***

He says his team is in check, but I want to make sure my damn self, so I take it upon myself to do a little private investigating since my freedom is at risk. I'm unwilling to leave my daughter. Hell naw! My instinct tells me to search, and I'm ready, 'cause it's never told me wrong. Ced has to understand what I'm doing is for us and our children.

I've had a bad vibe about this nigga on the team named Worm, so I follow him around for a while. On the third day, the nigga gets pulled over by the boys in blue over on Polk Street. I park in the church parking lot nearby so I can watch what happens.

They've' got police dogs all around his car barking their asses off. They cuff Worm and put him in the back of one of the police cars. Then they rip Worm's car completely up until they find what they're looking for. Whatever they find, they put it in a brown bag. They drive away with Worm in their car. One of the police officers drive Worm's car away like nothing even happened.

Explaining the situation to Ced is hard.

"That nigga ain't gonna crumble," he sounds so certain.

"Shit, we'll find out, but I have a bad vibe about this nigga
"What you thinkin' of, Sweets?"

"I hope he ain't tellin', but if he is, I'm gonna mute him."

The very next day Ced calls an emergency meeting to see how everyone's doing, and everyone's there except for Christopher Lee Woodson, AKA Worm.

"Loyalty is a code that should never be broken, no matter what situation you are in. When you die, your reputation lives on."

Out of the blue, Worm walks through the door. Ced continues his speech.

"If I was drowning, I would never pull any of ya'll under, NEVER! I hope the feeling is mutual."

Worm takes a seat by the door. I'd gathered basic info on him already. He's 5'7", 262 pounds, but for a big nigga, he's got killer swag. He's got a honey brown complexion, short curly hair, gray eyes, and a nice smile. He's got two baby mas and four kids, two boys and two girls. He seems like an overall okay type of nigga. Clap interrupts Ced to ask Worm a question.

"Damn, nigga! Where you been at? I tried callin' you last night, but you never answered. I left you the code lettin' you know that we had a meetin' today."

Ced's already put the team on to Worm. Little does Worm know that I had seen the entire show.

"I know, yo! Me and shawty got into, it real bad and shit, so I just cut my phone off and chill," Worm answers.

"That's all that happened yesterday, Worm?" Ced questions him.

"Yeah."

It's crazy to me how this nigga gonna sit right here and lie like nothing happened. I know for a fact that he's working now.

Ced ends the meeting by telling his crew to chill out. Then he walks over to Worm, and whispers something in his ear. Ced nods his head at me.

***

“Drive up to Liberty mountain,” Ced tells Worm once we’re all seated in Worm’s car. I’m in the backseat, Worm is driving, and Ced is riding shot gun. No one says a word.

When we get to the top of the mountain, Ced tells him to turn on Hucker Road and park under a tree. As soon as we’re parked, Ced starts talking.

“You know, loyalty is all I live by in this game! Trust is somethin’ that I give so that I can receive it, ‘cause betrayal is nowhere in my lifetime.”

Ced’s talking way too much.

“Fuck that,” I say. I shoot that nigga in the back of the head, throwing his brains and head juices everywhere as he slumps over the steering wheel.

“Damn, Sweets! I wasn’t even done talkin’!”

“Baby, don’t worry! He got the picture.”

We drag his ass out of the car, and put him in the ground. The hole was dug last night. Too bad Worm didn’t know it was for him. After we cover it back up, I empty the .45 into the ground.

“I hate a fuckin’ snitch!”

Ced just looks at me with one eyebrow cocked up a little, so I speak my mind.

“I mean, he wanted us to drown.”

We clean the car up; Mr. Clean himself ain’t got nothin’ on us.

Once that's handled, we drive the car to Clap's crib, to get his truck so we can go trash Worm's car.

I drive Clap's truck, and follow Ced in Worm's ride. All the way to the chop shop, all I can think about is how I came to be caught up in this lifestyle. I hustle hard to get out of this game alive and still have my freedom, but I wonder if I'll be able to do that successfully. Yes, I'm glad that I have Ced, but I'm not a woman who is in need of a man, and I never have been. I am a woman that a man is in need of, but the two of us together are unbreakable, and unbelievable, 'cause we know way too much about each other. Physically and emotionally I'm stable but mentally, I'm all fucked up, and I know it! Too much time on my hands has got me thinking all kinds of shit, real crazy shit!

I watch Ced talk to dude about the car, and then he pays him to burn and crush it. Today was a productive day. We found and killed the snake before he even had a chance to attack. Can't get no better than that!

Chapter 35

Real Recognize Real

Business is good, great if you ask me. Everyone is playing their part. All the work in the city is coming from "Our Team". We're getting nothing but love and respect. Motherfuckers know if they try to disrespect us in any way they'll be handled, so they stay in their own lane.

Traymon's finally gotten his money up, but he's still fucking with that bitch Regina. I guess she's his main joint, 'cause I've seen him with this super high yellow skinny bone bitch named Quanet. I've heard through the grapevine, that old girl is a ho; every nigga and their daddy done hit that shit.

She's got hood pussy, no walls in that shit at all. What the fuck is he doing with a bitch like that? She must be licking his ass for real! I've got to give it to him though; his little side of town is on point. He's the main man around the Bridge, but if the nigga wasn't my sperm donor, I would touch his ass my damn self.

"Damn, nigga! You eatin' heavy around here?" I ask him.

"Naw, I'm just tryin' to get to where you at!"

"Shit! I'm broke, strugglin' to see tomorrow, and just tryin' to survive. You know the world we livin' in, so I'm just livin' it one day at a time."

"You really gonna start a family with that nigga, Sweets?"

That question came out of nowhere. Now I'm just looking him up and down. Damn, we would have been one hell of a couple, but he hadn't wanted that. He gave me a baby, and then ran off to that other bitch.

"Let me worry about that. My life ain't your business."

"You right! I have enough problems in my life now. Regina hollerin' how she think she pregnant, and even that is too much for me to handle right now."

Pregnant! Mane, he just crushed my feelings to the dirt, but I refuse to let him see it.

"Damn! You that lucky nigga then!"

He wants a reaction, and I know it. Instead I gave him a compliment.

"You know that nigga Jay comes home in less than a year?" I change the subject.

"Yeah, I heard! The question is, how you gonna handle that?"

"For me to know and for you to find out, nigga!"

I brought him what he wanted, four bricks. I hand it over, get in my car, and drive away.

I can't help but think about how things are gonna turn out, 'cause truth be told, I know Jay isn't to be played with, but shit... ain't no need to stop living my life either. Who the fuck is Jay?

"Nobody," I tell myself out loud.

He's just another nigga who can be touched.

Chapter 36

Put On...

I put Ced on, just to keep him updated, 'cause I don't want him in the dark.

"Baby, I'm glad you tellin' me this, but to be honest, I am not scared of that nigga."

I know he means what he says. Our words are all we have, so if we say something, then we have to carry it out.

"By the way," he says, "My father comes home tomorrow."

"Hell yeah, I'm so happy for you! I'm excited 'cause I finally get the chance to meet him!"

"I got him an apartment over there on Old Forest Road, plus I have somebody doing some shopping for him. I'm giving him some bread, so he can be straight for a minute."

"That's what's up! At least you have him back in your life now."

Damn! What the fuck! I have no mother, no father; my only

brother that loved me is gone. Beauty is all I have of my blood! "Yeah, I'm glad he's finally coming home."

"Do you think he'll wanna take the business back over?"

"I don't know, but if he wants it back, he can have it. I ended up with what I wanted."

Fucking multi-millionaire.

"And what is that Mr. Williams?"

"You! I got the best gift ever in this game!"

That night, the sex was amazing! I know life can't get any better than this...

Chapter 37

Home With Drama

Ced's father is a clown, just funny as hell and they look nothing alike! You can tell that time had turned him into an old man fast, but gray hair aside he is a handsome man.

"Damn, boy! I left you with no kids! Come home and you got three and a model on your arm! I raised you right I see" He says smiling at his son.

"Glad you'll be able to enjoy your grandkids and your freedom. I want you to be a part of my wedding also." Ced tells him.

"Congrats to you, my son's sweet lady."

"Thank you, Mr. Williams."

"No need for Mr. you call me Steven. We're family now."

"Thank you for your blessing, it means a lot to us" I tell him.

"Yeah Dad, thanks! I wish mom was here to see it for herself, but I know she's looking down on me smilin'." The pain in

Ced's voice says it all, he misses his mom.

I know my father's looking up 'cause he's damn sure in hell, but I didn't miss that mother fucker. I know Ced's missing his mom though. She was his best friend, and he was her only child.

"Look, Cedrick, I have something very important to talk to you about. I can't keep it a secret any longer, 'cause it's going to eat me alive." Steven said.

What the fuck? Now he wants his business back!

"So, Sweets, could you please excuse us?" Steven asks me.

I'm ready to walk away, but Ced speaks up.

"Whatever you have to say, you can say in front of her. We don't hold nothing from each other."

I look at him and smile. I am fallin' in love with him more and more. For him to stand up to his father like that for me even on something little like this shows me everything. Thank God he made me stay, 'cause I wanted to know. It sounds serious.

"Cedrick, I have another son"

What the fuck?

"What?" Ced says backing up a little.

"Just listen son, let me explain. Your mom wanted me to tell you a long time ago, but I couldn't. I ran into him in prison, and I knew I had to come clean with you."

"You want me to stand here and listen to how you disrespected my mother? You had another child and say she is the only woman to possess your heart, but let me guess, not your dick. Listen to how that shit sounds, I know she begged you to tell me, but you didn't." Ced is fuming. This is some real Jerry Springer mixed with Maury shit for real.

"I did your mother wrong, but she forgave me and stayed with me. She loved, me, and I loved her back, 'cause she was a real woman, the realest woman God ever created. It kills me every day to know that because of my ways she died."

"You damn fucking right! You killed my mother before her time! The love from her heart ate away at her soul, and because of that she ain't here."

I walk over to Ced to try to calm him down.

"Baby, let's go" I tell him.

"Naw, fuck that! He's gonna hear what I have to say! You ain't even my father no more. You Steven to me. If you want the game back, you better get the lookin' for a team, and a new contact somewhere else. You are not gettin' that shit that I've lifted up, and you better move to a different state, 'cause Virginia is mines." He gives his father the business alright.

"Boy, you don't scare me. I brought you into this world, and I'll take you out if I want to."

Now Ced is face to face, nose to nose with the man he called, Steven.

"Ma gave birth to me, she raised me, you just the water that helped her egg to hatch. You put no fear in my heart, and if I die today, I'll die a real nigga, somethin' you can never be and when I go you better believe you going too. Sweets, let's go."

Damn, how could everything turn upside down just like that?

"And the money that's in the room, just look at it as a gift from my mother, 'cause if it wasn't for her, your ass wouldn't get shit." He says to his father, and we walk through the door.

Damn! That's all I can say. Damn!

***

"Sweets you remind me so much of my mom. You're as strong as she used to be and you go just as hard as she did. She killed every nigga who told on my dad herself. I know for a fact that she is happy that you're in my life."

I'm lost in my thoughts. It's crazy!

"We would have been a hell of a team if she was alive."

"You damn right!" He says smiling broadly.

"Well, you and your brother will probably get along. See how shit works out and try to forgive your father. You have to remember we're human, and we're far from perfect. Everyone makes mistakes. We just have to make sure they don't become our habits."

"You right, Corona."

"Whatever you decide to do, Ced I'm down to ride." I tell him and he knows I mean it.

"Oh, I already know. You stay ready and I love that about you. I could never go wrong with you by my side."

I can't hurt this nigga. Cross over on him? NEVER! And I damn sure ain't gonna let anyone else hurt him. So, that shit his father had to say, I took it personal! 'Cause I'll ride on his bitch ass...

When we get into the car he breaks down and cries. He needs me more than anything, and I want to let him know I am truly here for him.

"Baby, if you want me to handle him, just say the word."

"Corona! I love you girl. You are one of the realest!"

"Remember, Real Live Trill Ass Niggas don't cry!"

"Cryin' is good for the soul, and I miss my mom to the fullest. My dad couldn't do any wrong in my mom's eyes, even when he used to beat her, she stayed with him. When he cheated she stayed right there with him, playin' the scene like a real woman. When he got on drugs real bad, she took up the slack and took control. She found my dad a connect, she got him clean, and put him on top. But look how he repaid her."

"Damn. That is some cold ass shit for real."

"How about a small vacation, just us and the kids?" I suggest.

"Where ever you wanna go, let's go!"

***

Atlanta's beautiful. Between here and New York, I don't know which one is better. We stay in Atlanta for an entire week and the kids are so spoiled it's a shame. Between me and Ced, they get whatever they want.

Growing up I didn't have shit. It hurts me to my heart to know that I had parents who just didn't give a fuck. When I do run across my mother, boy oh boy, do I have a surprise for her. My past alone eats me alive, that's why my daughter will always have everything she needs.

Cedrick spoils me, treats me like I'm a queen, so I spoil him back, and treat him like the king that he is.

On the way back to Virginia, Beauty tells me, "Ma, when I get older I wanna be just like you!"

I want to tell her no, but how can I tell my child NO, don't be like me? So I just tell her "I'll teach you whatever you need to know baby."

Yea, and that means pulling the trigger.

No Visitors Allowed!

Ced had put Clap, his right hand man, in charge while we were out of town.

"Mane, business is slow! Word around is that four Philly niggas visitin'," Clap tells us over dinner to catch us up on everything.

"What's the word?" I ask.

"They don't have what we have. They got somethin' better."

"Better?" Ced ask.

"Yea, they moving that PCP, also known as boat. Even the damn crack heads smokin' that shit; and let's not talk about the local small time drug dealers."

"Word?" Ced asks.

"Word!" Clap assures him.

"So what's the deal with them?" I ask.

"They getting mad money and they stuntin' in our city right in our face like this their shit. All up in Club 2 every night like they ready to take over Lynchburg."

"No visitors allowed! No niggas disrespect our foundation." Ced's angry about this situation, but it's okay.

"I have a plan" I say.

***

Club 2 on Wednesday night is wack; but with me in it, it's a different story. Dressed in some 8732 jeans and shirt with some J's, all I'm doing is chilling. No need for attention, 'cause I'm just coming in and going out.

I see my targets as soon as I walk through the front door. You can always tell out of town niggas, 'cause they try to stunt on the niggas of that city.

Two with braids, one with shoulder length dreads, and the other rocking waves, I bet the main nigga of the crew is the one with the waves, 'cause all six eyes are eating up what he's saying. As I said, I came to see. Now that I have seen what I wanted, it's time for me to leave.

***

It's Friday night, and Club 2 is pack from front to back. Ced, Clap, and Trappa are already in.

As I walk through the door all heads turn to look at me. I see Ced and the crew. Hands down, I'm the shit. Bitches hate, and niggas wanna taste. I walk past Ced and his crew like I don't know them.

I know Ced's watching all these other niggas watch me and knowing that I belong to him makes him feel like a king.

As I get closer to the bar, I see my visitors sitting in their favorite spot.

"Can I get a Jamaican Lizard please?" I ask the bartender.

"Sure!"

I watch him mix my drink and wait for it to be served to me.

"Excuse me, sexy, can I buy that for you?" I don't even turn around to answer whoever the hell it is.

"No, thank you!" I decline, but I can tell that the person is still standing there waiting for me to face them.

As I turn around with my drink in my hand, I can see Ced watching me. Just as I said, out of town niggas want everything in another town.

"Excuse me, please!" I say to the man standing in front, of me blocking my path.

"A beautiful woman like you shouldn't be in a place like this."

This nigga's acting like he knows me.

"Really? You shouldn't be in someone else's city tryin' to start a war."

"Excuse me?"

Now I have his full attention, so I'm going in for the kill.

“I am asking you nicely to take your crew back to Philly…”

“Do I know you?” He asks, cutting me off.

“No, you don’t, but I know you very well! This is not your turf and you’re fucking up my business. Once again, I am asking you in a very nice manner to pack you things and leave.”

“Orders coming from a woman! I pay those no mind. You need to be at home watchin’ television with some kids.”

“Well, this is my order for you! You have forty-eight hours to leave my city!”

“If I don’t?”

This nigga really don’t know who’s fucking with.

“I’ll show you that I am not a woman who needs to be in front of a television with some kids. Now can you get out of my way?”

He moves and I walk towards the dance floor with my drink in my hand.

I know for a fact that he’d never had a woman talk to him like that before, because his eyes bout popped out their sockets.

No need for attention, I drink my Lizard and exit the building.

The entire Philly table watches my every step.

***

“Damn, T, what’s wrong with you?”

I know this nigga hears me.

"T, what's wrong with you?" I ask him again.

Him, and a couple of boys, are posted up on Holland Street.

These niggas look funny; even acting funny.

"Why do you look like a zombie?"

"Baby…ma…you…beautiful."

What the fuck is going on with him? He looked over at his boys in slow motion, and wave for one of them to come here. A short light skin dude walks over.

"Baby…ma, …this…my…nigga…BU."

BU, I've heard that name before, but where? BU extends his hand to shake mines.

"Nice to meet you." I say.

"Likewise; heard nothing but good things about you. Sorry we have to link up like this, 'cause this nigga out here tripping" he says pointing to Traymon.

Now I'm curious to know what he's talking about.

"What you mean?"

"This nigga is wet!"

"Wet?" I am so lost.

"Yea, he smokin' that boat!"

“What the fuck?”

“Same thing I said!”

Damn, these Philly niggas done come down here, and now my baby daddy’s a boat head? Oh hell no! I look T up and down and shake my head. How can he choose a drug like that to do? Yea, he’s tripping fro real. I walk off feeling completely sick to my stomach. As I got in my car, I call Ced.

“Babe, you won’t believe this shit.”

“What?”

“Traymon fuckin’ smoking boat!”

“How you figure?” He asked with no emotion.

“Cause I am looking dead at him as we speak!”

“Damn!”

“His home boy BU told me.”

“BU? Describe him to me Sweets!”

“Light skin, short, has a scar on the left side on the bottom of his chin.”

“Where you at?”

“I am on Holland Street. Why? What’s going on Ced?” Now I am trying to get to my best friend aka my gun.

“Get away! That’s the same nigga that shot Clap up!” He screams into the phone.

I knew I had heard that name before!

"Say no more!" I tell Ced and end the call.

I roll my window down so I can holla at BU.

"Yo, BU, come here."

I watch him walk over.

"What's up, ma?"

"What's your number so we can vibe?"

"434-907-9807."

"A'ite, I got you."

Don't worry, I got you alright.

***

Twenty-four hours left, and these Philly niggas still in the Burg, I know exactly where they're laying their heads, so I'm a step ahead of them.

I had called BU and told him to meet me over at Peeks View Park off Old Forest Rd at 7pm.

I'm dressed in all black, so you already know what I am about to do. It starts getting dark around five, so by seven I'm invisible.

He calls to see which side of the park I'm on.

"Yo, ma! Where you at?"

"By the basketball court."

I see him before he sees me.

"Damn, you out here in the pitch black dark with black on?"

He asks when he finally notices me.

Just knowing that his life is about to end has chills running up my damn spine. I am mad 'cause I am not doing it.

"Black keeps me cold, 'cause I'm always hot." The look on his face says he's confused.

"Damn, home boy!" Clap says from behind him. Fear settles into the lines of BU's face.

"Mane, it wasn't supposed to be like this, huh?" Clap asks him.

BU is in such a deep state of shock that he can't even speak.

That's why it's good to always keep your laundry clean. This is one body I will not add to my belt, cause I know Clap wants to handle it himself. I walk way and leave him to his business.

Bop! Bop! Bop! Bop!

I know they're straight head shots. Time waits for no man.

***

Fuck giving these Philly niggas forty-eight hours to leave my city. I gave them an option, but they refused to follow, so now I have to show them exactly who is Boss.

1927 Lakeside Drive!!! They're in a trailer in the cut, all the way in the back. They have one of the crew members outside in the car watching at all times.

He doesn't even see or hear me coming, who would at 3:00am in the morning if they're already sleeping?

Bop! Bop! Bop!

Straight to the dome. I play no games! Tonight I am carrying my P89 with a silencer and a 17 shot extender.

The doors open, so I creep my way into the trailer. A nigga on the sofa.

Bop! Bop! Bop! Bop!

Straight head shots. I am not playing games with these niggas 'cause they way too disrespectful. Two down!

I hear shower water running! At three in the morning, one of these niggas is showering. What the fuck? I open the door and let loose.

Bop! Bop! Bop! Bop! Bop!

I don't stop until the body finally drops.

Where the fuck is the other nigga at? He must be in the bedroom asleep. I open up the door really slow and see him. I watch him for a second before I shoot the lamp off the stand to wake him up. He tries to reach for his gun, but I stop him by shooting him in the upper body.

"Agh!" he hollers out in pain.

"All I asked you to do was to leave my town, but you refused."

“Shawty, my forty-eight hours isn’t up!”

“On my clock it is!” Niggas play way too many games.

“And by the way, I don’t need to be sittin’ in front of no television, especially when I have a job to do.”

Bop! Bop! Bop! Bop! Bop!

All these niggas had to do was take their asses back to Philly, but naw! The boss refused to listen to a COLD HEARTED bitch like me. That’s a mistake he won’t make twice.

I'm Just Too Nice!

Ced wakes me up with the high ass volume on the TV.

"Neighbors this morning found bloody water in their driveway when they went to get their paper. The police were called to the scene, and they found three males inside of 1927 shot to death. There was another male in the car that sat in the driveway also, shot to death. No witnesses have yet to come forward, nor family members to claim their loved ones. This is a very sad story." The anchor lady reported.

"No niggas or bitches are gonna disrespect my man and think I ain't gonna check them. I'm just so nice when it comes to you, Mr. Cedrick Williams." I tell him before rolling over, and going back to sleep. Sleep maybe for the weak but, I need my beauty rest.

***

Everything is going well for us. The money practically counting itself, and we're just living. Me and Traymon are beefing hard, 'cause half the day this nigga is high on boat, and the other half he's trying to track it down so he can get high again.

So instead of Beauty staying with him, I've been letting her spend time with her grandmother, Bella. She enjoys being over there, 'cause Bella had her other grandkids there. When I need a babysittter for Beauty, Bella's door is always open.

Traymon calls to check on her, but only every so often 'cause he had found a new baby; now the love of his life—BOAT! That shit smells just like death. He's dipping his weed and cigarettes and then smoking it while it's wet. Sooner or later his ass gonna be smoking crack. I know for a fact that nigga ain't getting shit else from me for free! He's got money to buy boat, he better have money to buy work and whatever he needs. I am gonna treat him just like any other nigga from here on out.

Chapter 40

Time Stopped!

Nine months later, Ced and his dad are on ok terms. They're trying to make their relationship work, and I am super proud of them both. I'm a full time mom now, and I'm loving it 'cause I'm the queen of my kingdom. Just don't push me 'cause the killer in me is just sleeping.

Steven invites us over to his place so Ced could meet his step brother. I'm excited for them, 'cause truth be told, I didn't want to kill anyone in their family.

Ced drops his kids off at their mother's house, and I drop Beauty off at Bella's for the night.

***

I'm dressed in all black, but no, killing is not on my mind. Once we arrive at Steven's house I tell Ced to go on in 'cause I want to check on Beauty before she goes to sleep.

"Don't make me come look for you."

"Just make sure you leave the door unlock for me, Ced!"

“You know I will!”

He kisses me and gets out of the car. I call Bella’s phone, and talk to Beauty for a few minutes. Just hearing her voice puts me at ease. I know I have to get out of this lifestyle, ‘cause Beauty is my world, and I want to see her live a beautiful life.

As I open the door and walk into the house, everything sounds peaceful and it seems like everyone’s getting along. I’m so glad to hear them all talking. I close the door, and head to where they are.

Time stops when I see Jay’s face, I feel a sharp explosion of pain in my chest. It feels like my heart has stopped beating, and it scares me, everything goes black but I hear Ced’s voice.

“No! Baby no!”

I can’t open my eyes.

***

“Welcome to Street Heaven, Sweets!” Says a loud booming voice. No! This can’t be happening to me, I’m trippin’!

I am tripping really hard.

Beep…Beep…Beep…Damn!!

ABOUT THE AUTHOR

Julian James, known as Jamaica, was born and raised in Jamaica, West Indies. She grew up in Brooklyn, New York and lived in Virginia. Currently, she is incarcerated in a federal prison and is trying to be world-wide with her thoughts on paper…

Julian James #16692-084
F.C.I. Aliceville
POBox 4000
Aliceville, AL 35442